STATE OF GRACE

STATE OF GRACE

JOY WILLIAMS

SCRIBNER**SIGNATURE**EDITION

CHARLES SCRIBNER'S SONS · NEW YORK
1986

First published in Scribner Signature Editions in 1986.
Copyright © 1973 by Joy Williams

Williams, Joy.
State of grace.

Library of Congress number 86-1880
ISBN 0-684-18645-4

Published simultaneously in Canada
by Collier Macmillan Canada, Inc.
Copyright under the Berne Convention.

3 5 7 9 11 13 15 17 19 F/P 20 18 16 14 12 10 8 6 4 2

Printed in the United States of America.

Cover painting "Backyard, Echo Park April 1984"
gouache, 61" x 44¹/₂", © David Hockney, 1984.
Courtesy of the artist.

STATE OF GRACE

BOOK I

Ah! don't you see
Just as you've ruined your life in this
One plot of ground you've ruined its worth
Everywhere now—over the whole earth?

Cavafy

1

There is no warning of daylight here. It is strange to know that it is only twenty miles to the Gulf of Mexico and all that dizzying impossible white light, for here there is such darkness. Here when one can see the sky, it is almost always blue, but the trees are so thick nothing can make its way through them. Not the sun or the wind. And the ground never dries. The yard is rich mud with no definition between it and the riverbank. Tiny fish swim in the marks our feet make. The trees are tall and always look wet as though they'd been dipped in grease. Many of them are magnolias and oaks. Pods, nuts and Spanish moss hang in wide festoons. The river is the perfect representation of a southern river, thin and blond, swampy, sloppy and warm. It is in everyone's geography book. I was not shocked at all when I saw it. I was not pleased, although it is quite pretty.

The moss is smoky and dreamy-looking. We can thank the Indians for that. It's the hair of a girl who killed herself after her father murdered her lover.

The moss feels like Father's hands, which were always very rough although there wasn't any reason for their being so. So many textures are the same. So many views. Almost all arms and noons and lips and anger are the same and love. It's no wonder we're all testy and exhausted, trying to show delight or even a polite interest.

This silence is beautiful but it makes my head ring. If I awake at the proper time, I can sometimes see the mist rising from the ground and floating down through the trees to the river. I sometimes feel I live in a dangerous place. The river is only the mist moving down it.

I wake early, as a rule. I try to remember what I've told him. There's no way of being sure how much he knows. Sometimes, when we are walking through the woods together, I am quite at peace and even believe that any terror I previously felt is merely an aspect of my parturient condition. I know that he is thinking. I know that he is trying to decide what to do. I wait for his decision as nothing can proceed without it. It is the choice between life or death, between renewal or resumption. I have no fear of him. We are in love. Of course I could only hope that he would kill us, that is, Daddy and me, because I have a feeling, though I know it's mad, that we are going to go on forever. But it's too late for that now. I must be realistic. Even if he traveled there, he would not find Daddy. Even if he did, even if Daddy made himself available, he would not be able to deal with him. God and the Devil are the whole religion and Daddy has both on his side.

I have not offered to leave but he does not think of this. Several times he has suggested traveling together far away. I would agree to anything but he dismisses his suggestions instantly, almost before they are uttered, as though he was not the one who made them. No possibilities are open to me. As I say, I wait. What is going to happen waits with me. We have always been reluctant companions.

And in the meanwhile, time, as always, passes or fails to. To the eye, we have proceeded with it. We have our little willfulnesses and quirks. For example, I have terrible eating habits. He eats almost nothing now. He used to saw away at a huge side of pork that he brought down himself and prepare that in a variety of ways. But the hog is gone now, as is the reason for his killing it. Or at least we have always liked to believe that the hog was the same that butchered our hound, though the woods are full of hogs, shaking the land with their mean rooting and rutting. But the hog is gone now and the dog and our hopes for living simply, on the land and on our love. Once he liked grits with syrup and pecans that we'd shake down from the trees but now he cannot even be comforted by memories. I, on the other hand, have a terrible hunger. I love awful foods. Children's cereals, cupcakes and store pies, that wonderful gluey bread Dixie Darling, yes, two long loaves for only 21 cents. Once, before I moved out here, I ate nothing for three weeks but Froot Loops. It became hallucinogenic after a few days. Anything will. If you breathe in too much basil, a scorpion will be born inside your head. If you eat too much roe, you'll probably die. Why not? I had to stop the Froot Loops. Everything was so enormous and I was becoming so small. My gums bled. The girls became lecherous and outraged even though I was curious about them as well. Everything smelled rancid in that big house even though the girls washed themselves constantly and all the food was kept in jars. They were so boring about their hygiene, their hair and fingernails. They were healthy enough I suppose. The lint-free pussy plombs employed! The cases of disposable M'Lady Tru-Touch Hand-Savers. . . .

Once, for an infraction of the rules, I was forced to clean the shower drains. I also had to change all the beds. . . .

I do little here in the woods. I assimilate the soundlessness. We pursue the meager life with a few garish exceptions. I have my Dixie Darling products, which, I might add, have never disappointed me, and he has his Jaguar. An old faithless and irrational roadster, black, and in perfect running condition. It is so fast and inside it is a warm cave and smells delicious. It is parked beside the trailer and often, in the afternoon, I go out and sit in it and have a drink there. It calms me. The leather is a soft dusky yellow from all the saddle soap he works into it. It smells like lemons and good tack.

After that singular Fourth of July, Daddy never had a car, although there once were two. Daddy and I walked everywhere. On Sundays, we would skate across the pond to church—two sweethearts, my hand in his, in the other glove, ten pennies for the offering plate. Slivers of ice flew up beneath my skirt, my eyes wept. We skated quickly, seriously, lightly on Sunday mornings, barely leaving a mark behind us. . . .

He loves the Jaguar—the skill and appreciation it takes to enjoy it. He is Grady. I shall make myself clear. Grady, my husband, a country boy with brown face and hands and blond matted hair low on his brow. The rest of him is long, white and skinny. He knows a great deal about hunting, fishing and engines. He loves the Jaguar and he also takes an abashed pleasure in this dank trailer which is his. It cost $10. He bought it from Sweet Tit Sue who now lives farther upriver. She wrote out a bill of sale which we keep in Rimbaud's *Illuminations*. At the moment, it happens to mark the spot you know, Andthenwhenyouarehungryandthirstythereissome-onewhodrivesyouaway. It is not always there. We move it about for amusement, to tell our fortune. He used to enjoy that. All those words with their imminence and no significance. He always saw luck in these woods.

He gets angry at me often now. I'm afraid it's the way I keep house. I don't keep house. His face becomes rigid and he speaks so softly I can barely hear him. The place is so soiled that nothing can be found. It smells. It doesn't bother me. What is the purpose of order?

Each morning I am ravenous. I eat with a lamp on and my

feet in a pair of his socks. The mice have left their turds all over everything, in the sink and in our shoes and in the dog's dish. It doesn't bother me.

I am chewing on this bread. . . . I must admit I eat this garbage because I want to insult myself. We think as we eat. Our brains take on flavor and scope. What I want is to slow down my head and eventually stop it. I strive for a brain friendly and homogenized as sweet potato pie.

In the early morning, alone, eating, I push back the curtains and watch the birds. The curtains are old and streaked with the sun. They must have been brought here from another place. The cloth is rotten. It seems to come off on my hands. I use our binocular. I recognize the osprey naturally, the little blue heron, the flicker, titmouse and kingfisher. I have difficulty with ducks and hawks. I have a guide book. I have lists and charts and know proper terminology and range. Nonetheless, I am able to identify very little. The birds I often see can never be found in the book. The eye ring is incomplete or the shading of the primaries is wrong or the pattern of flight. Everything might be in order except for the silhouette. It is annoying but not surprising. Perhaps the artist who drew all these colorful pictures that appear in my book is untalented or anarchistic.

I like birds although I realize that they are dull-witted. That is part of the reason. Birds are uncompromised by their surroundings and never react differently, an ideal, I believe. I am like them with my inflexible set of instincts. It seems I cannot improvise. For I have been through this before. I have seen these things. . . .

. . . The important thing is to consider the significance of things and not to worry about their authenticity. This is the way I have lived my life but I really cannot comment about the efficacy of the method. It's difficult to tell at the end of the day whether it was theory or need that got you through it. I try not to judge or feel responsible for events. I try not to make decisions. This often causes problems. For example, I'm five months pregnant. It's only as big as a man's palm, it's true, but it turns and feeds inexorably. I don't look at all pregnant and never would have thought of it myself, but I've been told firmly that it's so. I peed into a paper cup and now I know.

I would like to go off with Grady, to be with him while he is going but I lack the courage or even the ability. He has a journey to make as does the baby. I will not accompany either of them. I remain, as I will say, still. I try not to be intrusive. And I conduct myself not only carefully but hardly at all. Who could prove the life of such a creature? And who would think it necessary to deny it?

Yes, Grady and the baby, all those people with things to do, moving through their landscapes, victimized by their sceneries. Even Daddy once took a trip. Even I years ago made a trip, which it is difficult for me to reconstruct as I was quite sick, I believe, at the time. It was on the bus. I slept for forty-seven hours on the bus. Abandoned in the seat beside me was a plastic orange, filled with disgusting perfume, purchased at a roadside rest. Also a complimentary three-inch bale of cotton. I changed seats several times, usually to free myself from unpleasant companions. One was a man with a tan reading aloud from his Bible. A real doppelgänger though cruddy and with a speech defect. "Oh remember that my life is wind," he kept bringing up like yesterday's breakfast. Wind, wind— we've all heard that line before. Well, I want to tell you something.

Here there is not even wind. There is scarcely any air at all in these woods where Grady and I live. There is no wind or sound and nothing moves. My boy husband lies flat and prim beneath the sheets. He looks two-dimensional. When he opens his eyes, I may find that they are painted on his head. Perhaps I can dress him myself, cutting out paper trousers, shirt and Levi jacket, bending the cardboard tabs to pass and cling to his ankles, hips, waist and shoulders. Perhaps I can press some tea down his throat or drive to the coast and place him in the sun. I don't care to watch him sleeping and always leave the room immediately. It confuses me, his lying there, his mouth dry at the corners, foam from a punctured pillow gathered round his damp cheek.

Time does not move here. I do not change. Only the baby changes. I want to be rid of them all. I want to be rid of this terrible imposition of recall.

One wants and wants . . . I used to lie constantly, but now, I assure you, I've stopped.

2

I listen to the radio. I sleep only a few hours every night and spend the rest of the time listening to the airwaves. It is very tiny, a transistor, and rather weak. I can only get one station. From midnight until six, I listen to "Action Line." People call the station and make comments on the world and their community and they ask questions. Music is played and a brand of beef and beans is advertised. A woman calls up and says in a strangled voice, "Could you tell me why the filling in my lemon meringue pie is runny?" These people have obscene materials in their mailboxes. They want to know where they can purchase small flags suitable for waving on Armed Forces Day.

There is a man there that answers the question, almost always right away and *right on the air*.

A woman calls. Yes. She asks, "Can you get us a report on

the progress of the collection of Betty Crocker coupons for the kidney machine?" The man can and does. He answers the lady's question. He complies with her request. Astonishing. I think sometimes that this man can help me.

3

And I live by the airport, what is this that hits my house, that showers my roof on takeoff? We can hear it. What crap is this, I demand to know. My plants are green, my television reception is fine but something is going on without my consent and I am not well, my wife's had a stroke and someone stole my stamp collection and twenty silver dollars.

Yes, well, each piece of earth is bad for something. Something is going to get it on it and the land itself is no longer safe. It's weakening. If you dig deep enough to dip your seed, beneath the crust you'll find an emptiness like the sky. No, nothing's compatible to living in the long run.

Next caller, pulease.

See, look, I begin, we can see it all. I want to flatter him. It's all prerecorded. They can cut it out but now I have his ear, he's mine. I can't make you out, he says. I speak more firmly. See, look. There's the chamois running, the cutlet nursing, the sandwich cropping grass. The bleeding baby seal capes. And the smells are overwhelming as we know. The limbs adrift in hospital incinerators. The race horse pies at the yearling auction swept up by those men in tuxedos.

Right, he says.

All those trees being made into publishable lies, I say. The mucus under the leaves . . .

I must correct you there, he says. That's humus. Essential
to the fertility of the earth. Humus.

I know I don't have much time left with him. He's getting
off the track. Listen, I say, the spinal tap was only a partial
success, leaving me dead from the knee to the foot and the
waist to the bridge of the nose. There's no recourse for they
never made me any promises, although they spoke frequently
and in depth.

You'll acclimate, he says.

But the death I thought I'd died is back now for a slight
correction and they've given me a cornea injection and now
I'm only useless in the eyes and the loving parts. I'm perfectly able to do all the things I couldn't do before. I can eat
and drink, bite my nails, take a walk and bend for prayers
and toilet. They're pleased.

I can well see that, he says.

I was immediately released, I say hurriedly. Not for one
day was I in Intensive Care which is reserved for outpatients,
ordinary seamen, phronemaphobiacs and the like.

Un-huh, he says. There is static and humming. On the radio,
while he is listening to me, he is playing *the mystery tune*
which I can tell him is "Sapphire" and win myself two free
tickets to the drive-in movie. But I don't want admission. I
want to know my hour! When is the fatal hour and when will
the truth come to me?

Why it went when you were sleeping, he says. It come and
saw you dreaming and it went back to where it was.

4

Some memories have no past. This town for example, this setting. I have mentioned the frame that held Grady and I. There, goats were often seen climbing in the trees. They preferred live oaks because of the low sturdy branches. This is not peculiar. It is an invisible landscape. Everything, more or less, is invisible upon it.

Don't sulk. Everything is over. Here is the place. There are Grady's woods and river. Then there is the logging road. Rattlers slide down the colored gullies. Great cattails rise from clear yellow pools. There is the blacktop that meets the coast. Black people live here in low and fragile houses with tile roofs. Sea grape shields the windows from the sun. They farm. There are a few calves and chickens. Some of the livestock are hobbled to the docks at low tide. The cormorants rest on the pilings, drying their wings. Everywhere there are glistening unnatural mountains of oyster shells. They spill into the road, cracking beneath the car's wheels, shining like oil. Then there are palmists, bars and spaghetti houses. There is a sign that points the way to BRYANT'S BEASTS. There is a sign that points the way to the college. It is futile and oppressive—the entry to a southern town. It is hot. The streets are empty. Huge fans move the air in restaurants. You watch the blades turning as you pass. The town is irreconcilable to its space. Dismiss it. If you must, think of the cheap motels, the drugstore luncheonettes, the hospital. Once there were more cats in the corridors than doctors. Think of the bars, the empty De Chirico train station, the grassy subtle tracks that fade to the north. Think of the highway that moves to other places.

Don't become impatient. Here is the time. It is late in the year but summer will soon follow. My friend Corinthian Brown comes out of a small café. He is digesting their week-day special which is pizza, chicken, roll and potato. The time is shown in a clock set in an electric waterfall on a wall beside the pies. The water is a shiny neon blue falling from shadow-box mountains. The scene clicks and hums from the current that keeps it operating. Corinthian patronizes this café because of the waterfall clock. It is popular with others as well and a source of speculation. "It's the Adironeracks," someone is saying. "I been in that area in 1953. It's the Adironeracks for sure. Water'd freeze your pecker off."

It is early morning. The pizza is still cold from the day before. Corinthian carries a book, *Heart of Darkness*. I will have given it to him. He walks toward his job at Al Glick's Automobile Junk Yard. Now the job of guarding objects that people no longer feel the need to molest is far too much for any one man. Corinthian realizes this. He realizes that, in particular, guarding junk should be the job of presidents, of congressmen, of those with far more power and influence than himself. It is not the task for one with no resources, no persuasive menace, no continuing stake in the eventual out-come. Nonetheless, those who could perform the function best are not called. Or do not answer. So Corinthian serves. In return, Al Glick allows him to sleep anyplace he wants to and to use his hot plate. Corinthian hardly ever takes advantage of the last benefit because he doesn't want to be pushy. Some of the wrecked cars are quite well-appointed and it is a joy for him to sit in the plush seats, particularly on a rainy day, and read a good book or two. Corinthian has become at-tached to some of these cars. He is broken, after all, and these machines are as well, although he realizes that he is still using himself up whereas someone has finished them long ago. This is not to say that he deals in endings. Who could claim that? He simply protects the things whose defeat and destruction have already occurred. Like us, he keeps a feckless guard, one with the resting objects.

But objects need not detain you. Forget them. Remember instead the picture of Corinthian Brown. He is running now, he is late. His mind is on the menagerie that he has just left. Corinthian labors continually. He works at Bryant's Beasts as well. It is a terrible job that affects and grieves him. He worries that he has not given the ostrich enough water. He loves the bird's eyes which have long thick lashes. He loves its poor wings. Think of lovers. That's where stories lie.

It is morning in the South, on the Gulf Coast. On the empty beach there are two girls. They are eating powdered donuts. One is bare chested and pretty. She is lying on her back and eating. The sugar crumbs fall on her chest. The other girl removes the crumbs, sometimes with her moistened finger, sometimes with her mouth. It is an obvious attempt at an unspeakable practice. The pretty girl has a dogged and sincere expression. The other girl is charmed. Her name is Cords. She kisses her friend's hair wryly. A helicopter beats toward the coast from inland. It flies low over the girls, turns, hovers. They can see the Navy men inside it. Cords raises her middle finger and waves it stiffly. The chopper clatters angrily above them.

To the north, a train is moving toward the town. Everything is amiss on southern trains. There is no ice water. There is no meat, no flowers. There is no service at all. The train does not speed but it's never not arrived. There's no timetable available but it is never late. The train bears doom and Daddy through a swamp. Part of the swamp is burning. There's a smell of toast. People are filing into the dining car.

The sun moves up a mite, startling no one. Tradesmen sit on the curbs outside convenience stores and eat their snacks of raisins. In the hospital, the new babies are wheeled out of the nurseries for their feedings. They are like fancy pastries offered in their aluminum cart. The mothers in the wards try to be clever with one another but what is there to think? Down in the basement, in the emergency room, a few college students are being given tetanus shots by a moody intern. The intern is brooding because he is monorchid. The college girl that he had had a date with the evening before had been discomfited when he had pulled off his boxer shorts. She had been coolly disapproving throughout, but her surprise had not curbed her speech. "Well, that's really interesting," she had said. "At school, they're always putting the vegetables on my plate that look like a man's parts and everyone teases me about this, but never in my life have I ever seen anything that could be construed to look like that." He had bought her all the shrimp she could eat and then he had bought her five brandy alexanders and listened to her ballad of interminable immutable opinions. She was a girl with a great deal of gorgeous wavy hair and she wore expensive clothes. Her aunt owned the controlling interest in the country's most popular baking soda. He learned that her aunt had sent her to Venice in, as luck would have it, the year of the flood. "It was beyond belief," she had told him, "I couldn't buy Tampax. No one anywhere had Tampax." She was so beautiful and he had taken her back to his apartment and pulled off his boxer shorts. "Well, that's really amazing," she had said, but not in a special way.

The intern angrily inoculates another student and entertains grisly notions. His patients have punctured and scraped themselves with nails and chicken wire while building the floats for the college's big Homecoming parade. The injured are predominantly waffle-thighed energetic girls with dazzling and insincere smiles. The floats are lined up in a dead-end street, covered with parachutes, waiting for tomorrow.

The sun is getting white and old. Grady double-clutches as he rounds a corner on the woods road. He slows still further and the Jaguar thuds across an old wooden bridge. A boy about his age is fishing with a drop line. The river is purple with water hyacinths. The boy's car, a broken-down Ford with a smashed rear fender, is parked on the bank. OUCH is painted on the fender. Grady chews on the sweet end of a blade of grass. He enters the town and finds a parking space before a movie theatre. There are no pictures on the poster advertising the film. There are black stars painted on the sidewalk. The day yawns before Grady. He might go to a movie, perhaps not today but soon. He feels aimless and wasteful and anthropomorphic. The theatre seems a greater orphan than he. The walls are mildewed. The entranceway smells like a recent excavation. Grady moves off, combing his hair with his hands.

The morning's almost behind us and loss is the less to notice. A group of 4-H children are sitting on a bench outside a supermarket, drinking chocolate milk. One of the little girls raised the steer that brought top price at the county fair. They have just returned from a packing plant. One of the children says, "There was your old Scoobie-Doo hanging there." "There he was." The little girl giggles.

Noon is opening to your touch. Two ladies in Day-glo housedresses are driven into the Garden of Repose by a small man whose smooth head is barely visible over the car's seat. The Garden has no headstones or vain statuary. It is a deep and grassy reprieve on Main Street, dotted with handsome trees. The car stops. Its occupants scan the impressive acreage. The women get slowly out. One holds a piece of paper but its information seems useless. The traffic files by on the street. The living are kept at bay from the dead by a hedge of oleander. It is highly toxic but attractive. Children have been poisoned by carrying the flowers around in their mouths at play. It makes an efficient hedge. Behind it there is almost silence. The women wobble on their high-heeled shoes. One sings a few words of an old gospel hymn:

"But none of the ransomed ever knew
How deep were the waters crossed,
Nor how dark was the night that the Lord passed through
Ere he found his sheep that was lost."

She coughs. They are Baptists come with a pot of geraniums
for a distant relation. An attendant floats by, seated on a purr-
ing motor. They extend the paper to him. He studies it and
turns around in the seat of his mower, pointing in the direction
of a tree that's been pruned to a profile of an agonized prayer.
The women wobble off and place their plant on the ground.
Its color is lost in the brilliance of the grass.

Be grateful that everyone's accounted for. Intentions are
being pursued although nothing is being presently instigated.
Everything began a long time ago.

5

. . . *Imagine the happiness of voyaging there to spend our
lives together.* That's not mine. I'm doing my lessons. Translating. Poorly, but pretty all the same. Actually, I'm considered quite good at this re-rendering, a talent that grows in
direct proportion to one's life. You can imagine how troubled
I was to discover, and only recently, that Father's scripture is
based on consonants, the vowels in the original Hebrew not
being clearly indicated. It's clear the problem *there*, although
in itself, it explains almost everything. *To love to our hearts
content, to love and die in the land which is the image of you.*
My ear, however, is terrible. As is my tongue. In France,
I would sound cretinous. I would be misunderstood. My

simplest request would be denied through fear and puzzlement.

You know the old joke—a gentleman goes into a store and wants to buy *une capote noire* out of respect for his recently departed wife. Oh, they still laugh at that one, you bet. I first heard it at the age of nine, a little darling with a bottle of valve oil and a coloring book in her trumpet case, the only girl in the band. We were playing patriotic songs and the story was rendered interminably at the time by the Exalted Ruler of Sebago Lake Lodge of Elks, B.P.O.E. No. 614. It was not intended for our ears of course. Even if it was, how could we have understood it? I'm just recollecting the moment is all.

I played second and almost never had the melody. The boy who played first later blew off his lap on the Fourth of July. *Aimer à loisir*. Lovely, isn't it. I'm dawdling on the porch swing of the sorority house. A sister lies folded messily on the other end, reading a volume on necessary proteins and table settings. She has pimples on her upended thighs but her face is as smooth as a waxed car bonnet. Under her blouse, she has rigged a complex padded harness to her bra so that the sweat won't show. The sun's like lemon juice, splashed across the sky. It's so prevalent, it's really nowhere to be seen.

The sister is eating maraschino cherries from a jar. I have told her many times that they'll be the end of her. They're our only words with one another. I tell her that because of them, someday, someone will sadly have to cut it all out—sphincter, kidney and ovaries. Inside, she'll be all smushy like a pear. She disagrees. She likes them because they have no pits. The porch is littered with ants and stems.

I'm having difficulty *ton souvenir en moi luit comme un otensoir*. I close the book and idly watch the avenue that winds up into the college buildings. I am content here, warm and dopey from the sun. Inside the house, the fans are turned on and small balls of dust and hair float out the open door.

The light pours through the leaves of the orange trees. The mail is delivered. The housemother appears, collects the letters and sorts them. She turns her head carefully and then swivels her shoulders around after it. It is as though she had bones webbed in her throat. I get no mail. No one knows where I am. The housemother has received a tiny box of detergent and a Corn Flakes coupon. She's enormous. Which brings to mind, "Inside every fat man is a thin man trying to get out" . . . which I've never understood. Not only that, I would go so far as to say that it isn't even true. It's not a question of getting out at all. One's true nature must be considered. It's a question of performing one's role.

The housemother's dog is eating ants. She pries him away with her foot and they re-enter the house side by side. Her dress is as big as a bedsheet. As Father said, *it is not we who live but the god who lives within us.* The housemother and her skinny god retire.

I swing on the swing. I'm a little bored but that's acceptable enough. It's my second season here. I'm a fugitive, you might say. A vacationer from the future. I'm taking time off and may never take it on again. I'm getting my strength back and don't want to discuss it. I'm in an awkward position, you see. The first thought I had as a child was not an enlightened one, thus all my subsequent thoughts have been untrue. I'm doing very well now though, thank you. I'm getting back my sense of reality. In the sorority house, the girls wash one another's hair and play cards. Bridge, which is supposed to be good for the mind. We have parties and dances and so on, and we have meetings in the cellar which are conducted according to parliamentary procedure. Our colors are maroon and white, our pin an inverted triangle, a sliver of diamond at each tip—moral, social, intellectual, good deeds, femininity, order—a plastic pubis, respected by none. Our motto is

THAT WE MAY BE PURE ENOUGH FOR HIM

All the sisters fuck like bunnies.

They work out after supper, splashing and panting. Trying to find themselves. I've tripped across them many a night, practicing. A rolling eye, a shaking wrist, a tapping foot . . . It's enough to scare the pure yell out of you, the earnestness with which they go about it.

They tried once to bring a boy in, to service us all. The first of every month, along with the bills and the grocery order. A pleasant enough boy, though his nostrils were overlarge. The hairs blew like wheat as he'd come down for a kiss. Distracting. And there was a whistling noise, a sound like plumbing. I don't know. The sisters complained and soon ceased to use him altogether. It just didn't work out. These girls have to be in love, after all. They kept him on but he grew surly. This was before my time. Now he's gone. And we're back to the old mitt and hiss.

I've been away for a year and a day, just like in the fairy tales. That first month, the heat was marvelous. I was fainting constantly. My soul cringed before it, my heart sweated and shrunk in my chest. I became all matter, lush and blameless, turning into the sun. I had been the perfect child—motherless —and now I was the ideal young woman. All tanned meat, carefree and compliant. Yet I find myself performing as he would want me to, though I hardly ever dwell on Father any more. I use the doggerel, of course, which can't be helped. But he is so constant! His pursuit in my head and my heart stops only long enough to show me that it is going on still.

Yes, I'm going into my second year. Like the alcoholic, I'll age myself through abstinence. I've even learned a harmless thing or two. In the summer, I worked in the dirtiest little Dairi-Whip in the South. The practices that went on there! My God. I left to become a cocktail waitress in one of the town's finest restaurants. Where even more terrible things occurred. Why, I've heard them pissing in the Rhine wine. Jizz in the béchamel. Running sores in the cherry flan. I let

it all ride. Who am I to bubble the globe of the ordinary life?
My only concern was that Father would enter and demand
to be served. He sent his surrogates, I know, but never himself. What's a girl like you doing in a nice place like this,
they'd say. Actually, I've never seen a man who resembles
him in any way, but if Father's the Shepherd, then we're all
his willing lambs.

You've a nice face, dear, they'd say. You bring to mind a
girl I loved once and lost, and what are you doing after this
place closes and you've washed your lovely hands?

When you think of life's routine . . . They'd always have
to make a remark about Entree Six: Red Snapper, Hush
Puppy and Cole Slaw, our luncheon special all for only $1.35.
They'd have the same attire—seersucker jacket, black pants,
white shirt—and the same amusements in their linty pockets.
Comb, nail clip and a roll of Life Savers in assorted flavors.
I believe that 98 per cent, if not more, of all Life Savers in
America are sold to middle-aged men out to turn a trick. I
can't understand why God made every tiny snowflake differ-
ent and all these men the same.

Yet I'd attend to them for I'm passing the time while I
recover. I'm just taking this opportunity to get better. Yes,
we'd go out, these patrons, these consumers, and myself.
Down to the race track and a bottle of Mums. Scratching at
me beneath the clubhouse table as though I were a flea. Each
time they got up they shot their cuffs and grazed me while
passing. Father sees all this. He imagines that I'm doing it. I
must confess, I used to see him everywhere. On the phone and
in my sorority sisters' heartshaped lockets. On some mornings
when the air is very clear, windless muggy mornings when I
feel my head earnestly trying to repair itself, I can hear him
tracking me. It's a sound like a hymn. Pale. Full of rectitude.
And I'm distressed because I see that even when I cheat, I'm
losing.

But the summer vanished and now it's the fall. I'm rocking

on the swing as though in my dotage, watching the students leave their classes and spill across the lawns, a pretty amoeba washing up the walks, cutting across the grass, which is cut out like cookies in the shape of Greek letters.

It's accurate grass, not a single weed, all the roots and rhizome stacked in the gutters. This whole estate, this college acreage, once belonged to a madman. He had a circus quartered here. You can still see the lions' paw prints on the concrete rim of the swimming pool, and stranger things still and some not so strange. What acts! Elephants, bears and Siamese twins truly from Siam. Silhouette artists and palmists. A man with a tattooed eye and another with an organ growing directly from his ear. Actually it looked more like an infant's pacifier, but who would come to see that? They billed it as his organ.

He's around still, a soldier of fortune.

Many of the old performers return. Dwarfs and gorgeous ladies. Noodle Man came back before leaving for Fez forever. Nine feet tall and one hundred and three pounds. He went into the Student Union and had a cup of tea. I missed seeing him, however. Oh yes, they love the returning, even though it breaks their hearts. The place is a tomb. The menagerie is buried everywhere. Even so, all the structures are in gay colors. You can see it glowing beneath the fresh cheap paint that the maintenance men have applied.

Now I see an aerialist, walking his Doberman bitch. The bitch is in heat, flagging everything in sight. The aerialist is old, bald and handsome. Perhaps he is a juggler, he has a sequined groin. He passes very closely to the house. He has pierced ears but no earrings. The dog pulls him along enthusiastically. She'll outlast him. I wonder what will become of her.

There's quite a mob in the streets now. Boys with bright bandanas like apaches. Girls in tennis skirts. The noon siren on the firehouse begins to blow. Everything is drenched in sun. It's like a festival! In the air are chemical experiments and kites and tennis balls. And in the middle of it all walks Father. He's walking slowly, as though for amusement. I'm not startled for I knew he'd come. Redoubtable Father, it's him all right. Ablepharous Daddy. There's no need to ask anyone whether my recognition is true. I leave the porch and run up to my room, and come back down again with my camera. No more than half a minute has gone by. I'm not a year old now, no, I haven't gained a day. I'm just a tiny thought now, rocking in his sperm and then I go back even further than that. I'm nothing but bloodless warmth like the hot yellow beak of a bird.

He's looking at the porch, at the still trembling swing. There's a red claim check tied to his small and battered leather bag. His coat is rumpled. He turns his lidless eye on me.

Le temps gagne sans tricher. C'est la loi.

I go to him once more, coyly as a bride.

6

In by seven and out by eleven, as the laundress says, and we have to be out of here by noon or we'll be charged for another day. From the window there is a view of the street. This is the parade route when there are parades, which there is about to be. It is not a fashionable place. It is lodging for those who seek relief and not amusement. It is a way station for those who haven't traveled for quite some time. It's in a different class entirely from the motels on the beaches with their Hawaiian bars and their swimming pools. Off to one side of the courtyard is a ping-pong table. Over

the door to the office is a sign, WE ENCOURAGE YOUR IN-
SPECTION. Which is curious, for surely, many times over in
America, there are those good people who check out before
in, but they do not come here. This place is inhabited by
men who lay tile, newspaper reporters nightly eating chicken
and drinking wine on the tufted bedspread, the boys who
bait the hooks on party boats. This is no place for gifted
lovers like ourselves.

All the lights are orange to keep away the insects. Father
doesn't unpack his suitcase. He draws things out of it se-
cretively. I never had a secret of my own. They were all
Father's and he kept them for both of us.

Where is Grady? I am not acquainted with him yet. He
is down in Artifact I, on the campus, studying. Soon he
will want to love me. His hands will grip my waist, his lips
move across my stomach. . . .

Pardon me, I am so inept at identity. Why is this girl
here? Was she a foundling? Had she been ill? She sat on the
edge of the bed. Father stood by the coin TV. Was he a
visitor? Was she? The veins in her eye pits were white, her
cuticles colorless. She'd been sick. Not blood enough to even
hemorrhage. Presuppurative puberty. Spreading decline like
a citrus tree. Would take years to run its course.

And Father says, "You come on home where you belong
and stop this crazy dreaming. You're from me and of me."

"Yes, Daddy," I say, "you know me better than God
himself."

"I do," Father says. "You're my pretty darling dreaming
girl and I was with you at your hour of birth and know
all about you." And he looks at me so sadly disappointed,
with a bleak cheer and a meek look. He brushes his long
fingers against my cheek, removing, he intimates by gesture,
a bit of sleep from my eyelashes. "What's your liberty worth,
bringing us both to sorrow?"

I look hungrily at the basket of fruit which is, for some

reason, in the motel room on the window sill, crowding the venetian blinds. Father brought it. The sort of thing you give to dim relations or people in sick chambers. Bananas, apples, grapes, pears, oranges, all injected with coloring, lying dumpled in their bed of paper grass.

Also included is a bottle of champagne. Father doesn't drink himself, but he will open it for me.

We are sitting in Fred's Sunnyside Motel. Outside, Fred is examining his collection of air plants, which are hanging everywhere.

Father says, "The truth removes the need for freedom."

"Oh yes, Daddy, I agree."

"What could you be looking for, darling, to go away from me?"

I'm brief. "I'll tell you, Daddy, I was looking for love."

He's looking at me so kindly, but he's weary from the long train ride. One eye closes, but the severed one remains and wanders over me with a vague and sleepy touch. If only I knew now what I knew so long ago . . . And what could one expect from one's own father's gazing? It's the touch of a shadow on the papered walls of the mind. He shakes his head so slowly, I know that I could capture it on film and I fumble for the camera which is all I've brought along. Just me and my broken camera for I've come into this room ownerless as a newborn babe. I had to brush my teeth with mine own finger, I had to trim my nails on the concrete wall, and I'm sitting here in my underwear, for all my little washables are hanging to dry on the shower rod.

Oh, he looks at me so generously. If I could only get this on film! The development of trysts. One could make a fortune, once the processes were perfected. I have my camera but there's fungus in the lens—parabolas of muttony fur both hidden and revealed—which comes from living in the damp, too close to the sea. I still carry it about with me, hoping helplessly that it might correct itself. Even the film in it is no good. It's dated. I was duped. BUY ME FIRST, I'M RIPE. I always do. I have a conscience. I bought it from a failing store, from a failing little man, all blond in the face and the head from his liver, shaking like an aspic as he bagged my purchases. Six rolls and a 35mm used Yashika and all of it useless. The moment I walked out of the store, that film was past its prime and wouldn't print a buttered muffin. And from what I haven't heard, this happens all the time.

Next door, a toilet flushes and there's a giggle and a rustle. We've seen them both, from Number 6, two grinning teens, wearing the same outfits, goofy Geminis. What a job in these places, just to keep the plumbing in repair!

Father steps up very close to me. I feel the chill from his frozen eye and he says, "You'll only do harm here, sweet. This is a terrible town, a town of waste and hate. I saw it immediately. Something is going to go wrong here. I can see the expectation on their faces. Why did you stop here?"

"I was going to go on."

"You were waiting for me." Father puts his hand on my hair. "I took care of you. You were such a lovely child. I used to wash and brush your hair. You always asked me to brush your hair. Would you like me to do that now?"

"I was waiting to go on," I say.

"You come back with me. There's no place to go on to. It's all happened. They're all dead, our little family, all gone." He strokes my hair. He wraps it around his fist. "We only have one life," he says tonelessly.

"I haven't had mine yet."

"You're my sweet little girl," Father says.

I push away from him. My hair runs out between his fingers. My clothes are dripping in the shower. I had hung them up and they were dry but then I'd taken a shower with them hanging on the rod and now they were soaked.

I look through the venetian blinds at Fred. He is an old man, beating on a mourning dove with a garden rake.

"Come over here and sit beside me," Father says. I do. I lie between the bedspread and the blanket. He takes a brush from his suitcase and begins to brush my hair. "When you were born," he says, "I brought you phlox in a white china mug."

"There aren't any phlox down here," I tell him. "The climate's not right for them."

A clock is ticking on the dresser. It lies face down and works only when it is placed like that. I dropped it myself as a child and it broke in that manner. In Spain, I hear, there's a place full of old, expensive clocks. A palace and a room in the palace where they bring all the clocks of value that don't work. The room is zealously guarded. They have guns. They'd kill you if you tried to steal one of those clocks. Father always used to say that keeping time was an affront to God. I am surprised that he has brought this with him.

"What are those flowers outside the door?" he asks.

"Bird of Paradise. Century plants," I say. It is an erotic desert flush against these rooms. A little joke.

"You've been here before, haven't you," he says convincingly.

"Oh no, Daddy."

"Yes. You're one with the art of harlotry and self-deception. You came all the way down here just to prove that you were common as any of them."

My head bobs with the pull of the brush. His hands are long and cold, with a tumble of veins visible. He is ageless. Once I was young but I am growing so quickly now . . . soon I will be of his time and then hardly linger there until I am beyond it.

"Haven't you," he says.

"No, not this one."

"You don't know anything about love. I've tried to teach you but you don't know. What do you think you can give to a man? Or woman? Your mother was . . . the only thing your mother gave me was you."

"There's nothing I can give, Daddy. I was just hoping that I could take a little. A little warmth for a little while."

"You're everything to me," he says. "You're everything short of dying."

"Dying's not so much," I say.

"To those that don't do it. You killed your mother."

My hair is snapping and curling around his fingers. He raises his hand. It follows him.

"Why of course you did, sweet," he says. "She died because she had an evil heart, a vicious jealous eye. We're all weak, I won't deny it, but it was the Devil himself who gave your mother strength to curse me the way she did. I won't accuse you of it, really. She died of rage."

"I think she died by her own hand, Daddy."

"No, love," he says, "she died giving birth. She died by God's own felon's fist. She was always wanting to have children. Can you imagine, she wanted to start them in accordance with the planets. She wanted someone to avenge her, but your mother got no relief and why should we, darling? No relief and no release."

Beside me on a little table is my gum from the night before. I put it in my mouth. In moments it's soft again. Quite usable. With this and a stick I could muster a quarter out of any grate. Were there a grate. Were there a quarter. What would I do with so vast a sum? My thoughts are a child's thoughts. I am a child, lowered into Daddy's lap.

My head rocks backward with the brushing. Lips brush my ear anonymously. I cannot see him. I see instead the open bathroom door where my clothes drip wine-red drops onto the concrete block of the shower stall. The dye gathers in unsightly puddling. I have arrived in this place. All my eclectic studying, worthless. All my babbling with the girls, the bleaching of my black-sheep ways. After my year of earnest infidelity, after scooting my body under the chassis of strangers, under the cologne, the Camel and Lavoris flavor of their case, I have been restored to the death that is all mine, to Daddy in this place. After all those strangers . . .

All those men. Bloodless little charmer aren't you, they'd say. Yes, I'm deep as the Styx. Think you're for special occasions don't you, they'd go on. By any means deliver me from special occasions. I must say they never took me to a place like Fred's. The bedposts did not have the taste of Pine-Sol. Nonetheless, how did it go? they'd ask. They'd kiss with all embellishments. I thought for a moment you'd chipped my tooth, I said, but I was mistaken. It was fortifying, thank you. It was peachy. Never did they offer compensation as far as I could see. Now once a boy had given me a silk tassel of his hair. It was blue. I counted the strands. Thirty-one. I wanted no mistake. The next time there were twenty-nine. I showed the curl to Daddy. He lost it though he wasn't angry. He simply lost it. The wind swept it onto the rocks. You mustn't mention this to anyone, the blue-haired boy had said. I'll send you a can of syrup from the store, he had said. You can make all the Coca-Cola you want. We didn't do anything but play but you mustn't mention any of it . . .

The men were never so poetic. Never a hank of hair. Just a piece of their bone. Oh, later they offered food, it's true. They were always starving afterward. Steak! they'd cry. Oh, steak and beer and hash-brown potatoes! One mentioned blintzes but he didn't mean it. You'd think a man who mentioned blintzes would be an honorable person but he was simply idealistic. Besides his ideas of a gracious life, he had in his pocket the broken part to a piece of his wife's washing machine. Bolts Breach Blintzes. One of Life's Drab Laws. If I treated you supper, he was reduced to say, I'd have to break a fifty-dollar bill to buy the speed nut for the

washer. And when a bill is broken it's shot as far as I'm
concerned. Same time tomorrow?? At the sign of the sleepy
bear with his nightshirt and candle?? I'm so afraid not, I'd
said. Tomorrow it's my turn to close the windows and take
in the flag in case of possible showers.

But this was the exception. Oh meat! my night companions would shout. Onions and gravy! A man must satisfy
stomach and sex and for the time being the last is a happy
fellow. So gracious. The time being what, I'd said. You're
peculiar, they'd tell me gravely, but you're not as bad as
some. My wife irons my underwear, for instance, but she'd
be the last to know what's in there. What about the soul,
I'd say then. I want satisfaction for my soul. The what?,
they'd say. What a live one. Come off of it, you're peculiar,
but I'll try to be of assistance, you just tell me where it
is. We have to get into a state of grace, I'd speak not quite
hysterically but with a nervous edge. I'd speak honestly for
I was not selfish. I wanted to arrive there. What matter did
it make who the driver was or what the vehicle. Why sure,
they'd say, having their little joke, it's just west of Corpus
Christi, but you're confused, you're a mixed-up girl not
knowing her geography, it's right here inside you and we've
been through there before. They'd push their hands inside
my panties. They'd put their own scrubbed knuckles on top.
And what's a funny girl like you doing asking for more. . . .

Father, I am far from home.

"Your mother . . . ," Daddy is saying.

My voice rattles. I begin again. "We haven't spoken of
Mother for eleven years."

"But, darling, she's beside us. She ages with us. Can't you
bring her to mind?"

My clothes will never dry. How can we leave this place?
If we should open the door, we would simply find this room
again. A bed and a man in black brushing a young girl's hair.
And in that room there'd be no door. Just a bed and a man

in black brushing his broken lover's hair. I put my hand behind me. *Trompe l'oeil*. Daddy's face. Never had I seen him take her in his arms.

"She's passed the years with us. No, death never saves us, darling. It would be unnatural for it to save us." His voice is halting, the voice of a fortuneteller, groping.

I reach for a pear. I swallow my gum. The clothes are still dripping mercilessly. Water enough to irrigate a steer. Why did I ever shower after the night? Once my hands were stained with blueberries. Once my hands were brown and wound round with the long pattern of reins. Mother had always bathed me, locking the door. She scoured me, so small and unrepentant. You are a sick and dangerous little animal, she had said. The tub kept filling. The water ran onto the floor, over her slippers. I joggled beneath the washcloth, the clear water turning brown. You should be treated like an animal, put in a stall, in a barn like your filthy horses . . . Strange impassive child. My skin pink with her rubbing. My riding clothes lying in a sour heap. I was so innocent with my pure and perfect love but Mother was weeping. The water dimpled with her tears. You know what you're doing, she had said. It's hideous, unspeakable. She plucked me from the water. She wept and wept, smelling of linen. Then she scoured the tub, down on her hands and knees. Again and again, after sister died, the door was locked, the water drawn. Mother had washed me so many times, so long ago, why would I shower here? I woke up here. Daddy was watching me sleep. And I remember. It was the first evening of the day that Daddy came to get me. We were celebrants. Daddy had found his little girl again and he's begun to bring me home. The champagne was opened. The cork flew into the ceiling. It flew into the rotting roof of the sad motel, and the soft roof split, just enough for an eye to see it, to hold the ball of an eye, and my protection from the starless night sifted down around us.

"And yet still her eyes would be flooded with darkness," Daddy says. "Her knowledge would still be empty knowledge because it was corrupt. She continues beside us, still in the error of her ways." He puts down the brush.

"Live without a suspect, sweet. There are no criminals. Only God's largesse and plan." His voice stirs, rises. "When you were a child, I would hold your hand while you were sleeping. You never had bad dreams when I watched over you. Your tiny curved hand. A baby rabbit. Such a blessing. You were my child."

Mother had dried me with a thin striped towel. Her hands were brief upon me. The water went down the drain sluggishly, as though there were truly substance to it, as though she had actually washed off some of my sin.

HOW LONG WILT THOU FORGET ME O LORD? FOREVER?

I do not interrupt. Daddy is addressing me.

"Such a sweet deep sleep with never any dreams at all when I was beside you, but I couldn't stay there forever. Each night I had to leave and then there was no way of knowing, there was no way I could tell, what rose up to trouble you, what words you heard, what wicked lies came to seem real in the dark."

Yes, Mother had spoken then. I would creep through the house. I would watch them together under the modest glow of a single lamp. They would be in bed side by side. I am ransomed to that vision of comfort, of safety. Mother faced the door behind which I was concealed. I have forgiven her that which I accused her of, she had said. I have no courage left. I have nothing. Once I wanted to save her, to take her away from you, but it doesn't matter any more. I don't even want to save myself any more. I want to suffer. There's nothing else I can do. I want to suffer terribly. I have forgiven her that which I accused her of, she had said, the words hardly words at all but some endless redeemless anguish falling, say-

ing, Why is my child so far away? how did I go into such a
different land . . . but he did not reply. And never had I seen
him take her in his arms.

"I'm going to buy you some new clothes. Nice clothes to
travel in. We'll stay today and go back tomorrow morning."
His voice is bored, uxorial. He goes into the wretched bathroom, takes my things from the rod and stuffs them into
the wastebasket. He opens the door and puts the wastebasket
outside. I am surprised to see the daylight, the street, folding
chairs set up in a rigid row in the distance. In the distance
also is a singular fellow standing beneath a light pole. He
looks like the gentleman on the Beefeater's bottle. Flowered
red jerkin, hammerhead shoes and a kindly self-conscious
beard. He carries a staff. It is all totally reasonable. He is a
float marshal, waiting for his float. I have always wanted to
go off with the fellow on that bottle but this was not my
chance. Daddy shuts the door.

"We have so much to talk about," he says. "Up home, the
herbs from your mother's garden are still growing. The
mint is particularly strong. I think that even now, my shoes
smell of mint." He does not look at his shoes. "Who gave
you that camera?"

"I bought it myself."

"You must come back with me, sweet. I'll absorb the harm
you'd bring to others."

"I never hurt anything," I beg. "I would take the moths
out of the house in my hands, remember? I was a simple
child." The room seems all the darker since he shut the
door on the street. Everything is black. He is in black as he
sits beside me once again. I can almost smell the chemicals,
hear a hose draining in the soapstone basin. Where my clothes
had been, there are now curling photographs, still wet,
dangling from wooden pins. Everything has been recorded.

"How can you forget, darling?" he says. "Why should you
ever want to forget?"

7

I protest, don't I? "Daddy, let me be. There's no one I can hurt." I want a new clear picture so badly I could cry but there is no light in this dingy room. All the pictures there are going to be have been taken.

. . . When I was a child, I also had a camera which I had sent away for and which came directly to me. What a thrill when Mr. Bolt the postman stepped off his red white and blue bicycle and waded through the damaged daisies to our door. I was a darling dangerous child then with my little crazes and habits. Oh, she adores her father, Mother would say as I scampered down the street in his shadow. And only the obtuse would fail to detect the note of sadness there though perhaps I erred on hearing an entire symphony. But what if I should have fallen from Father's silhouette? The sunshine was a pit to me. And even though it was a game, my mouth would fill with drool, my chest would ache as though I'd dropped my heart if Father strode away from me. Daddy's little girl, Mother would say, though it was just words that she was using. As Father would use the holy writ and I, my too literal love, and poor sister her sweet adjustment. Oh poor sister, she never heard the coded humming of the world . . .

Yes, the day of the postman. The sea was all white and furious that morning from a storm the day before and was beating up the rocks and filling the air with a fine spray . . . I accepted the package reverently. It was almost consumed in Mr. Bolt's huge hands. His fingernails were tan and thick as hoofs, shiny and smooth but at the same time a bit

maimed, as though they'd all been crushed. His thumbnail
leapt into an orbit all its own, his one significant feature.
It was half again as long as his thumb. A lovely ocher and
shiny as a writing slate. Perhaps there was something en-
graved thereon. And doubtless from the Scripture. I WILL
MAKE THEE A TERROR AND THOU SHALT BE NO MORE? It's
really not for me to say. Etched with a pin? A reminder
of something that hadn't happened yet. For why else such a
coarse and local epidermis? But then, perhaps it was he who
had the hidden vice. Perhaps he worked with crayons or
played the guitar. Of his face, nothing remains today. Just
the impossible hand bringing me my plastic camera from
Battle Creek, Michigan. And down by the water, on a folding
chair beneath the salt blasted pines, sat Daddy.

Mother was absent then and sister was gone. Just me and
Daddy, like it was and like it would be in a little while, forever.

And I am running in my hand-me-down dress, a dress
that contained far more incident than myself, having belonged to two town girls and then sister before being passed
on to me. A drunk exposed himself when it was worn by
little Lola Roebuck. We had the longest winter in fifty-seven
years when it adorned Jackie Fucillo's ratty frame. And I am
running with my new possession which is shooting out car-
toon images on cardboard the size of a movie ticket.

The moment was mine, I knew, because I grew up all
intuition and no curiosity. There's not a curious bone in my
body. Like clockwork, I grew up with an innate sense of
the proper order of things. I left it to the others to discover
their egotistical sexuality. They were programed for impulse
but lacked true desire. I recall my own schoolmates professing
to enjoy the dopey pleasures of the Tip-O-Whirl in the
bleached grassless playground of kindergarten as they wrapped
their little thighs around the banana seats. I was not affronted
by such behavior. How could I be? I was up to Jeremiah in

my insatiable quest for order. THE HEART IS DECEITFUL ABOVE ALL THINGS AND DESPERATELY WICKED: WHO CAN KNOW IT?

But I was a child and I was running and I've never been prettier than I was that day as I ran so sincerely thrilled, on my long white legs, to Daddy. The world reflected me, the symptom and the disease, as I ran so childishly simple toward him. The sea smoked with its foam and the sunlight fell bone white on his head as he sat beside the leaping water, all rumpled and harangued as he always seemed when he was by himself, wrestling with the Lord. "Daddy!" I said, "Let me take your picture." And of course it is so innocent. An incorruptible request. He shields his lame eye from the wind with a piece of scarf, for it couldn't help itself that eye, it lay open continually, gaping at the world. It has never rested but has only watched, tireless and constant, blazing and cerulean, thick like a muscle.

"Daddy," I cried so adorably.

And he kissed me then, didn't he, he drew me to him as guilelessly as he does now in Fred's Sunnyside?

8

Everyone that has ever loved has loved this way. There is no other way.

9

Father and I are eating in Woolworth's. I am in my new clothes. There is still tissue paper in one of the sleeves. I pull it out.

"We are not going to return to Fred's. We are going to a beach-front hotel. This is our first vacation," Daddy says. "I am not a worldly man, as you know, but I want you to enjoy yourself. We'll take a small vacation every year if you'd like. You look very nice. I remember that you often wore that color. Your mother dressed you in that color because she said it did so much for you. That was her term, but she was quite right. You look lovely."

"Thank you," I say. We are eating a turkey plate. The cranberries come in a microscopic fluted paper cup. They taste like peas. It is not Thanksgiving but it seems that the meal is a return to that sacred gala occasion of home—a perversion of it, a transubstantiation. Father blesses the food, then he gets up and puts the plate on a tray of dirty dishes. He is gaunt and elegant. The hollows of his cheeks had thrilled me.

"In the year when you were gone from me, there were frequent periods when I went without eating for days simply because it did not occur to me."

"Speaking for myself," I say, my mouth full of fowl, "I am hungry all the time."

"You have a very slim and attractive figure."

"Thank you," I say.

Someone knocks my arm and launches my fork against my molar. It's very crowded. We're crammed like mullet in a

net. Beside us is a couple with a baby. The baby has a
I SLEPT ON HOLMES BEACH FLORIDA T-shirt on and is waving
his legs, firing off his legs as though he'd like to be rid of
them. He farts. It's long and bubbling, very satisfactory. The
baby crosses his eyes. All motion ceases. The first sound in
the universe and this baby has made it. "For chrissakes," the
father says, "get him away from the butter." The young
mother does nothing. She picks up a french fry and puts it in
her mouth.

"You know what I want," she says. "You know what I
really want?" The father pushes the seat board away from
him, to the very end of the table. The baby regards us all
furrily and falls asleep, mustard on his knee. "I want one of
them deluxe facial beauty mist saunas and one of them O'Nite
cases. You owe it to me at least for what you've done."

"Where you going overnight," her husband grumbles.

"I intend to do some traveling. You and me are going to
travel right on out of this town."

"Set thine heart toward the highway," Father says dryly.
"Find grace in the wilderness."

"Philemon," I say too quickly.

"No." He is cheerful. "You are trying to be exotic, aren't
you? My little grown-up girl." He pats my hand. Our fingers
make a little bridge. The counter girl sails a rancid rag
beneath it. "Nothing will ever be Philemon," he says.

"A dull letter."

"I suppose you found my letters dull."

"I wouldn't imagine so," I say.

We leave the counter and walk through the store. The
floor is wooden and warped. I feel that I am nailed to a set
of wheels and am careening across it. Father strolls easily.
We pass notions. A fat child bumps into me. "Could you
tell me if I have a stamp on this postcard," he says, "I'm
blind." His friend is bent double over the nougatines. "I'll
sell it to you for a quarter," the chubby says. "Give to the

blind." I careen along. "Hey, blackhead," he hisses, "are you a boy or a girl!"

We reach the door, the sidewalk. The sheriff's posse prances by, leaving shit all over the street. They are followed by an enormous paper and paste alligator. His eyes are telephone spools. The crowd roars.

"What is this," Father asks, realizing the unlikelihood of a satisfactory answer. There is a marching band, composed, it seems, of dandruff. The parade is sad and ambitious and extravagant and mean. There is a dangerous and desirous mentality at work on both the viewed and the viewers but it is so heavy-witted and humorous that no one feels subject to it.

"It's Homecoming." We squint up the street into the sunlight, into the traffic of gargoyles and beasts and athletes. "They march to the bay and they have a ski show and a slave auction and a gourmet booth. They have a barbecue and a bloodless bull fight and a calliope. Then they release twenty-four hundred balloons into the sky."

"We can walk to the hotel," Father says. "I was told it wasn't far." We turn down a side street and, after several blocks, turn again. There's not a soul visible. Some of the shops' doors have been left open. A telephone rings and rings. "It seems as though the trumpets have sounded," he says, "and everyone has answered but ourselves."

"This event is not as popular as the Crowning of the Queen in summer," I volunteer. I see the town suddenly as feckless and sweet, generous and hopeful, wanting only a little spectacle and a sauced pork rib. Nothing's going to happen here. "Last year a national magazine sent several photographers down to cover the Queen pageantry. It was said that they took over one thousand photographs. It was said that they drank over five hundred pineapple gimlets. Nothing was printed, however."

We walk and walk. We can hear the Gulf of Mexico

plopping and smashing, bringing frantic things in with the tide. I am hot. I roll up the sleeves of my blouse, extracting another piece of tissue. Father holds the camera. My hands are damp from holding it. The camera looks unsafe. He is holding it distastefully. It turns its foggy eye. The setting's wrong for sunlight. Everything is wrong. My lungs seem frozen and I am hot.

"Race disappeared, you know," Father says. "He was old and had arthritis so badly. He'd have to be helped to his feet and when the poor dog was up, he'd stay standing until someone laid him down again."

"That happened when I was there, Daddy. It's been a long time since Race died."

"I think he was down by the water. He was probably following a bird and went into the water and the current took him down."

"Well, Daddy," I say uneasily, "that seems as good a way as any other. Actually it could be considered nicer than most."

"You invested in this camera, did you? You've become interested in such things?"

"I know the terms," I confess modestly. He puts his arm around my waist and ushers me forward. The hotel is ahead of us. Decorative boulders. Restful sago palms. Three men are playing bocce on the beach. They wear snug stretch trousers in Easter-egg colors.

THE VOICE SAID CRY. WHAT SHALL I CRY? ALL FLESH IS GRASS.

"It's all a question of chemicals," I say. "Potassium hydroxide, sodium sulphite, phenidone. It's a matter of accelerators, preservatives, restrainers and water."

"I can't imagine why you waste your time on such things," Father says. "I find it most depressing. I have heard that film can be developed naturally in certain highly polluted bodies of water. I have seen the results. The eye of God enraged. A camera is simply not relevant."

"No," I say sadly. AND WHEN THEY AROSE EARLY IN THE MORNING BEHOLD THEY WERE ALL DEAD CORPSES. My camera teeters on his fingertips but he doesn't let it go.

"Let's dispose of it," he says, "this poor substitution of resurrection." He puts it in a planter of succulents. There is a red wasp in one of the yellow flowers of a succulent. The camera appears all pocked with scale. It is a piece of junk.

"Yes," I say. I seem somewhat heavier than before and my hands are uncertain as to how they should handle themselves. We enter the lobby of the hotel. It is spacious and cool. The desk clerk gives a key to Father. Beside him is an extravagant bird chained to a perch. Below the bird is a drink tray with a circle of newpaper cut to fit. On the newspaper are flashy compotes of half-digested fruit.

"If you get too close to Thalassophilia and she bites you, which she may," the clerk begins in a bored voice, "don't . . ."

"Thalassophilia, that's wonderful," I say, rousing myself. I must make the attempt to keep witness. Daddy and I are here and that's all there is to it. Tomorrow will be different but as for yesterday we have been other places and as for now we are here. My womb turns to face its star.

"How can it be wonderful?" the clerk says without surprise. "It is part of the hotel's policy. The owner has other properties in Puerto Rico and Nassau and they too include birds named Thalassophilia. Now if I may continue? If you get too close to her and she bites you, pretend you haven't noticed. Then she will stop."

The clerk and I look at each other with distaste. "Shall we go up to our room and freshen up?" I ask Father primly.

We ascend to our room. It is on the third floor and soars out over the beach, which is empty except for the men playing bocce. All three seem to have achieved an identical degree of skill at the game. No one is winning. They yell at each other without passion in Spanish. There's a knock at the door and Father opens it. "Would you care for luncheon or a beverage?" The tone is intense, funereal. An old man stands in the hall in dyed black hair and milkman-white.

"Yes," Father says. "A bottle of gin and a bottle of lime juice. Water biscuits, paté and a good Brie." He closes the door. "Do you find those young men attractive?" He walks out to the balcony.

"I was watching the porpoises." I point to the water. Between the long sandbar and the shore, shadows move in a complex rhythm. Two rise, rolling their wise sweet heads.

"I wish I had been a very young man for you. I wish you had known me then."

"I have known you always, Daddy," I say dully.

"Why don't you go for a swim? The water looks so inviting. I'll watch you from here. When you were small, I would watch you enjoying yourself and it gave me great pleasure. The water looks so refreshing."

"I don't have a bathing suit." One of the bocce players paws at the beach with his foot like a horse. He throws the dark ball beautifully and it lands dead in the sand.

"You go for a swim and when you come back our refreshments will be here. The towels here are extraordinary. Did you notice them? Like rugs. Do you remember the poor towels we had at home? Your mother was always mending them. And the sheets as well. Tiny stitches. Starbursts of thread. Roses and faces of colored thread. You made up a story for each one and you would tell them to me. But these towels look brand new. And so white. No stories there."

I go out of the room and down the stairs into the lobby. The clerk is standing beside his desk, bouncing on the balls of his feet. The bird is sleeping, folded up on its purple talons. I walk onto the beach, past the young men. Two are standing close together. One is standing farther away, measuring distances with a cloth ruler. I hear a voice, speaking in perfect, musical English.

"John, I saw a muscle of yours on that last shot that I swear I have never seen before."

I walk into the water and continue until the sandbar. I walk over the sandbar and instantly into water up to my neck. My clothes expire. I turn and face the hotel but do not try to find Daddy on the balcony. I stand there for a while. The nice porpoises have vanished. I wallow back to shore. The young men never glance at me. I take a turn around the desk.

"We prefer that swimmers use the service elevator at the rear," the clerk says. I go to the rear. The elevator obediently exposes itself.

"Hey," the clerk says. He has a borrowed, uneasy face as though he chose it off the television. "This bird can shit seven feet flat across the room."

I return to Daddy. Our snack is laid out nicely. Daddy is fixing the drinks.

"That's fine," he says, "that's fine. I want you to have a good time." He calls for someone to pick up my clothes for cleaning and pressing. He rubs me dry and wraps me in one of the sumptuous towels.

"You certainly have developed a way about you, Daddy," I say.

"I want everything to be pleasant for you, darling. I can control it all if you allow me to." He hands me a drink, expertly prepared, gorgeous with crushed ice.

"Drinketh damage," he says, smiling. His jaw twitches. His jaw is clenched. He wears a handsome, expensive jersey. His face and thin arms are hard and white like marble. "It's pleasant here but not for us. You can see that, darling. The sun is bright with malice."

We sit on the balcony. The sun sprawls scarlet across the Gulf. The sea birds are going home. The plovers, the pelicans, sanderlings, terns and ibis stream across the sky. He

slips his hand inside the towel. It falls from my shoulders.
A breeze swims across me and stops.

"This is not my favorite time of day," I say. "Speaking
only for myself, I prefer dawn. Birds drop their eggs at
dawn. It is generally more a time of hope and promise."

"All the promises have been kept," Daddy says.

10

I am swinging in the dreadful hammock of a dream. Whatever woke me has stopped but it will come back again if I am
still. It is the sound of birds, beyond the board and metal,
in the woods. And my foot aches terribly. In the dark, I
reach beneath the blanket and touch it. It is hot and spavined,
the toes spread out in a cramp. For some reason, the baby
needs something that is in that foot. The baby makes strange
demands. It is stronger than I am. *I* am being housed by *it*.
I am being fashioned in the nights that will bring it to term.
And it is I who feel the exhaustion of journey. Not it. What
would it know? It is myself who lives in darkness, slowly
becoming aware, and it is the child who moves resplendent
in the sunlight, beyond restitution in the sunlight.

The child is my dream of life. I harbor its progress and
am victim to its whims. Gestating is like being witness to a
crime. And I am furtive, I must admit. We all look furtive.
My suggestion is to confess to everything. Once, on the street
here, shortly after I arrived, the FBI spotted me in a laundro-
mat. I thought the manager was giving me the eye because
his machine was acting oddly. Clanging and banging and
taxiing around its filthy slot. I tried to ignore his mean and
greedy eye. He thought the reward was his. I maintained my

poise by reading an agricultural bulletin that was available
for patrons. The article I was engrossed in concerned the
rat

Eat—hide—gnaw—scatter filth—start fires—gnaw—eat—breed
—hide! THAT'S THE LIFE OF A RAT!

And then these fellows slipped around me, crisp as pudding.
Smith their names were, and Smith. When Smith showed me
his card, he exposed the weighted exercise belt around his
middle. Smith, on the other hand, was not a vain man. He
conducted the questioning. "Howdjew find Jessup the last
time you was there," he said. "They sure changed that town
some."

"Jessup?" I say.

"You let your hair grow out," he said. "I gotta say it ain't
becoming. But a girl like you. I can't imagine you traveling
alone. Where'd your boy friend be? The boy what done the
carving? I'm sure a little thing like yourself wouldn't have
done that carving."

"Sheeit," Smith said, "I bet a little girl like you can't be
aware even of the enormity of her crime."

Unfortunately, something or other had run in SOAK. My
clothes were the color of gasoline.

"Whyn't we just check up on your little niceties here,"
Smith said. "Blood's harder'n tar to get off your clothes."

Smith tugs a bit at his crotch. "We might add that your
boy's caught now. It was him that told us where you was.
He's up there in Tampa spilling the beans and he don't give
a pig's piss for you at this point."

"Wrong girl," I say. And of course I was. They wandered away. The manager said that he wasn't responsible for
clothes left in the machine and if I didn't get them away
he wouldn't be responsible. Of course I knew what Smith had
been referring to. A dreadful story. Chopped up someone's
lover and sent him to Coconut Grove in a casserole dish.

But that was when I first arrived. I am sought after, accosted, but never found. Is that not how you find it?

In any case, now I am here rubbing my foot, twisting my toes and wearing a spotted nightie. I can see nothing in the room, but outside the birds are singing and so it must be morning. Or perhaps it is the afternoon of the day before for I can't place falling asleep. I can make out shadows in the room. There's a small window over an easy chair but it is stuffed across with webs, hives, cocoons and silky sacks. There is also a large X taped on the window with adhesive as though the window were condemned. Almost no light enters, but there is enough, for the moment, for me to see Grady in the easy chair, sitting with both feet on the floor, his knees apart. I like seeing him there and perhaps the knowledge of Grady being there is what woke me. The first time we met, I woke up and he was there. Most people that later one discovers are significant to one's living are met through glimpse and carelessness, through stumbling brush and grope. They expose themselves gradually in serial form. Not so with Grady, my groom. He rose beyond reproach in the stink of the old movie house, his voice in my ear an overcurrent to the thud and pound of repair within the walls (for they were renovating the old movie house, redesigning it for a more sophisticated and lucid audience) and his hand on my shoulder was strong . . .

I want to have him love me. The fact that he does already troubles both of us. I prop the pillow behind my back and begin a conversation. The room is close. I've spilled some scent and it's in the carpet. I open my lips and the words enter my furred mouth.

I begin to tell him a story. Many times I have talked but I have never finished what I wanted to say. To be frank, I have never begun what I wanted to say. I have discussed something else. But now it is as though my whole life has fashioned itself for this moment which is, of course, true. It is as though my whole life is dependent upon the reply to this moment, upon the recognition of it, its application and success. When I complete not telling this story, my life will begin.

"An annal of crime," I say and curl up within my stained nightgown, comforting myself as though it is I who am being told the tale rather than being the taleteller. There is a glass of cold coffee on the floor. I hear it fall as the bed, on its casters, grinds against it. The child redistributes itself, opening and closing itself like a butterfly. I say,

"In the French mountains in the sixteenth century, an eleven-year-old girl was married and some years later the wedding was consummated and she had a baby boy. She was very much in love . . ." I stop and inquire about the hound, whether there are any indications that it's returned. I fall asleep but in no time I am up, pummeling my foot. I mention a party we went to at the home of one of Grady's friends. There were twenty people there, the same little band that are always present at the parties we attend. Expecting little from these gatherings, it nevertheless gives us no pleasure when our suspicions continually prove correct. Some of the people are students at the college but they do not recognize me for I've removed my sorority pin. All that remain are two tiny holes on the right side of every blouse. They don't know that I am pregnant and they don't know that I am married to Grady. At one of the parties, a man fell against me and knocked me flat. I had hoped that something might come of it, that the baby would be expelled. Nothing came of it except that now the man comes to me at every party and speaks to me earnestly. He wears tight jerseys with alligators on them. Tiny alligators like jewels. At the party most recently, he came to me in the kitchen where I was drinking gin and eating from a shallow dish of hamburger relish. He was an older man from the college, possibly even an instructor. He had sweat on his hairline, above his lip. He embraced me and I turned rigid. A camouflage. I became part of the sink and tiles. He pressed his mouth against me and wedged the plastic glass of martini between. Beyond his head, on rough drawing paper, I saw crayon renditions of a child's moon, house and railroad train. I pushed him fretfully away. He was the host. He pushed me back, slightly.

"Well, kiss my coccyx," he said. He left with dignity, his ass high up his back, like many basketball players I have seen, playing in their prime.

I tell Grady this and slump down in the bed again, turning on my side. The sheet's pulled back and I rest my cheek on mattress ticking. My mouth moves against a small cloth tag attached with a safety pin. Contents Unknown. Well.

At the window, tiny dots of light shine through the mess. A spider pushes a leaf out of its web. Grady's told her that there's something in a spider's web that mends a cut. Something in the spinning juice. If I should smash one of my limbs through this window, there'd be nothing that wasn't fine. Damage and repair would be simultaneous. The healing is working out there before any wound that needs it. This is the way it's always been, I suppose, but never, before Grady, has it been true for me.

I move raptly on the bed. I am an impediment to our lives together. I want to tell him. The moments pass. None of them are correct. The baby goes about its mysterious business. It has formed eyebrows, a lung, certainly a sex. I want to tell him. I will say, "Perhaps the baby isn't yours." That is nothing. He suspects this, I know, and yet he has said nothing. My womb is a disease, a benign tumor. I despise my womanliness which carries its sickness about with it, inherent and innate, as though it were success. How can a man know such dyscrasia? I move back against the pillows. The light is so bad that it obscures my speech.

If I begin the story and do not finish it or if I begin it and do not tell it properly in the way it happened, in the time and the place and the circumstance, in the correct sequence of results, will it not then persist like a drowned man, going on to haunt the sea?

I am trapped within this monstrous child. Each day I become precisely less what the unborn has become. If I tell Grady, will I release myself like a virus upon his loving world? The child is not Grady's. That is nothing. That will cause no conclusion. He assumes responsibility after the movie house, not before. I know this. His pride lies in acceptance, renewal and life.

I am shivering for now I am fully awake and it is cold here. I reach down and turn the dial of our small electric heater. Its red grille and smell and clatter give the impression of warmth. I am only a nest and so cold. The child rocks in its sunlight, warm and breathing in its egg.

"I almost died the other day," I say.

"That's ridiculous," Grady says.

"No, I had some bullets in my pocket and I forgot about them and I was baking chicken and the oven was very hot. I was working around the oven and the bullets were in my pocket."

"That's ridiculous," he says, "they never would have gone off."

I get out of bed and limp toward him on my aching foot. Grady does not sit in the chair at all. It is his jeans, his sweater scattered realistically in the chair. I pull on his jeans, retaining the nightgown over them, and limp into the kitchen, skirting the dog's dish. I heat a pan of water, making some coffee with part of it and using the rest to soak my foot. The dog hasn't been at the trailer for days. He sits a mile away, at the juncture of an overgrown logging rut and the blacktop that goes into town. He sits beneath an enormous tree. When we slow the car for him, he regards us pleasantly enough but he does not get into the car, nor does he look after us as we drive away. The hound is waiting for his owner to come pick him up because he is a good redbone. And good redbones are trained to return to where they were released and to stay there forever.

I miss the dog. Only yesterday or so, I walked to the blacktop and brought him some food—fatty ribs and mash that we feed the ducks. He sits in the shade beneath the tree. In front of him is a deep ditch that catches and holds the afternoon rains. He had been very happy at seeing me and he'd eaten the food like a fellow of means and leisure and he had taken time out to watch me as I sat watching him. But he didn't follow me home. And I know he never is about to. He has his own fidelities and they don't include us.

I dry my foot, and go outside. Grady has built a fire in an old washtub and is sitting before it, throwing straw and dead branches on it from time to time. Beside him are four ducks, rearranging themselves continually on a patch of straw. They are dull barnyard ducks of unstable numbers for some wander off across the river and are eaten. At times, I collect their down which is bleakly sensual and useless in quantity. They set up a terrific racket as I approach and fly off into short trees.

It's cold and the fire burns cleanly in the air, without smoke. Sometimes, sharks come up this river by mistake. I lumber toward Grady, awkward as a cub, bumping against him remotely, an unburnt branch on a cant from the fire, snagging my nightgown. Some things cannot be forgiven. Grady is not the one to forgive.

I crouch behind him and put my arms around his chest. Grady stirs the fire and the flames snapping in the weak sunshine are blond as his eyes. "How are you two this morning?" he asks.

"We're fine," I decide to say. "We're coming along nicely."

He shares a piece of bread with me. I take it and push it into the shape of a pony. Just as I crimp its mane, it trots away.

11

Don't look, Father says.
I struggle for effect but my intention never lay in looking.

12

I say to the ducks, "Weather cold enough for you?" My
life is prudent, recessive and dark. Every day is Christmas Eve.
I talk to the animals but they do not talk to me.

"It's going to warm up," Grady replies instead. "Move up
twenty more degrees by noon."

Noon. The threat of another pretty day with my Grady.
He speaks with joy of little things. He tosses his head and
laughs.

"Cold's what makes the orange orange," I say positively.
I can learn anything.

Grady's hands are warm from the fire. He turns. He unzips
the jeans I am wearing and rubs his hands across my stomach.
"Little fish," he says.

I smile. For a moment there are just the two of us. For
a moment, this is the way it is going to be. Daddy dies with
our happiness. The baby dies. Poor baby. Rather he curls up
like a flower, he goes back into his impossible night.

We are smiling. This was before the accident. Before he
was corrupted and our life together lost. He did not want to

touch upon my past. He did not want to know if my favors had been freely given. He was not interested in the life I had before him. Instead, he tried to take me with him, through each day. He used time masterfully. It minded his whims. He spent it conscientiously, for both of us. We never returned to the movies after we met. I dislike movies, he told me that very night. Everything takes so long, he told me. He wasted nothing. Nothing was spent on him without ample reimbursement. I see him as a little boy watching fireworks. Oh, they are stunning, grand. He approves of each one. He gives all his blessing. He does not allow a single one to bloom and fire without his breath of praise. He never allows his attention to wander. He sees through to the finish. I see him as a little boy, very grave, tireless in his respect.

No, nothing escapes his notice and he studies, in great detail, everything but me. He is in love with me. I am beyond his code.

Look at the deer, he'd say. We would be soaring in the Jaguar under a cathedral of trees. It would be night. The lights would find everything, but not for me, never for me. Look, he'd say and slow, but they'd be gone. They love cigarettes, he'd say. They're after the stubs that travelers throw out.

Look, he'd say. Look. He squeezes my shoulders. His tongue darts lightly down my neck. His eyes burned with happiness. He is proud of his wide smooth sex. It is fragrant with soap. He is assured of the sweetness of life. It sings to him.

Look, he'd turn my head gently. An old man drifts down the river in a white wooden boat. He wears a big flat straw hat and three sweaters, buttoned to different levels. He has a deep canvas bag for the fish hanging from his shoulder. He moves regally by. The line flicks lightly through the water flowers, into the deep pockets of the ancient river.

Everything is pleasing. There is a Ferrari. There is a mule.

There is a tiny Mennonite girl at a Whopper-Burger. She
has been picking fruit. She wears a bonnet and a long brown
dress and she smells of citrus. She eats her hamburger with a
knife and fork. It takes forever. There is a woman wetting
the stones that ring her flower garden. That is the most satisfactory chore, watering the stones. There is a drumfish,
pounding on the water each night. We go out in the boat.
The fish rises beside us. It sounds like a gigantic frog. He follows the boat, he nudges it. It is a magical fish, an enchanted
fish that will grant your wish. Grady wishes for nothing.
I always wish that he had taken me that night after the movie
house and never looked for me again. We were silent. More
so than I'd ever been with the strangers. I thought that I
would never see him again. We drove, we drank, we stopped.
We drove again. He lay me down gently in the darkness
beneath some sweet smelling pines. His hands trembled. We
drove by water, I could smell it. We heard the chuck-
will's-widow. We went back through the town. Tomorrow,
he said. I was startled. Tomorrow, he said. Tomorrow, next
week. But I was so weary, so lost. I did nothing to prevent him
from saying . . . it's true I wasn't paying attention. My mind
was going home with Daddy . . .

Just hours before, Daddy had boarded the train. Behind
the coach he'd entered was a snow-white refrigerator car
bearing orange juice for the rickety North. He was the only
one departing. I was the only one left behind. Now, once this
station had been one of the busiest in the state. There were
huge crowds coming to see the circus. And an elephant was
killed right here on these tracks though there is no plaque, for
it was not Jumbo who was killed in Ontario but another elephant.

But there are no crowds at the station any more. It was early
but the heat was rising. You could smell the fertilizer they'd
packed around the sidewalk lily plantings. The town was dirty
and had a milky cast. The street was trashy from the parade of

the day before and as we waited, Daddy and me, the work crews were making their way toward us slowly, cleaning up, the prisoners of the county in their gray trousers and shirts with the wide blue stripe down the side. Daddy was holding my hand in his. My hand was empty. Or rather, I was not holding his hand in mine. He brought it to his lips but did not kiss it. I could see our image in the locked windows of the station. I was in a position to notice this. Come with me, he'd said. There's nothing here for you to leave behind, he'd said. Come with me while it's still that way . . . the image of my hand moved back. The train wound through buildings and appeared abruptly and then wound through buildings and departed abruptly as well. The train didn't even come to a full stop. Daddy glided on. The train sank dreamily away. The crews came sweeping and bagging up the street, nice boys, fresh faces, up for stealing copper wire or beating on their women's fellows.

"Yo," the captain said to me. He smacked his shotgun against his thigh. The boys phalanged by, leaving everything pretty behind them. I could hear birds beginning their day. The street lights went off simultaneously and the morning became a healthier color. Opposite me, the proprietor of a U-Rent-It-All put out his wares on the sidewalk. Mowers and beds and automatic nailers and hoists. And then he brought out an aluminum ladder that he would rent you too and he climbed up on it and put a new combination of letters in place on his glass marquee, a new message on his fresh new day. RENT YOUR CONVALESCENT NEEDS. His little boy came out and voiced some easily accomplished desire in a piping screech and the man descended, folded up the ladder and leaned it against the storefront.

And the letters there you know, the portable letters there so ominous and . . . took me home again. Yes, I was home, waiting for Daddy. It would take him two days and three nights to return but I was there already. Years ago. I am a

darling toddler assisting him with the slate letters on the
church bulletin board. I choose from a sturdy box that still
smells faintly of apples. A remarkable box. It can make any
word that anyone can think of. It is limited only by me. I slide
the letters along the rusting runners, following Daddy's directions. He is my only consideration. It is summer, it is
spring. Daddy and I seduce the mornings. I weigh forty-one
pounds. Fifty-seven. The earth shimmers with the yearnings
of God. Daddy guides my hand. I LAID ME DOWN AND SLEPT I
AWAKED. My thoughts were his thoughts. Psalms, I would say.
Yes, darling. It is raining. It is a day of high cool sun fading
my hair. Song of Solomons, I say, Genesis. Yes, sweet, he
would say. Life's simple as it seems for we love but once,
darling. The rest is dissolution.

I walk across the street and into the rental place. Something
clicks as I cross the threshold. Something's counting me. The
little boy sits on a rental hide-a-bed. What time is it? I ask.
His mouth is full of jelly. Ten till, he says eventually. That's
wonderful, I exclaim. And what's your name? Rutt, he says
peacefully after a long pause. The proprietor emerges. Am-
brose, he says, what does this lady want. The time, I intercede.
He jerks his head in the direction of a big wall clock. Feast
your eyes, he says. I go out onto the street again. I walk a
little. I buy some coffee. For lunch I buy some wine. I know
the time. I spent the day in darkness. And at the end of it, I
met my Grady. But as I say, I wasn't paying attention.

Look, he said to me then, I'd like for you to stay with me
awhile. I have a place. He talks to me in darkness. My hips
rub on grass. I have everything for you, he says, or I can get
is tomorrow. Tomorrow. Next month.

Grady.

I did not demur. I entered his life. Coma calling. Now
Grady sits on the riverbank. The fire sparkles. He gives my
belly one more caress. It's sculpted and heavy as a wooden
pear.

"Come to school with me today and at noon we'll go to the beach," he says. "We'll swim. We'll buy some bread and cheese. We'll swim and eat and sleep."

"At noon. *Juste milieu.* When the sun is up."

"And so am I," he says.

The fire burns. So do all of God's children.

13

Grady enjoys going to classes. He wants to make a fine life for us. He works very hard. There is going to be the baby. He sees other babies. He sees a fantastic tree house on his beloved river. He will design it himself. He will build it himself. Inside it will be leather and wicker and aluminum and wood. We will have pet otters that will bring us fish. We will have lime and lemon and grapefruit and orange trees and ladybugs to eat the aphids. We will have a telescope and study the stars. We will have an herb garden. We will have a Land Rover and a De Tomaso Mangusta. We will live in our fantastic house. Then we will travel. We will get a motor sailer. Go to Greece. The Pacific. Go everywhere. Then we will return. Our children will be loving and handsome. The orchids will grow on the trees. Everything will always grow around us beautifully. We will always be in love.

Of course this is in the future.

I tell him, "Love, love, I have no future." I say this. I say, "When they were casting the Weird of my life, that third sister was out on an apéritif."

Naturally, he does not agree. There is the future of this day, for instance. I've promised him I'll go to school today and I've dressed and I have. We are in town, going to school,

but first we stop in a hardware store, for he has to buy a tool
or two, for his Jaguar, for his class. I wander off to the seed
bins. They're lovely. St. Augustine, Argentine bahia, centi-
pede, zoysia, Tiflawn bermuda. I plunge my hands into the
bins. It's wonderful. I worm my hands around, up to my
elbows. Tiny slippery busy beads. A clerk comes up. He
points to a sign. "They'll have to be baked now," he says
angrily. "You've contaminated them." Insulted, I buy fifteen
pounds. I turn out my pockets. I give him every cent. "A good
choice," he says, handing me a sack. "Low maintenance.
Will survive total neglect." Grady's at my side. He's bought
a picnic basket. He puts my sack inside it.

"It's pasture grass," he tells me as we leave.

"Let's make a pasture!" I am so enthusiastic. Where will we
plant it? Who will come to watch it grow? I imagine already
friendly beasts following us down the street, birds and bees
and grazing things. But I become weary. My feet lag. What a
responsibility, this grass! What a burden! I have poisoned it.
The man said so. I am so destructive. My hands are hatchets.
Daddy had told me this. He'd said, AND WHERE THE SLAIN ARE
THERE IS SHE. Job. He'd said, It's happened and it's ahead of
you, forever and ever.

We enter the college grounds.

I sit down beneath a banyan tree though I only want to be
back in the trailer or sitting in the Jaguar, at rest, resting.
Grady kisses me good-by and enters the chemistry building.
He turns before he opens the door, his hair all smacked
askew with water, heartbreaking as a grebe, and waves at me.
I wave back, grateful for his familiarity. He drops from sight
into forestry and mathematics.

He has a theory for the animals, with which by equation
the earth can be saved.

I have a malapropism or two.

The leaves on this tree are long as baseball bats. Many of
the roots haven't rooted yet but stick out stiff as wires, at

eye-level, from the trunk. Everything's so colorful and fecund. A bellowing order and thoughtful rhyme. Noah's Ark. A path for every foot to trod. A trot for any taste. Students move heartily by with the faces of winning contestants. Everyone's a winner here! The South is Cracker-Jax!

"Hello!" they cry. I blink.

"Hiyew," a girl says cutely as a comic book. "Why we haven't seen you for quite some time. My boyfriend's sleeping in your bed."

"O.K.!" I cry cheerfully. I am speaking too loudly. I know this girl. Debbie Dow. Before I'd gone off with Father five months ago and then immediately with Grady, five months ago, I had known this girl. A sister. With a pin and a barrette of hammered silver weighing down her head.

"Those your sheets?" the girl asks. "Or are they from the service? Better get yourself some new sheets when you come back. Are you coming back? Jean's wearing your clothes. Half of them are in her closet now."

Her teeth do not grow out of the gums but are perched there as though in afterthought. Other than this, the girl's face is wealthy.

So many questions, so much news. "OK.!" I cry joyously.

"Those sheets certainly have had their lives," the girl says. "Those pussycat sheets."

I know this girl. I've seen her squatting for the soap. Rump bumpy as an ugly lemon. I know the boy as well. A baseball player on a scholarship. A pitcher with big ears. What's all this talk about boys and beds? A whore is a deep ditch and a strange woman is a narrow pit. A youth's a rictus and an aging man is ruinous. There's no turnpike to love. Just snares and snaffles. I want to go back, back. But to what?

I will tell this girl instead. I will whisper in her ear's veranda. The girl's head tips expensively, from the barrette. She speaks first.

"There's been some mail for you. One or two letters. I saw them just the other day but they were gone this morning. I suppose you picked them up?"

The girl seems to be shouting at me. From a distance. I look down at the ground, expecting to see a cheeping creek separating us, an unfordable crinkle in the earth. It's almost there. There's a plastic straw on the ground. I pick it up and put it in the new picnic basket. A straw's as good as a cup. One never knows what the day will bring.

"Was that your daddy I saw you with? Down for Homecoming? Down for the water show?"

"Oh, but that was a long time ago," I shout.

"Yes, but that was the last time I saw you," the girl says confidently. "Why wasn't that the Homecoming though? With our float winning and all? What a time Cloyd and I had! We fell asleep and the tide just about took us out."

I think of replies. I discard them all.

"We had champagne in the House after the parade," Debbie persists. "Why weren't you there?"

"That certainly would have been the time to be there," I agree.

"You bet!" squeals Debbie.

"We saw the parade," I say.

"You and your daddy?"

"Pardon me?" I say.

"I find older men sort of frantic myself," dimpled Deb confides.

"What a parade!" I exclaim.

Thousands and thousands of tissues stuffed into chicken wire.

"Better than the Rose Bowl," Debbie ventures.

All that paper! Three thousand trees vanish from Big Cypress Swamp.

"The Toilet Bowl!"

The girl's face is smooth and silly and kind. I am so exhausted now with all this conversation. I want to lie down and put my mouth on the grass. It is a beautiful day. Grady was right. Blue pours through the trees. And it is so still. I wear my bathing suit beneath my clothes. They are wrinkled and old, clothes that Daddy bought me, things I wore years ago when I was with him, walking across the brown crisp ground in the springtime. I try to blink my eyes. Someone's rolled a stone across them. Why is this girl talking to me? Why does anyone ever begin anything when none of it can ever end?

"It's really mostly crepe," Debbie is saying. Of course she does not care for weird stringy me. But she is a sister and the sisters are bound in the solemn ceremony of Omega Omega Omega, linked one to one by their knowledge of the secrets of Catherine who was not only a virgin and perfect in every way but also had her paps burnt away and her head smote off.

Debbie is being gracious. She is exercising her southern self—that is, she does not see rag-tag unpleasant me. She sees no object specifically. She works utterly on a set of principles.

The stone rolls back across my eyes. I open them and then I close them firmly. I would like a glass full of gin and cold orange juice and a few drops of Angostura bitters and I would like to be under the sun on the beach, getting hot and clean. The thought of gin makes me sick but I persist in its conjuring. My stomach turns for I am really afraid. My stomach is no longer my own. It is the baby that my thought of gin repels. I think of Sweet Tit Sue. I am deliberate in restoring her. She didn't touch me. She smelled of shade and wild tarragon growing. She wouldn't touch me. She stood with her arms crossed over her enormous chest. There were plants everywhere, growing in red dirt out of potato chip cans. You're Grady's girl, she said. I'm not about to do anything to mess him up. If you're messing him up it's best he be shut of you, she said. She wouldn't put her hand on me. *Where did he touch you*, Mother had said. She was weeping, she had lost her mind. *Was it here? Here?* Something flew from her mouth and dropped wetly on my knee. Mother was crying. *God.* She shook me. A bubble of sickness rose in my throat. I knows that good boy Grady, Sweet Sue said. It's him I'll do the favors to. You come back here with Grady if you want. The baby was twisting and clawing inside of me. His fear took up the oxygen. Her cabin has one room. Someone drops an egg—a brown one with a tiny fluff of feather stuck to it. It falls and falls. It's not for me, I said. I don't care what happens to me. I sat down on a corner of her beautiful brass bed. Sue made a small rude sound. The sheets smelled of onions. She made me go away. *Tell me,* Mother had said. *Tell me what he did.*

"I must be off," Debbie is saying. "See you round like a donut."

The swollen banyan bloats out around me. I sniff my absent repulsive and wonderful gin. One can feel only so sick after all and I am not really sick. If anyone ever leaves this world alive it will be me, or someone like me, a woman and a lover, bearing a bad beginning in my womb. Kate fecit. When will the bottom be? What joy, the bottom of the pit. BUT HE BEING FULL OF COMPASSION DESTROYED THEM NOT . . . FOR HE REMEMBERED THAT THEY WERE BUT . . . words, words. I must only be silent as Daddy said. I must not tell. And what is the pain of this moment? I am a young thing gripping a picnic basket, waiting for my man. All is sequence and little is substance . . .

"Hullo, Kate." The voice is too familiar. I would know it anywhere, as though I had never had to relate it to a form. "Come back, have you? Had an adventure?" Cords stands over me as though it was she who laid me low. Doreen stands behind her, a pretty little doll with glassy eyes. Cords has bitten her nails down to stubs and wears gloves, trying to break the habit. They are black vinyl gloves and their pres-

ence, so close to me seems apocalyptic. A BAD ANGEL. AN
ANGEL OF DEATH.

"Well, Cords," I say, "you're cutting an impressive shape
this morning."

Doreen looks empty-headedly down. Her hair swings
around her hips. She passes her hand across her neck in a
precise gesture of languor. She smiles at me. Then she smiles
more anxiously at Cords.

Cords says, "You definitely look peaked. Think a picnic
lunch will really perk you up? Picnics aren't for you, Kate.
They're for those with lighter hearts."

"I am waiting for someone," I say.

"So are we all," Cords sighs, "but you do it so drably.
You've dropped out of our sights for months and now that
you're back, you're the same."

"More of the same," I correct her wittily. *Oh, Grady, I
cannot right myself.*

"Yes indeed, you've got all those things you keep thinking
about. All in the past. And you keep chewing on them.
You're choking on them."

"You're right," I say. "I had a bird once. He was a toucan
and extraordinary looking but everything about him was for-
gettable."

"We are speaking of your problem," Cords says, putting
her little finger in the corner of her mouth. She immediately
jerks it away. There is a look that is almost pain on her face.
"These goddamn hands of mine. I've abused them too long
and now they're just blood waiting to spill."

"Icchhh," Doreen says.

"Tender as hell," Cords complains. "Like some of those
poor mammals born without skin."

"Icchhh," Doreen cries.

Vivid Cords. Today she wears a black suit, a mauve linen
shirt with huge soft cuffs. She is striking. The heat has made
tight ringlets of her hair. She is the leader of our sisterhood.

As in most things, the real leader is not the acknowledged head. Our head is a girl with a slight mustache whose mother sends a torte from Cleveland monthly. When motorists scream *dimyerlights* at her while she is driving she thinks that they are from Ohio too and acknowledges them with a cheery thump on her horn. She is seldom heeded, even on her own terms, and has a continual expression of candid disappointment. No, it is Cords who's in the saddle, as it were. It is she who plays big brother to all the little sisters. They run around her thither and there, cooing in their Italian underwear. One size fits all. They do not discuss her with each other. They want her to themselves. She is fashionable. She is smart. The sources and supply of her insults and praise are inexhaustible. The girls clamor for her attention and authority. When she leaves them they feel lovelier and luckier than they had before. They feel relieved and knowledgeable without being wise, like bunnies escaping from a snare.

She exhibits her profile to me. It is as cold and inarguable as a knife. She has never been touched by a man and makes no attempt to conceal her success. Each year she chooses a girl for herself. The choice is never questioned by the chosen. They are without exception beautiful girls. They are usually rich. It was apparent that the moment Doreen walked on campus, Cords would want her. And she got her. Which was not to say that Doreen didn't enjoy the boys. Cords urged her to, for Cords was out to make her the Golden Rain Tree Queen, queen of the town, of the state, of the country.

Doreen is looking up into the branches of the banyan, alternately tossing her hair and twisting her fingers around her necklace. It is a mustard seed in heavy-duty plastic, crouched in the dimple of her throat. It really is.

"I have a notion that we are akin in many ways," Cords says to me.

"Don't be forward." I try to rise in one long and confident motion to my feet, but fail.

"Where have you been?" Cords muses softly. "Canceling issue?"

"Ahh," breathes Doreen.

Cords shakes her head. Her skin is eerily matte flat, lacking blemish or shadow or curve. "No, I don't think so. You're the one with one foot in religion. Think all the little babies are stars in heaven waiting to be plucked out to bless earth."

"That's not me. I'm partial to the thinking that they're glowing wee embers in hell."

"My poppa always used to tell me that I was the brightest whitest star in the Milky Way," Doreen exclaimed sweetly.

"It hasn't ever been the same since and that's a fact," Cords says, but doesn't take her eyes off me.

"I thought it was a real pretty thing for Poppa to say, him being such a busy man and all," Doreen says. "I think . . ."

"Don't try to think now, sugar," Cords says smoothly. "It causes a hardening 'round the mouth. Besides it's not the time. I'm just talking to our lost Kate here." She raises one of her gloved hands and pats Doreen's mouth with it. "I'll hear your thinking later, sugar." Doreen's mouth is generous and a little slack. She smiles again at me, faintly and dismissively, in the way that Cords has taught her.

"I don't know why you're troubling yourself with me," I say, looking over at the forestry building for Grady.

"I take an interest in you," Cords says. "Seeing you is useful to me. It musters out my most helpful and endearing qualities. I have seen you riding about in a discontinued but very impressive car with a blond young man. I gather that you are looking for peace and safety in his company but he looks a bit frail to me. You have a clumsy way about you, Kate. I'd be careful that I didn't press too hard. My single memory as a child was of my own clumsiness. It all seemed collected in my hands. They continually broke or worried things. They were very strong and big as well and should have belonged to one of my brothers. But they didn't, they belonged to me.

They were my protective mantling, I believe. A tool of survival, you might say. I was the last of thirteen children. My family insisted that I was the fourteenth. There was no thirteenth. They wouldn't think of having had a thirteenth. I have heard that they've done that with the floors of hotels, the knowledge of which was not a consolation to me at the time."

"You do go on," I say.

"I apologize," Cords says airily. "I meant only to make myself conducive to your distress. And, of course, I want to welcome you back."

"I don't live here any more," I say. "I come back to classes only occasionally. We probably will never bump into each other again."

Cords looks amused. "But that's just not the way the world works," she says cheerfully. "The same people are forever cropping up in our lives. Besides, we can be of assistance to each other. I'm sure we could have some nice talks that would make you feel better. As for myself, I can be easily obliged. I've heard that you know that black boy that does something or other in the menagerie on the bay. We need one of their animals, a cat of some sort, for Doreen's Queen Serenade. It will be spectacular. I have it all planned. They have a leopard there, I'm told. I would like that. That would be best."

"I wouldn't be able to help you there," I say worriedly. *Trouble.* Daddy had said, *The snare and the pit will follow all the days of man. It always will.* I see the darkness of Bryant's Beasts. Dim. Brackish moist. The surface of the fish tanks breaks and glints and moves in silver circles across the animals. Their shadows are swollen on the walls. The leopard does not pace. He waits.

"We'll see," Cords says. "But it troubles me the way you drift off. You were looking back then again, weren't you? A terrible weakness, memory. Memory's just a hole that fills a lack."

"I wasn't remembering anything," I say,

"I can see your problem, Kate. Really, I'm very sympathetic to it. You were born nicely, weren't you, and were christened like Doreen here and you wore a little frock and you had white sturdy shoes. Your daddy told your mama to raise you so that you would love that which was good and hate that which was evil and you grew up hating and loving all the right things in all the right places and that's dandy but it doesn't seem to work out in the long run. Now it's easier for me because my mama was nothing but a tumblebug. Rolled up a little ball of dung and laid her egg. And I hatched right there —surrounded by shit."

"Icchh!," Doreen is insistent this time. "You're gonna make me sick, Cords. You're gonna make it impossible for me to eat any lunch."

"At the very least," I say. "I'm going now," I say. My simple statement sounds much too aggressive as though I didn't know I didn't mean it.

"I think you unsettled her even more than me," Doreen whispers as I stride away.

"Don't be stupid," Cords says.

14

"I think I changed my mind about the beach," I tell Grady. We are in an eddy of boys with slide rules slapping from their belts in holsters. Part of the wall in the first hall of this building supports a piece of redwood the size of our trailer. It is dirty and stained, with a tragic and breathless presence. THIS SLAB IS OLDER THAN CHRIST, a sign says. In part.

"Do you want to go anywhere?" Grady asks.

"No, nowhere." Our legs seem trembling in a pool of pink from the redwood.

A POISONED HOST PREVENTED HER FROM DYING. I shake my head to try and clear it. *Grady, leave me.* I cling to him, forcing a smile. We walk back to the Jaguar.

Had Cords always appeared to be wearing a nylon stocking on most of her face? There is no assurance. Had Father ever bought me a sugar cone? And was it sherbet or a cream? Daddy never did. Had Daddy bought my napkins? Who else would I have asked? I was shy but he proceeded. Shameful tactics not of my invention. *All grown up,* he said. Before, Mother had always told us, *Carry two safety pins and a dime for a telephone call at all times and in case.*

The baby turns his big remora head and fastens on my heart. Grady has one hand on the wheel. He clutches his chest with his other. I cannot tear my eyes away. He gathers up the cloth of his shirt embarrassedly over the hole in his chest. I can see his quiet lungs . . .

"Look here," he says, taking out a piece of paper from his pocket and handing it to me. "Would you like to go out Friday night for dinner?" There is a name on the paper and a number and an address. I can see the letters. "You remember them," he says. "You've met them before."

"Dinner? Of course," I say ambitiously. "I'll make a salad!" I am so grateful that Grady's chest is not open, that he is speaking.

"They are a pleasant couple although he sometimes becomes tedious on the subject of ferns."

"The Fern Fellow," I exclaim, remembering. "Very agreeable."

Right,! he would say to anything and then pursue his own dichotomous course. Right! We haggled all night. Small silky hairs grew from the palms of his hands.

We are on the road now, heading home. There is a truck

ahead of us, moving slow. The road is narrow and winding. It is a small truck, hauling mirrors. They hang from all sides in glinting sheafs. "Oh, pass him!" I cry. Grady noses around his bumper, but pulls back in. Seconds later, a logging rig hurtles by from the other direction.

"I can't for a minute," he says. "We have to wait until the road straightens out."

THAT WHICH HAS BEEN IS NOW AND THAT WHICH IS TO BE HATH ALREADY BEEN AND GOD REQUIRETH THAT WHICH IS PAST. The eye's our totem but mine's snapping and popping like a jacked deer's eye. There is nothing in the glass but ourselves. We are pinned like butterflies to the worn seats. Even the trees have been banished.

"Then stop," I beg. "Pull over and let him go on, past our road." My voice is weak. All my strength is in my feet, pushed against the floor boards. The Jaguar struggles to a halt. The truck sways skittishly around a curve and is gone. Before us is the world again, sounds settling in the void of the engine's silence. Grady's parked in a burnt-out pocket of woods. And it's then we can heard the sound of singing, very frail but determined, and see the sign of a penciled arrow on a butter box nailed to a tree.

"Revival," Grady grins. "See the tent?"

The black tree trunks seem to sparkle. The tent is brown like the dead forest we remain in and is strung up somehow between the trees like a poor umbrella. There are no sides. We sit in the car. Grady cocks his head.

> "There were ninety and nine that safely lay
>   In the shelter of the fold,
>   But one was out on the hills away,
>   Far off from the gates of gold—
>   Away on the mountains wild and bare,
>   Away from the tender Shepherd's care . . ."

"It's always that hymn," Grady says. "They have always been singing that hymn and if you came back here in twenty years, they'll be singing it still. When I was little and living with my cousins we would go to church on Sunday morning in a drive-in theatre and they would be shouting out that hymn. It was never my maiden cousins' favorite as it seemed too generous. They preferred texts that put the fear in a boy because they were certain I was going to turn out troublesome. But every Sunday we would sit in that ugly little pasture with the billboard advertising the week's movie, which was always something like *The Day Gongola Ate the World* or the like, and we would be forever singing that hymn."

He stops, thinking about his orphaned days, his cousins whom he has never discussed with me. They gave him nothing but the care they could and he's obliged.

He backs the Jaguar onto the road. The singing follows us. It slides over us and gets behind us and it stops us dead. Then Grady shoots down the road. There's only the snick of the gears. We do not see the truck again. We come to the trailer. Something crashes through the brush as we get out. In those mirrors I had seen my Grady tumbling headlong toward the light beyond their frames. *Don't be afraid it will work this car can still go ninety-five miles an hour it can work sometimes at ten miles an hour there won't be anything left of us there's hardly anything left now just enough to bury.* He was missing, then he was gone. I cannot stop myself. I tell him my story at last. The hounds are yammering in the woods. The hounds are tracking. No one's fired. We have a drink or two. I cannot stop. At last I say, "I must tell you about Father."

15

The class is already in progress. I come in late and must sit in the very first row. I find that I am wringing my hands softly, softly, as though I am washing a pair of socks. Grady is in the room. He does not look at me. There are thirty or so students here in French class. It is held in what was once the kitchen of the mansion. Of course now all the stoves and sinks have been removed and the room is equipped with the furniture of learning. All that remains of its former use are the big black and white floor tiles and the white pressed tin ceiling, dimped in a flower design, creamy and faint and deranged, like a wedding cake had blown up on it.

I watch Grady but he does not look at me. He ignores me without rancor. He is just not looking at anything. I am called upon to recite. A tick is crawling across my neck and up into my hair. I can feel it moving, even when I feel it stop.

I read—

And then I read,

> "Cet aveu que je te viens de faire
> Cet aveu si honteux, le crois-tu volontaire?"

The instructor shakes his head desparingly. "This is a terrible moment in Racine," he says. "Should there be a court order protecting him from sophomores?" There is a respectful titter. He sighs. "Go on," he tells me.

I say,

> "You think that this vile confession that
> I have made is what I meant to say?"

16

I have waited for Grady for nights. He is here but he does not come to me. I wait naked in the midnights. I know I am not attractive. My stomach has taken on crooked dimensions. My breasts have become all flat nipple. Nevertheless, one night he comes to me. He has made our decision. My phantom lover. I can see his outlines clearly. He sits beside me for a long time and then I feel the first touch of his hand. He wraps his legs around mine and enters quickly. His hands hold my hips without ambition, his mouth rests on my own without words. He takes me again and again with him into his new darkness. He is trying to wrest something from me. We understand this. I tremble like a branch. It does not stop. He probes deeper and deeper, cool like metal, like an instrument. We are drenched. We continue. Soon it will be the last time. The morning comes down.

17

I try to explain to the sheriff's deputy, but I don't understand it too well myself. I am walking along the shoulder of the road and he travels beside me in his striped Ford. I feel that it is up to him to speak first. At last, the car shoots forward and stops ahead of me. He opens the door and gets out. There is an enormous white light on the roof of his car, twisting hysterically. He's reluctant to turn it off. He's young and heavy-chested, his hair is cut so short you can see the white skull skin. His shirt strains and gapes across his stomach. Underneath, he wears a T-shirt. I sit in the front seat and we drive very slowly. Along the road, the eyes of dogs are blue in the dark and the houses are careless and painted in garish colors. We have not reached the town. Every time I touch my head, sand falls out of it, and there are a few pine needles caught in the weave of my sweater, where, I suppose, I might have been lying on the ground. He talks quickly and slyly as though there were a secret between us. His jaw is long and his face is thin. The stomach sprawling heavily above his belt is merely a part of his law-enforcement equipment.

I am trying to think. Mistrust all evidence. We were going to someone's house for dinner. I am still holding a bottle of wine in a paper bag. Grady is very conscientious—always the perfect guest. He remembers the name of everyone he meets and always brings a little gift, wherever he is invited. If he was about to be hung, he would bring the nooseman a stick of gum. It was he who insisted we continue on to our friends'. He said that they would consider us rude, that they would think something had happened to us. It wasn't far, a few miles, so we set out, leaving the beautiful Jaguar on the curve, all smashed and broken like a flower.

I am sure that this is how it was happening. I was following him in another car—I can't recall the make, such a tiring car, round and slow with great patched tires that someone had painted white—an enormous wallowing car with bad suspension and a compass bolted to the dashboard. He crashed right before my eyes. The car turned slowly in the air like something at the movies. He was thrown clear, landed on his feet and running. The lights were still on, the radio was playing a very popular country and Western song about love and subterfuge. In this song, the lovers have an arrangement by which the woman will raise the flag on the mailbox when the husband is out of the house. I stop talking to the deputy and swallow a few times. My head seems full of penny candy, garnished with a Melba peach. I realize that my problem is lack of discrimination. My head fills achingly, like a poisoned lung. I cannot stop thinking about the song.

The radio is playing and the engine is running still, in perfect tune.

Grady runs raggedly, crouched, as though he is in a war. Something disquieting has caught in his hair. He turns the ignition off and stands beside the Jaguar. He looks fierce and sad and lopsided. Perhaps the engine can be salvaged. Everything else is a ruin. The frame is bent. The pretty metal pocked like a waffle.

He loved his car. He loved the language of it and the feel of its oily gloamy parts. Once he took the engine out and apart, only for his edification. It fluttered from a tree for days in a canvas sling. The dirty jargon would make me laugh. Camshaft sprocket setscrews. Cotter pins and slotted nuts. Idler sprockets fitting to eccentric shafts. Starter jaws retaining with locking washers. Some madman went and named them all and expected me to follow along. It made me angry in a way. I refused to be educated to it. However, he did teach me how to adjust the carburetors—there were three—and I could also correct valve clearance for he bought me a feeler gauge. .006 inches for the intake, .008 inches for the exhaust. It is so depressing to know that this knowledge will stay with me always.

He knew the Jaguar perfectly. It was his only inconsistency. Stalls and shelters dotted the yard, housing soaking parts, tools, fluids and hoses. I remember him working on it on beautiful nights, the trees impossible ash, the river fat and white beneath the moon . . .

I remember him working on it the last time. I called to him but he only pressed deeper into the engine. His only movement was when he exchanged one wrench for another. When he was finished at last, he came in, smelling of soap and kero-

sene. He went to bed. We did not kiss the last time. We
gripped our bodies as one learns to. Feeding cutlery.

But why do I speak so myopically? There has been an accident. The deputy looks at me as though he would like to hit
me. He lights a cigarette that seems absurdly long. I wrap my
fingers more tightly around the paper bag that rests in my
lap. "Let me rectumfy something . . ." I begin and know I
have made another mistake. "Rectify," I say. There is a
big star painted on the hood of the Ford as though we were
part of a circus train. The deputy seems not to be listening.
He pulls up to a White Tower and glares angrily inside for
a few minutes at the people bent around the counter, eating
fries and eggs. He puts the car in gear again. He seems displeased with everything.

He says, "There was only one accident and you left it.
You wasn't about to report it. There was only one accident
and only one car."

I agree with him as much as possible. "I saw the whole
thing." It was true. It wasn't happening to me for, after all, it
was Grady's accident. I can't be expected to assimilate everyone else's events. A suppository of junky remembrances is
pressed upon me by them all and I can't forget a bit of it. I
can remember everything and no one fact complements the
other. It feels the same whether you've pretended it or not.

"You're lucky," the deputy says. "I seen accidents where
nothing on the vehicle is broke save the headlight but the
people inside is deader than bricks."

He is so bewildering, this angry man. He is driving with
prideful slowness through the town. He lingers particularly
outside Mr. Porky, Mahalia Jackson Fried Chicken and
John's Bar-Bee-Q. We cruise in and out of the parking lots.
The deputy breathes through his teeth and taps his fingers
against the steering wheel.

Why am I lucky? I don't understand. I am unable to make
inferences, but nothing ever seems to come to a conclusion

and that isn't my fault. The deputy doesn't mention Grady.
I try to think of him, once and for all.

It is warm and the top of the Jaguar is down. I am following him in the other car, passing and falling back again on the
thin blacktop road. I feel like a little girl and happy. The
night is warm and smells so good and we are going out for
dinner. The Jaguar rockets down the road, the wind puffing
out his shirt like a sail. He moves his head up and down to
the music that he hears.

He has washed in the river. His chest and arms shine like
a fish but the parts of his body that are covered with the river
are yellow and dented like a chewed pipestem. I interrupt
him and he drops the soap. It floats down into the mud and is
lost. He hoists himself up onto the dock and walks naked
to the trailer. Water splashes from his hair onto my hands.
It feels like nothing—the same temperature as my skin—but
it smells nicely of weeds. The woods in the dusk are dappled
like an appaloosa. There are shadows everywhere and splinters
in my hand. I try to work them out with my teeth. Everything I touch hurts.

On the road, he is driving very fast and well. We travel for
miles and see no one. The Jaguar flows tightly around corners.
The air is cool and damp on my face but our hips and thighs,
pressed against the transmission tunnel, are warm. The engine
throbs so heavily and the wind noise is so high that we would
not be able to speak to each other even if we wished to.
There are so many dials and needles, all telling him that he is
progressing well.

. . . I will admit I'm not stylish, but I want to tell you
something further. Intimacy brings its own alleviations. It
substitutes for a great deal that would otherwise have to be
carefully worked out. We are young and secret newlyweds,
cutely expecting a baby. I am allotted a certain recklessness
of feeling in such circumstances and I might as well use it.
The wreck was spectacular and I enjoyed it. I know it's not

stylish but I refuse to chastise myself for this as I might have at a more impressionable age. I felt a sort of sick exultation, as in making love. Now I feel merely sickish for it's quite apparent that I am in some frame that is in process after the accident, that the accident did not include. The wreck was interesting while it was going on because of its promise of finality—graceful, very honest and so soundless, for Grady did not once touch the brakes, which was commendable. I see it all now—flying, turning, settling—in black and white stills. As though taken from an exhibition. But now I realize . . . that is, it seems apparent . . .

He tries to shield it from me, although this is quite impossible for the car lies in several sections on the curve. The top half of the steering wheel has disappeared into the ground. The exhaust system lies in the road but one tailpipe has become embedded by its pointed end in a tree. It falls as I approach. I touch Grady's face. He tries to assure me that what has just happened doesn't matter. Of course I know this but he is so insistent that I have to pretend to disagree so that he can convince me. I touch his face and it moves oddly across his jaw . . .

The deputy drives faster and faster as we approach the courthouse. We tear around a corner with two wheels in the air and lunge into an underground parking lot. He strikes the brakes and the tail of the Ford leaps up into the air and settles with a grind. There are prisoners down there, working on motorcycles and sweeping the concrete floor. They do not even look up as we roar in. One has only one eye and is drinking an Orange Crush. The deputy leans across me and opens my door. I step out with my paper bag of wine.

We walk to an elevator and soar softly upward. Everything is very new. Modernization begins here and tramps southward along the coast. South of the courthouse is the college, the pretty bay, yachts, condominiums and dazzling subdivisions where no tree grows. North of the courthouse, the country shifts and simplifies. It is noisy and brackish, the shoreline messy with skiffs and abandoned appliances and pickup trucks. We arrive on the second floor but nothing happens. In the elevator is a picture of the Governor and a small rotating fan, mixing the air. I smell like a cheese for I didn't have time to bathe once Grady was through in the river. The deputy kicks the door with his boot and it slides back and we step out into the sheriff's department. Three young boys shivering in plastic chairs look up. They are all rib and muscle and long bleached hair. Each has a generous cluster of pimples on his cheek in an ornate and purple curve, like a tattoo.

I sit down in a chair by the window and look out onto the street. My deputy is talking with some other men, all in uniform, and writing something down in a notebook. They talk very softly except when they are calling each other by name, then their voices boom and roll toward the surfers and me. My deputy is named Ruttkin. There is Tinker the jailer and Darryl at the desk. They call out their names and laugh and answer to them. They are solid presences in the room, more solid than the soft drink machine, certainly more solid than me sitting by the window and watching the wide white street. Ruttkin brings me a form to fill out and a folded newspaper to write on.

I want to say, "Besides I'm true, so why do I need an alibi." I would like to tell them that good-humoredly but they would never know that it came from Mae West and it would be wasted. Besides, they don't ask me for an alibi. They ask me if I would like a glass of water.

I fill in the blanks the best I can. The questions seem extraordinary even though I have seen them many times before. The ink from the pen soaks in a widening dot as I hesitate. Age Blood Address Kin Make and Model, numbers intentions past employments and explanations. All of these forms insist upon excuses as though life were only a succession of apologies, an aftermath of error. I would like to depend upon memory rather than instinct at times like these, but if thoughts are acts, as so many maintain, my answers would be just as useless. I am true but guilty, ready to admit everything. I grip the pen fiercely. I am misspelling words and wrinkling the paper. It's gone all damp beneath my fist. I am unable to recall my birthday. They were in the winter months. Snow, blizzards blue in the morning . . . and I making myself sick each year with restraint and decorum. Once Mother ordered magicians but Father barred them at the door . . .

I suck in my breath and try to co-operate. The point of the pen sinks wetly through the paper. I concentrate. I simplify.
. . . I see myself barefoot in a short cotton dress, carrying my food stored in my cheek, abroad at dawn and afield in winter, and . . .

I discard and reject. There are hundreds of reasons for the wreck, even more for Grady's absence in the county courthouse. If he were here, he would reply imaginatively, taking into account what happened, but I am trapped by the immobility of events. I cannot shuffle them about or alter them. That's not up to me. The answers remain the same when the reasons for them being true are gone. If Grady were here, the pen would move determinedly and fill this form up with signs. Somewhere, Grady is being polite and respectful. His mouth is wet and sweet and his hair the color of sea oats. He said that before he met me, it was true that he had kissed other girls.

Outside, a Trailways pulls up to the curb. The driver jumps out and runs into the building. Underneath CAUSE OF ACCIDENT I write, *The rubber grommet on the steering column was not replaced, causing the wheels to lock. The box was not topped with oil the track rod was loose the curve banked improperly the road greased with the fat of a wild animal struck down before we came. A clear case of*

*metal fatigue of misadventure driver passivity and a choked
fuel line.*

We are young marrieds, wed almost yesterday. Grady looks
at me lovingly and I strike him down with my fabulous eyes.
Like the basilisk. The Jaguar soars off the road and into the
scenery.

I am writing faster and faster, blushing and panting with
relief. I am thinking as Grady would, abandoning myself to
possibilities. A deputy that I have not seen before walks out
of the building and into the bus below me, reappearing a few
moments later with his arm locked around a black man's neck.
The man is small and slight and wears tight bright clothes.
He seems to be strutting with his spine arched and his head
flung back against the deputy's chest. His sneakered feet paddle slowly in the air and he strikes awkwardly at the deputy's
hip with a pillowcase. I halfway get out of my chair and
watch them as they cakewalk beneath me and out of view.

I resume. *Refitting is the reverse of the removal procedure
and perhaps Grady left something out of the car when he was
putting it together.* Why not? Someone left something out of
Grady. His face is a bit out of focus. He fell too soon from his
mother's womb, being born beside a gas station on a Labor
Day jaunt to Key West. The family had planned nothing
more than a picnic lunch and some bonefishing, but there
came my husband, perfectly formed and scarcely breathing
but smarter than they knew. For if he had waited six more
weeks as he was supposed to have done, his mother would
have already been dead for two. It cannot be surprising that
he is obsessed with time and chance and orphanage and fell in
love with me. Such thoughts make him gentle and grateful.
He thinks of Time as his chum and accomplice. He is a
swimmer swimming in his element. While I . . . It is a black
and steel diving bell anchored to the bottom of the sea.

I am feeling a little giddy and would like to raise my hand
and ask to be excused. The Jaguar turned on its nose and

Grady popped up like bread from a toaster. In the trailer, the sheets are damp where Grady wraps his mouth, the thin cotton full of holes where he has punched his feet.

Under ADDRESS, I write *Hemo Globin Rho House 122 5th St*. That is a good joke I think on the sheriff's department even though they will never be able to puzzle out my wretched penmanship. Everything asks pretentiously Where Can You Be Reached? I see *Hemo Globin Rho*, which I have made, and I feel my mouth widening in a rubbery grin. I look around for someone to smile at. The surfers could be smiling but they are not looking at me but at the elevator. They look wolfish, flat and opaque. The arrangement of their lips could foggily evaporate should circumstances allow. Tinker the jailer cocks his head and sniffs like a deerhound and the elevator door is open, the deputy that I do not know is wading across the room with the black man from the bus. His wide red arm is squeezed tightly across the man's neck and he steps on the heels of the man's sneakers and raises his knees high as he walks so that they punch the man's buttocks. I cannot see his face. The pillow case that he carries is dirty on the bottom and heavy with pointed objects.

Sweat drips from my armpits and falls down my sides. The air is full of ozone, like it was before the accident. I could smell it then—something about to let go—and it has come back. My eyes float and bump against the scene, trying to organize it, for I am afraid that freakily this is my friend, Corinthian Brown. I cannot see his face. I get up from the chair and step solidly on my paper bag of wine, our party gift. I drag my foot up quickly but the wine is gone, the bag flat, a hole in the bottom and the brown paper stained. Beneath my sandal straps, my toenails are broken and my feet ache. I sit back down again. This cannot be my friend, Corinthian Brown. Though his arms beneath the plum blue jersey are a honeycomb of scabs, though his hands windmill wistfully in space, it is not him at all.

"John here has been messing around all the way since Chiefland," the deputy says. "Ain't you?" and he jiggles the black man, rearranging him to face us like a sack of feed. The man's face is round and middle-aged, his chin and eye pouches pale, two stringy lines of white descending from his mouth and his lips jammed shut as though he were holding a jawful of milk. "Drunk and stinking up that pretty bus. Bothering them nice people."

He looks serene and amused and grips the pillowcase like a strangled hen. He is not Corinthian. My friend is young and morose, lovely with his nervousness. He is sick, Corinthian. He would never be traveling on a bus.

I should be relieved but I'm not. Something flutters in my stomach. The baby moves and jabs my spleen with his watery head. I touch myself there. My belly is crooked and there is a hard ball on the left where it has settled for a while. At night, I lie with my stomach against Grady's flank. It beats against him and makes him dream. Sleeping, Grady moans and trembles like a dog, ill from the straw and dust he has eaten under the impression that it was marvelously delicate food. No one mentions him here.

"You nothing but a bother to us all, John," the deputy says and drops his arm. He walks over to where Darryl is sitting, reading the Sunday comics. The black man looks around the room, swallowing. Swallowing, it seems, once for each thing his busy eyes rest upon. There is an open door and behind it the cells. The windows are single high plates of glass. There are filing cabinets, a tree in a pot bearing real oranges. The floor is a set of different colored tiles, like a game, and the man sets one sneaker down lightly on a new tile and then brings it back again. He spits between his feet. He shifts the pillowcase from his left hand to his right and swings it around like a bat, hitting the departing deputy in the ass.

Darryl drops the funnies in the paper plate of food he's

eating from and my man Ruttkin's face turns gray as a sheep on the spot.

No one makes a sound and no one moves except the surfers who back their shanks deeper into the bucket seats. They stare and look adventurous, as though they'd been brave, squinting and hunching their shoulders like gangsters. I would like to say a few words or make a noise of some sort, a cough, hiss or clap, but something seems to jam me up. The thing slips membranous over my head and my mouth fills up with air. It is too late, it is ritualized. The moment turns from chance to rite and the four deputies are together now, for Darryl has run from behind the desk. He has an enormous torso but tiny sick legs and there is a stain on the fly of his pants. But they are all together now and circling the black man who still looks distant and bemused, who swings lightly the guilty pillowcase. He isn't even watching them—he is an audience like me, watching this in some far-off balcony—and they walk around him in a tight circle, walking faster and faster and I think perhaps that they might turn to butter like the tigers did and we will sit down to stacks of pancakes. We will swallow them up and later void them in the scrubbed latrine, over the scented bulb that is wired to the bowl, and flush them into the holes beneath the town . . . I smell a small smell of whiskey now and flame and the black man smiles and gives a happy growl.

"Mother," he says.

And the deputies fall on him, softly and without noise like dogs on a barnyard duck. There's a dull splash and smack and the man's ear begins to bleed, the pillowcase slides across the floor and out of it falls a clock,

a comb

and a can of pears.

I can't even see their hands moving, they're jammed so close, but I see the two white sneakers planted in the thicket

of professional country blue and Tinker's thighs churning up
and down as though he's peddling a bicycle. I tell you, I can't
feel a thing. I'm a wastebasket, and if you were honest, you'd
admit it too.

18

PHOENIX, ARIZ. (AP)

A collision with a horse as he drove home from the
race track left L. J. Durousseau, the nation's leading
jockey, in critical condition today.
Deputies said the horse bolted into the path of
Durousseau's car during a rain storm. He swerved
sharply, according to authorities, but was unable
to miss the animal.

I am reading the newspaper and I start to cry. They have
taken the man away now. His face was red, sealed and shimmering as though with the cellophane on a box of Valentine
candy. The surfers are gone too, leaving a puddle of sea water
behind them. Across the room are small signs. A piece of tooth
flew through the air and struck my hair, I thought, but I have
not been able to find it. And the tiles seemed trampled and
discolored where they beat him, but I know that this is just a
function of the surface of my eye.

The deputies have sent out for french fries and 7-Ups
and I am crying on the newspaper sports section. I have not
cried for so long, for so many years, that there seems something wrong with the way I am doing it. I used to think that
loving and breathing and crying were things that you never
lost the method of but this is just not so. There is nothing that

cannot be forgotten and learned in a different way or never learned again.

Ruttkin, too, seems to think that I am not crying but am in the process of something else. He stands beside me and runs the tip of his finger around the neck of my sweater, picks up my wrists and regards my dirty ankles. He has learned this maybe by heeding Dick Tracy's Crimestopper Notebook. He is looking for a chain, a disc, a tag.

"You ain't an epileptic? You ain't a diabetic?" Ruttkin is relaxed. On his knuckles are teeth marks. His shirt is wet where the black man has drooled. "The hospital," he says, "says there ain't a bit of change. You aren't wanting to go over there, are you? If you want, I'll take you but I'll tell you about them hospitals, they don't tell you a thing. You ask and they answer something that don't make sense. Or they answer you something you never asked."

I flap my hand vaguely at him. I want nothing in common with this man who is happy as though after a meal, who is showing his teeth at me in a commiserating grimace. I feel uneasily that his discoveries are the same as mine, that the methods he has chosen to get through the days, the weeks and into the years that he can put behind him are no different from my methods. The result's the same—we trample people in the eagerness to get on with our dying. Yes. I know what he says is true. I cross my legs and kick him in the knee, still crying. He crazily apologizes. *I don't quite understand your question but whatever it is the answer is no.* Yes. That's the attitude. That's the way of this world. The answers are all to something you've never even asked. Now Grady balked at this. Like some, he was more fortunate than most. When he wanted to know how to tune an engine, there were instructions for doing it. When he was young and wanted to shoot and sight and track, there were rules for that too and all he had to do was listen and learn them. He grew up trusting in the sanctity of the right reply. He was confident and hopeful and bright. And not without imagination. And honor. For when he found that I was going to have a baby, he kissed me gravely and married me in the afternoon. The ring was made of wood and too large for me. I packed blue tissue beneath it to keep it on my finger and when the tissue rotted, the ring fell away. I don't know when but now it's gone. Grady wouldn't mind. He traced my thighs and the sockets of my eyes, he was so in love.

Every girl remembers her wedding day. Excuse me . . . I have a cold and my tongue is green from flavored throat lozenges. It is raining, the sky is almost black. There may be a tornado. As I run from the car, I slip on wet pine needles and fall, catching my hand on the barbed wire fence that separates the chapel from a field. It is auspicious for my hand doesn't bleed. It lies snagged there as Grady helps me up but there is no blood and Grady laughs and kisses it and folds it up gently in his own hand. Gently, as though the hand had been severed, the ring, the marrying hand, and he were saving it, gently as though it were a wounded bird. There are big friendly mules in the field behind the fence and beside the chapel is the preacher's pickup truck with a brace of shotguns hanging in the window rack. For everyone is a hunter here, even the meek; everyone is prepared here for something terrible coming out of the black hot southern afternoon that they will have to protect themselves against.

Yes, every girl remembers, but as for the ceremony itself . . . The words, I suppose, would be the same that Father used although Father would first teach that loving is good preparation for dying. I was the only one who learned this. Everyone else seemed uncomfortable at the thought. Perhaps they believed that loving was what made a happy life. And I often wonder what became of those who Father blessed . . . ?

My eyes are breaking from this crying. Poor jockey Durousseau. I cry and cry. I sizzle and choke. A long time before this, in the time when I wept, I cried never for grief but from frustration. That had a pattern to it, a rise and fall, a stretch and slack, an end in sight, but this crying now can go on forever, like this day that goes on into continuing night. The land revenges itself upon us all, for I passed through that time as though through a dream, with no knowledge in my flesh of snowfall or handstroke, knowing nothing but dreaming those days in my head.

. . . We are going out for dinner. The Jaguar moves like a ghost through the dusk. A graven image, a negative, and us inside, leaning into the turns. Grady, my young man, all blond like wheat, takes the corner and falls out of love with me . . . *love in his watchtower darkling and in ambush is stretching his deadly bow.*

For it was clearly love, make no mistake, that met my yearning Grady on the curve. The falling hatchet loves the lamb and when bones ache, they ache for the breaking. It's love that starves and makes us murderous. And it's Father who is in the watchtower, watching from his steeple study through the snowy nights, with his hands folded across his eyes. I was so frozen, so embalmed then . . . I left, a pioneer with no tools for discovery, and not the sense to know that this made all the difference, traveling from the ice and cold and his abstraction into the South, the sun and reality. I was surprised at how easy it was at first. I developed a miming manner and was accepted everywhere. But all the while, he was knowing my life before I lived it, knowing that each step I took would only bring me home again. Oh yes, it was dark and obscure Father who struck my Grady down.

Grady was taken completely by surprise . . . His face didn't change, nor the muscles in his throat or arms. He is a good boy. I could see his mind beating, like a yolk dropped too soon in formaldehyde. And now I keep answering but he never asks any more. If I had told him a lie, we could have lived it better than any truth, but he had made me feel so hopeful . . . He wasn't afraid of anything. He was so ambitious then, and proud and confident. He thought that life was infinite and incredible and that for every question he might have, there would be an answer and the answer would be right.

Yes, Grady thought that there were only as many answers as there were questions in the world. He believed that, in the end, everything would come out in an implacable and just balance and pairing. Some things existed and some didn't and he told me he could tell them apart. He couldn't imagine there were people like me who had answers to questions no one would ever ask, that there were those who lived without a life, like moths without stomachs, lived for years with their lives beyond them someplace, dangling useless on a gallows.

In love, Grady wrapped himself around me like a twining vine. He didn't know that I had an answer for which there was no question. And that one day I'd give it to him. Yes. The very worst kind.

I cry aloud. Poor Durousseau. The tears splash on the newspaper and on my hip-hugger pants. They are of some cheap shiny fabric and there are marks all over them . . . a perfect paw print from the dog, quite old, coffee and candle wax and now these stains. Nothing washes out, I've found. I do not follow racing any more, although as a child, I had memorized the names of every Derby winner. The jockeys never interested me. In the photographs, they had the smooth faces of dwarfs, tiny waists and wardrobes. I was a child. They reminded me of evil playmates with terrible knowledge. I dismissed them and dwelt on the horses. I kept their pictures, tracing them out of magazines onto tissue paper. I knew their lineage, records and running times and could recite these statistics without error. Memorization then took the place of something else, something deep, deep, which I did not want to touch. I wanted order and it was everywhere. I memorized everything. There was nothing I could not talk about with vacuity. It was a masterpiece, my childhood.

Tragic Durousseau. Nothing unusual about it. Doom is accurate and vengeance is all the Lord's. Picture the horse galloping since a colt toward Durousseau . . . The thing that waits for all of us doesn't even bother to hide its identity or kid the survivors into thinking it was something else. In the Middle Ages, for example, I know for a fact that when dragons preferred to wear a human shape, there were certain discernible idiosyncrasies. They had wide mouths and flowing red beards and sometimes retained their horns. If you were paying the slightest bit of attention, you could avoid the dragon but this isn't the case today. No quarter is given. Endings never come outside our experience and there's no attempt at gamesmanship or artifice. Luck is not involved and wit or caution is useless. You catch up with it even when you're dragging your feet.

Father is right. Treatment is of little value except to prolong the illness.

Ruttkin kneels beside me. He has missed great swatches of his face in shaving. He hands me his bottle of 7-Up, trying to be friends. I accept it and tilt the neck deep into my mouth, trying to drool in it as much as possible. I would love to give him a bad disease. Hepatitis would be nice, but I've never had it myself, and anyone can see that such a sickness would be outlandish for him. I'm sure he's very clean, never puts his fingers in his mouth and drinks only beer. His distant end lies smugly on his face. In fifty years, he'll fall asleep behind the filigreed flamingo on the door of a concrete cottage and be buried two days later. He moves at a comfy pace toward death for he knows that he has time to satisfy his needs. God will send him niggers and the discovery of unnatural acts. Each day as deputy brings its own rewards.

He says, "You don't have to stay here any longer. I'll take

you home." He goes into the men's room and returns with a square of paper toweling. I hate him so much, I think I am going to be sick. It smells chloroformed. *Cloaca*, my dirty mind says. God only knows where Ruttkin found the toweling. Perhaps he is trying to kill me. I think of my friend, Corinthian Brown. It was only for a moment that I thought he was the black man, taken from the bus. This proves how tired I am, how wearying and confusing this continual watching and seeing and translating become. Corinthian does not travel. He has no pretty clothes. He wears shower clogs and the baggy gray khaki of the world's inmates. All night he works and he spends the days in the gutted cars of Al Glick's Junk Yard. He waits for beatings, I think, but no beatings come. Even the terrible Glick does not acknowledge him.

Tourists might notice him and exclaim, but the junk yard is off the highway and there would be no reason for them to be there. When I first saw him, he was sitting in the carcass of an elegant Buick convertible with a burnt-out engine. The Buick's canvas top was down and Corinthian sat in the sun, eating an apple and reading *Billy Budd*. Yes. He sat in the back seat as though he were being transported somewhere, his arms bare and scruffy in the sun, still as a giant discarded doll. The heat was extraordinary, coming in waves of rubber and battery acid. The sun bounced exotically off the metal and chrome. And no one noticed. Not the terrible behemoth Glick nor Grady who was looking only for a speedometer cable nor the half-breed shepherds who patrolled the junky pasturage. No one but me noticed Corinthian, my friend.

If the deputies have ever seen Corinthian, they have relegated him to the invisible. Corinthian could never be arrested. He would accept punishment gladly but it is not his to receive. You can see how confused I am, to have thought that the drunken victim beaten here was Corinthian.

Ruttkin says, "I'll take you home. Back to . . . ," he takes a piece of paper from his pocket, ". . . the sorority house. If you hadn't of been walking away from the scene of the accident like you was, if you hadn't have told me . . . ," he hesitates, looking for the right word, not wanting to be indiscreet, for he likes me now, he pities me and feels friendly, for I have been quiet this night, and then patient and finally crying, all the right things . . . "that thing, that shaggy-dog story about you not being in the wreck, about you being in another car, I never would of had to bring you here at all. It was suspicious, you know, you leaving your boy friend there and all."

I don't know what he's talking about. He is going to take me home, not back to the trailer, to the mobile home that never moves, but to the sorority house. No one knows about the trailer. No one has seen it except for the hunters tramping after turkey or pigs.

"That's right," Ruttkin says, "don't cry no more." I am looking at him wonderingly. He is going to take me back to the sorority house. It is incredible. I am going backward, the returning has begun. "C'mon," he says. And I stand up and step again on the paper bag that I thought held our bottle of wine. I pat my eyes and press my hair against the sides of my head like any girl and follow Ruttkin to the elevator. The picture of the Governor hangs inside. He looks the same as he did before. He has half-mad eyes and a space between his teeth.

We are back in the Ford, traveling across town toward the college campus. Ruttkin turns off the sheriff's radio. He is off duty. After he drops me off, he is going home. He says, "You know when I was called to the phone back there, after we corrected that problem with the nigger?" I am shivering. The night has turned cold and I can't find the handle on the door to roll up the window. "You know the time? Well that was the hospital and I'm a new daddy." He slurs the word hospital. I don't care. How can words hurt me now?

There are too many goddamn words in this world. As for the hospital, I have never even been inside one.

"It ain't the first time," he says, "but it's like the first time. It's a boy." He sets his hand between us on the seat. "I got three boys." He counts them off on his fingers.

I nod. I would like to ask him if his wife has a problem with caked breasts. I read a cure for it. The cure had something to do with warm pancakes. I think that was what it was, but I may be mistaken so I don't mention it. I am very hungry. I haven't eaten in more than twelve hours.

Ruttkin is so proud of himself. Smiling, he shakes his head slowly and chews on his lip. I am bored. I do not even wonder what his wife looks like or how sow-bellied Ruttkin makes love to her, I am so bored. We pass a drive-in movie. An enormous plastic sign on the roadway says

TONIGHT! BLOOD-O-RAMA!!
Four Fiendish Features

Blood Fiend
Blood Creatures
Brides of Blood
Blood Drinkers

Both of us bend forward to peer at the screen which is momentarily visible. Two women in evening gowns are sitting on a floor throwing letters into a fireplace.

"My wife wanted a little girl," Ruttkin says, "but I wanted a boy."

"That's good," I say.

"Name of Ronald," he says. "Already his name is Ronald and he ain't but half an hour old."

"Did your wife eat a lot of iodine before she had Ronald?" Ruttkin turns his face toward me and drops his jaw. "Iodine," he says.

"If she didn't get enough iodine, Ronald will be a cretin."

"Oh? Yeah, well," Ruttkin asks, "where would she be getting this iodine?"

"Fish." I don't know why I've begun this. If I had the strength, I would punch Ruttkin in the mouth, push him out the door and run over him with his sheriff's deputy's car. First and reverse, first and reverse, back and forward. Ironing him.

"Ugh," he says. "Fish."

I don't know why I've begun this and try to pretend that I haven't.

"She may have been eating fish, I don't know. I work nights and take my meals in town. She should know the right things to do."

It must be very late. Everything is quiet and there's very little traffic. The moon is small and high in the sky. On one side of the road is a long deep park and on the other, all-night convenience stores and empty shopping centers. We have almost come to the college. Near here, I remember, is a place that has one million baskets for sale. Another store sells towels and another, sixty-nine different kinds of sandwiches. It does not seem possible that I am being returned to the sorority house, but I realize that it's my own fault. I want to go back to the trailer and smell the good smell of Grady's clothes. I would fix the place up for him right away. He'd be pleased. I'd burn the brush that blocks the door, empty the wastebaskets, tidy and clean. I'd let the air come through. I'd wash the blankets and make him a nice breakfast.

Ruttkin is saying, "Iodine is a crazy thing to have to eat."

I close my eyes and fold my hands across my stomach. I would like to ask him to turn the car around and take me to the trailer, but I can no more ask him this than I can anyone anything. Change is beyond my range. I am in my black and steel diving bell anchored to the bottom of the sea. With my eyes closed, I can smell the oil heaters burning in distant orange groves. It must be close to freezing. The temperature has fallen by half since Grady and I began tonight. The wind blows coldly in my ear. My throat is sore.

The car slows and turns and stops. I feel that I have to remember all this. I am being kidnapped. I must be able to give instructions to those who will want to come after me. The car moves forward, turns and stops for good. He cuts the engine and opens his door. I do not open my eyes and he does not open my door. I sit in the dark for a moment and then my eyes flap open of their own accord. We are not outside the sorority house but in front of a little store. Everything is bright and clean. Ruttkin walks out with a paper bag.

"This here is milk," he says, and puts the paper bag in my lap. "When you get to your place, you heat it up and drink some. I seen people in shock before and you don't want any part of that. You drink this and go to sleep and tomorrow you'll be all right." We get back on the highway and almost immediately, off of it again, turning through fancy gates onto a gravel road. It is a small, smug and elegant college.

"He ain't dead," Ruttkin snarls, "and you ain't dead." He seems to be getting angry again. He accelerates. Gravel spins up from beneath the tires and across the hood.

"You don't understand," I say. "I don't appreciate this."

"They took the wreck to Glick's yard. You know where that is? North of town?"

"O.K.," I say. "Yes." The milk is cold in my lap. My thighs are cold.

"You'll probably have to pay the towing fee," Ruttkin says. "Ten bucks it is."

He pulls in front of a large stucco house, three stories high. It's faded pink and heavy with turrets and balconies. A rich man's nightmare, reeling in space. Once it was a mansion, then a bank, museum, church, rest home and dancing studio.

Descending like Dante's circles. All gone, all failed. Now, at this moment, it is the sorority house.

Ruttkin watches it with great distaste, watching it as though it might start to move toward him and he will have to shoot it. He is puzzled, he is exasperated. The house seems to float, to sway before us, breathing with the bodies of all the sleeping girls.

I am so tired. I concentrate on pulling up the door handle, pushing my feet over the ledge and onto the ground.

"Take the milk," Ruttkin insists. Childishly, I treat the carton roughly, knocking it against the door. He doesn't drive away until I am inside the house.

The main hallway is lined with mirrors. A clock ticks and the old house creaks and pings like a cooling engine. The clock is on a mantel in another room, a white and fading face set between the flailing hoofs of two bronze horses. Poor Durousseau. The horses are rendered in perfect detail, pricks, eyelashes, teeth, and the clock, they say, keeps perfect time. I don't see this but am remembering it. It is as though I have never left that tocking clock which really I have not been familiar with for very long. Grady had a watch with a black face and numbers and hands that shone in the dark. It might be comforting to some . . . so many nights I watched the watch on Grady's wrist. When he moved, it wound itself; while he reached for me in sleep, curling his hand between my legs, it fed off Grady. Yes, a succubus. Even when he removed the watch, the mark was there, a broad band of white that the sun hadn't touched.

The clock tocks. One can even hear it in the kitchen, where I go immediately. The refrigerator is full of remains—fatted, wilted, jellied and iced. Dishes covered with waxed paper and cinched with a rubber band. I quickly remove some and start spooning the contents into my mouth. The food seems harmless enough and bland. I drink Ruttkin's quart of milk too even though it would not be irrational of me to dump it down the sink or commit some terrible crime on it . . . as a gesture.

But I eat and I drink Ruttkin's milk, for I've been taught it's a sin to waste the food that prolongs life. What with all the starving bodies, I've learned to use everything up.

19

My radio is in its ordered corner beside my bed but someone has been using it. There's wax on the plugs. I turn it on right away. There is my old chum, my answer man on "Action Line," with the voice I've left him with. He is saying, "I am sorry, we do not accept solicitations. We only take questions offered in good faith and taste." I cradle the radio to my cheek. There is nothing for me to think about and I'll tell you, even when I could, I would never think about those woods we've left now. I couldn't understand them and I couldn't understand the people and the animals that came into them. When Grady was away at school, I spent hours in utter solitude and didn't learn a thing. At first I was alarmed, but then I realized that it was what I wanted all the time. My life was slowing down. Nothing was feeding it any more. It was draining like a wound and there was a possibility that soon I might experience true freedom.

Indeed, even now I have hopes that my only opportunities will be those I'll miss. I want to stall my life like a train on a track, perfectly midway, between what has happened and what is happening. First emission, then omission, that's the key to life and our success can be measured by the purity and bleakness of the bone of our existence. As someone said, *no one is going to kill you.* No, no one's going to kill you or even loathe or love you. Though this is not quite true, for we're told it has happened to some. Not us certainly but to some, people that we know.

Omit, omit and one day you will be down to a funny, white and quite lifeless seed. I see it as a sort of heart of palm myself. In the groceries, they sell them in tins at outrageous prices. In New York restaurants, I hear, they do the same. Actually the stuff is swamp cabbage, easily hacked from an ugly and useless weed that covers the ground of the South, common as pennies. But we're all game and gullible as tourists in this life. No one is able to tell us anything. The soul is a heart of palm and living is a messy salad with everything in it being similar but less interesting, less necessary as you proceed. The trick is not ignoring this discovery after you've made it. *Do not be a polite guest.*

BOOK II

What is a lost soul? It is
one that has turned from its
true path and is groping in
the darkness of remembered ways—

Malcolm Lowry

THE CONGREGATION was the town and the town made up the island. The cold was convivial to their natures but before the Reverend had come they had never been instructed in the bitter ways of God. It was true that once, before the Reverend took up his duties, there had been a suicide among them. Mr. Pardee cut his throat with an oyster knife. Mrs. Pardee, who was only seventeen at the time, was making cheese and refused to attend to anything else before the cheese was completed. This was an enviable trait exhibited and one which, all conditions being equal, everyone in town would have been proud to show themselves. Since that time, nothing more occurred—one dusk as they were out cutting greens for the Christmas mantels, each noticed the other had become middle-aged or worse.

Then the Reverend came and after a few years it appeared that God had found the island again, in the manner of putting a bad hand down upon it. When it appeared that the hand had come to rest on the Reverend's little family, the people came to the conclusion, without being aware that they had reached it, that the distribution of pain, at least on this tiny place, on this doggerel rock adrift in the sea, was as just as man could expect, because the man and the lone peculiar little child could bear it best. They handled it not only impassively but gracefully. It was almost their style. It was the mother who had always been wasted by it, who threw herself on grief's mercy. And of course now she was gone. There was the lesson. Everything exists to teach. Her haunted manner, her aching ways gone, at peace the frenzy she had shown in the last months . . . The Reverend was a difficult man, an exacting man. Perhaps he never should have married . . . but who could say? Needs are forgotten. Arrangements rearranged. Now he is alone, a father with the little Kate. Such a discomfiting child. There's something lame about her, something dark. There is the air of a sanctified crime about her—of a holy slattern. But she is only a child! She has the boniness of a child, the tiny features—they could be put in a cup. Heartbreak surrounds her, though she seems unaware of it. She moves through it like a leaf, like a feather, like a falling piece of soot. It is as though she is living out some event that is not part of her life. The townspeople, however, would not think of this. How could they? They live in the faltered rhythm and dip of the island. They listen to the telephone. Nothing happens here. The town has no possibilities and this is the only child now. The wombs are barren, the land cannot bear. They swim in conjecture, the time and the tides.

But how will the father and the little girl live now? The child seems an orphan, a ward of something vast and troubling. Of course they will remain here, she will go to school. The townspeople expect that the Reverend will continue to instruct her. Already she has developed great skill at recitation and vaguely terrorizes them, being able to recite long sections of the Bible with a dreamy and demonic exactitude, translating the sounds into something privately understood and then returning them to rote, to a maddeningly void and childish lilt. It's almost heresy for her to prattle so, so unmindful, the words so clear and useless like a mirror hung backward on a wall. She reflects nothing but her father. He is in her eyes, the way she holds her hands. Perhaps it is simply a stage the child is going through. They know nothing about children. The sister had playmates who would come from the mainland, who would tumble and yowl through the crisp black and white town, but now Kate is the solemn solitary child they must share and she has no friends who visit her. Even before the mother died, she was seen only in the company of the Reverend. At dusk each weekday, he would meet her at the ferry slip and they would go home together, flowing up the street, not speaking, her fingers in his big hands. The townspeople watch from their windows, eating bread and beans. They take an embarrassed delight in her inconsistencies, embarrassed because she is, after all a child, not yet seven years old, and they wish her no ill. She maintains that she takes no pleasure. That phrase. She has said it to almost all of them at one time or another when they wanted to give her a little something, make her a small and harmless present. And yet they have seen her eating ice cream. Tying ribbons in her hair. Climbing in the trees. In the winter she plays earnestly, skating, sledding, running with her dog. She obviously has rules, strict restrictions, self-imposed. The play is highly ritualized but it is play. Once the postman heard her singing . . .

"God's begun a state of grace in me
I'm the only one in town."

The sea wind carries such scraps of conversation, nonsense rhymes, dream images, for miles. Everything is echo. The townspeople are ashamed of the smallness of their thoughts but they are pleased that her actions belie the lie. She is a child, nothing more, small, dependent and without resources. *We are justified not without and yet not by our works* is the base they build upon. Is that not what has always been taught? And has not the Reverend himself said, scornfully, coldly, so that one could almost hear in his ears the frozen whistle of the fall to hell, "Works, a man get to heaven by his works! I would as soon think of climbing to the moon on a rope of sand." So they needn't concern themselves with their thoughts about the child. They are free to think them. The Reverend continues to remind them that they are worldly free. They are dismissed. Perhaps they are truly saved and safe. The child dismisses them with the gaze of her father. She is meek and even pretty, but unruly, a bit menacing. Sometimes her face looks withered as a crone's.

But her mother is dead, her sister is gone, transported so precisely that summer day, out of the moving car into the giant oak, that historical oak was it not? the one that had been brought over from England in a snuff jar? Yes, it could be the burden of death that the very young can assimilate but not bear, it could be merely *that* that makes the child appear so singular, so remote. And then the mother, the Mrs. being so odd at the end, bearing that new baby with such fury, being so unseemly, almost deranged.

Yes, they had not seen how any good could have come of her rage. For something had been in evidence, even to the town's slow heart. Something desperate and angry and even afraid. She was after something nameless, the Mrs. Jackson, or had already found it. How, they couldn't say. Where, they couldn't imagine on this simple island where everything lay like silhouettes flat against the sky. But she said the queerest things at the end, things that had no substance. It was as if already she had one foot in the other world. And half her mind as well.

SHE SPOKE OF HORRORS. She spoke to Mrs. Morrissey of giving her heart to horrors. This was difficult. For some reason, the Mrs. had chosen Mary Morrissey to confide in although Mary had once been Catholic and drank and couldn't be counted on to keep things straight. Had she selected someone more dependable to speak to, the town might have made more sense of it. It was the burden of a woman bearing, they supposed. She moved with hatred, moving hurriedly, heavily off through the ice, her chapped face wrapped up in scarfing. These were the only times they saw her in the last months, walking recklessly, out for the air, they supposed, but walking so quickly, as though she had a destination. But she visited no one and the boundaries of the town were the sea. Once, she had seemed quite ordinarily happy. Quite social. Enthusiastic. Kept herself up quite a bit more than the other ladies would care to. After the daughter's death, though, the only habit she kept was churchgoing. Three times a week for prayers and twice for Sunday service. Each time she left, she shook the Reverend's hand, her eyes averted, cast off into the umbrella stand. Except for these moments, she was never seen with her husband. He was always with the Lord.

The Reverend seemed such a loveless man. A dedicated man certainly. Wedded to God's work. But not one to give a woman comfort. They could not imagine . . . but their thoughts were frivolous, base. They had been shocked when they learned the Mrs. was pregnant. At first they had believed that their feelings were those of dismay, of fear for her well-being, but then they admitted to each other that they were oddly shocked.

She was in the seventh month when she died. She had taken to bed shortly before then, receiving no visitors (had it been her request or the Reverend's?—the question didn't matter—they were all barred, even Mary Morrissey, who undoubtedly would have been disappointing in her information anyway, having been married three times and divorced once, and having a penchant for unpleasant generalizations). No one could recollect the Mrs. ever looking as poorly as she did lying in the coffin. They can't understand what did it. *A complication of pregnancy*. They don't inquire further. They misunderstand medical terms. Their vocabulary is not one of disease. Nor is it one of health. What they do, always, is a compromise between death and living. They do know that no doctor was called. She died at night while the Reverend was sleeping, while the little child Kate was sleeping. They also know that the fetus was not expelled. It was tight within her still when she was taken away. Snug as a core in an apple. They do not like to discuss it really. It is not that they are not curious or bereaved or amazed. It is just that they lack the proper terms. They are embarrassed by their own references. The death isn't quite acceptable. It isn't quite . . . respectable.

They shuffle past the coffin, observing. Hair puckered up in tight ringlets. Not her way. A great deal of gray. They hadn't noticed. But very natural. With good color. Lipstick, which she seldom wore, prettily applied. *A good job* the man had done. Came over on the ferry with the equipment of his trade and set up in the parish house. Realistic. She looked as though she would get right up and walk among them, blinking her large mortified eyes, her hands spilling over them, making invitations and promises as she always did. She had loved to entertain, although the townspeople were not familiar with the accepting of hospitality. Once she had been giddy, nervous, eager. Twice monthly, she opened the doors of the parsonage, the finest house in town. They could depend on that like on the sun rising . . . the tea and cookies served in the pleasant rooms of the first floor, "strings" on the record player which they didn't care for. The afternoons began well but ended rather badly. One of the men would make a crude comment or break a cup. Fingerprints on the clean windowpanes . . . The talk would die down to almost nothing. And she would seem close to tears. She was always high-strung and expensive-looking. Once she had been from

the city. A flawless complexion, a charming laugh. All gone
now. Emptied her essence somehow. The mysteries of under-
taking. Who would want to? In the family's footsteps.

A lovely job. Though it was not the woman they remembered. She had lost an extraordinary amount of weight.
Her head was quite wasted. And her skin seemed much too
smooth. After all. He must have poured the makeup on.
Stomach flat as a frying pan, for the unborn child had been
removed and placed in a smaller box. Such a tiny coffin,
like a jewel box. She had carried the baby full and low . . .
wasn't that to mean a boy? The word was that it had been a
boy.

"Called back," said Mrs. Parrish, whose husband was in
feeds. "Called back because the loving Lord couldn't bear to
have him leave His care, not even for man's brief lifetime."
Her good eyes shook out tears.

The child did not even have the opportunity to be born
dead. As the Reverend said, for he was a man of order and
belief, even though he spoke of his own . . . "too imperfect
even for that." Sickly harbored. So sad. With its little untried
soul.

"My wife," the Reverend said, "had unnecessary thoughts
at the end. You could tell she was sick. You could tell that
something wicked had her in its grasp."

They all tipped slightly over the coffin, their hands twitch-
ing behind their backs. A button on the deceased's blouse
was dangling, the thread all ravelly. They all had a desire
to push it back in place. Such carelessness was inexcusable.
All pride gone out of craftsmanship ever since the war. The
blouse was brown silk, rather old, the thread of the buttons
was black. Two strands of beads; one of glass, the other
of clay. Like an Indian curio in a novelty shop. Almost a
toy. A child's necklace, for dress-up. Perhaps the child had
been responsible for this. A lovely gesture, though rather
lurid. Motherless Kate. Makes you cry. Looks like neither

the poor Mrs. nor the Reverend except in bearing. Little stranger. Black wool skirt on the deceased. A full skirt, as though for dancing. A plastic belt. Red and white pumps. Newly shined. The darker polish somewhat lopping over its bounds. The Reverend had picked out the clothes. You know the way men are. No sense of a woman's image. If the Mrs. Jackson could see herself, she'd cry. She cried for less when living. Her eyes were always brimming. Just before the end.

MARTHA'S COFFEECAKE was in a box tied on a little string to the front doorknob, the man says. His bulk is enormous. "She brought you a nice warm coffeecake this morning while you were still asleep. Did you eat it for breakfast?" Kate had not eaten it. "Yes," she says.

Everyone is there. She looks around at them all but their eyes are settled on something on the ground. She looks at the ground too but can see nothing extraordinary. The grave is a mess. The ground is frozen and the hole is ragged. The hole looks more like an act of God than anything men would think of doing with a plan and shovels besides.

The Reverend is talking about the grave, how deep and insatiable it is, just like the barren womb. It's never satisfied, he is saying. There are three things that are never satisfied and there are three things that are wonderful and there are three things which disquiet the earth and there are three things that go well. The child agrees, moving her small dark head as he speaks, making everyone want to cry out and rescue her from her false and awful comprehension.

But the child is thinking a harmless thought. The world's in her head. They've filled up the hole and the dirt on top is soft and black. They've trucked it here. The child is thinking about the land behind the gas station where the Hanson twins burn tires. The ground is springy from the rubber . . . it's like a trampoline. She is thinking about that is all, how nice it is.

The service is over. The child runs to her father. She rocks and dreams in her father's side. In the sea, the buoys ring and the sun slips from the afternoon toward warmer lands. She brings back the dream she has learned. It is delicate and brutal, brief and interminable; she can call it back any time she wishes. It lasts no more than a second, being, at the least, no more than one single shouted and preposterous word and being less word than the witless weight of joy. She stands on one boot on the bluish ice and dreams.

People try to interrupt her. Women in old furs are kissing and handling her. They make a ring around her and crouch, patting and joggling her, grasping her tightly. The child suffers this for she knows that they are inevitable. She knows that they are Christian and are being saved. When they go home after church on Sunday, they change into white gowns that are like wedding gowns and sit in shadowy living rooms, watching the door, waiting for the kingdom to come.

It is snowing. Everywhere an apocalyptic absence of light. A dangerous day of God's. The snow falls and shines in the women's fur collars. It falls upon the bright flowers banked upon the ground. The child is holding a flower in one un-mittened hand. She squeezes it again and again. It feels very odd; it feels very wrong like the soft rubber stomach of a doll. She plans to bring it home and place it in the drawer where she keeps all her treasures.

The wind howls in from the sea. The congregation would invalidate her dream if they could, but they don't know all the facts. The child is neat and polite, distant, old-fashioned in her manner. The people are uneasy as they wait and stamp in the snow. Perhaps they are even annoyed, even though the child poses no threat to anything except what they believe to be her own maidenish future.

The mourners separate and get into their cars. They travel up to the parsonage, meeting no one else on the road. Everyone is among them. They follow the curve of the sea which is high and yellow. It is the aftermath of a weekend storm. A flock of eiders move heavily into the wind and then change course, surrendering. The sky is white and the water is yellow. The birds vanish. It is an ugly day. The child sits beside her father, her hand in his pocket. He has some coins in there and his pipe, the bowl of which is still warm.

"Look at the ruin on the wrack," the child says, using her other hand to point at the beach. Her father smiles and the child laughs a little. It is an old joke that she has made up. She can't keep herself from saying it even though she knows that she has exhausted its possibilities. She looks at her father gratefully for having acknowledged it once again.

They arrive at the big house. The child follows her father inside. Relatives and congregation troop in behind them. Everyone takes off his boots and places them on newspapers put down by one of the thoughtful. Later that evening, several of the ladies present will insist that their own boots have been taken and strange boots left in their place. They will claim this because they cannot get their feet into these boots. Actually this is not what has happened. Their feet have swollen in the heat of the house. There are fires in several of the fireplaces and the big stove is burning as well. There are breads and cakes baking in it and on top are pots of coffee and soup. The place looks festive with all the lamps shining and the food and the women moving officiously about. The child lingers on the stairway. She feels invisible. She makes a face. Upstairs she hears a noise.

THE ROCKING CHAIR is rocking in the draft. No one's in it which means a death. The child thinks of her mother, up-stairs, in the month before she died. The child dabbles with the thought that she is still there but it doesn't really engage her imagination. The woman had been alone in that room for so long. What difference would it make if she was there still? The child sometimes had brought up a few toys and watched her. The woman moved around the bed, smoothing blankets. She moved about the room, breathing wearily, touching her breasts, caressing her stomach. Often, then, the child had seen the baby stretch, the head bubble up, the mother's stomach bunch and sag grotesquely. She had seen this before. Where had she seen the likes of this before? The shuddering yawn. The reluctant host carrying continence. When? She is a child, not even eight years old.

She had watched the woman in the room. Everything was bare. The light sockets were empty. The door had been taken off its hinges and was gone. The woman spent hours at the single window that overlooked the field. She pressed her breasts against the icy glass. She pressed her lips against the glass; she gnawed with her nails on the frost, putting down words, things, pictures. From the hall, the child saw them. They made no sense. Perhaps it had been an elaborate code, done in reverse, decipherable only from outside, from the field. Perhaps it had been mirror writing like Da Vinci's. The child had not investigated. It had been too exciting. She is just a child and she enjoys mystery and secrets and disastrous forebodings.

On the rim of the field is a snake fence. The field was always empty, one couldn't even see the wind move across it, but once, one morning very early, the child, again standing in the hall, saw tracks curving deeply across the snow there, as though something hungry but harmless had closed its jaws over the land. The day's ice storm obliterated them and they were never there again.

The child had imagined the woman behaving as though she were a prisoner in the house, suffering terribly and devising fruitless plans for escape. But how could this be? The woman was only her mother and she had planned to have a baby. She was merely "lying in." Naturally this has never been a prison house. It is a home. Like any other. There are cookies in the kitchen, for instance. In a china crock poorly rendered as a bear. There are little maxims scattered throughout: HANG IT HERE AND LET ME HOLD YOUR TEABAG and there is a spice and herb chart and a welcome mat and other homely objects, patent leather bags and night cream and paregoric and mayonnaise and seed bells for the birds.

The woman had always been free to go. Yet in that month, she never left that room which she had chosen for herself, except at night. They, the child and the father, had suspected this long before it became apparent in one terrible incident. She used her house then when she thought that they were sleeping. They would hear the toilet being flushed or note that some of the food was missing. They would never hear her actually. Only the sounds of her ablutions. Secretive. Functions. In the old house were many sounds. All of them could not be heeded. At night she wandered. That had been their conclusion. She did the small housewifely chores she felt were imperative. It had no doubt been relaxing for her. And respecting her whims, they had let her be and not confronted her with themselves. But they had never been certain that she rose when they retired until the night they heard the scream. It was in the kitchen. She had been ironing and there had been an accident. She didn't get enough sleep, she confessed. She was becoming absent-minded. By the time the Reverend reached her, she was quite in control of herself. She'd put a stick of butter on it. She had also picked up the iron from the floor. She worried about the burn in one of the tiles there more than she bemoaned the burn on her face. It had taken in a good part of her right cheek and chin. White as a flounder. The child had never seen anything so white. It went beyond sickness. It was the deep trauma of the flesh.

"I know butter doesn't do it, but it's all that was here." She moved placidly, curiously out of step with her pain. She put the ironing board back in the closet and went down on her hands and knees to rub at the blackened spot on the floor. She had been dressed up. A gray suit with a little velvet collar, a silk scarf around her throat, a gay hat fastened to her hair with pins. But her hair was combed queerly, slicked down forward and flat, ending in greasy rolls. The zipper on her skirt was broken. Her nylons were torn.

She rubbed at the floor, chiding herself gently. "How silly of me. How ridiculous. I was just pressing a few things. That basket is just full of things. The lid can't even fit. And they go back for years and years." She patted the floor one final time in commiseration. "The ones on the very bottom look like doll clothes. Little gowns. Tiny slips. I didn't want to move them for fear they'd break, but on top of them all the other things, in strata, you know, in histories. I had forgotten them and they're still quite good. If I just put them in order again I'm sure there's life in them still." She rose awkwardly. She still held the butter in one fist. It rose grayly with her, accompanied her as she moved to the big wicker hamper.

The iron had cut into the corner of her mouth as well. A few days later it would be black—a slim, fried shoestring of fat. "I used to imagine Kate and I doing little things together," she said abruptly, "you know, gardening, making cookies, Christmas candies. No, no," she said, although no one had interrupted her, "I had always wanted her to be happy. And kind. I wanted us to do little things together. Like in the stories."

"What stories?" the Reverend had asked, and his voice had been melancholy, surprisingly mild, gently respectful. His back was to her and to Kate as well. The night had been very still. They had heard the rocks rolling in the surf below, clopping like horses' hoofs. The child had crept to the stairs, had waited on the third step. She decided to run through one of her Bible quizzes. Thinking of puzzles, the Reverend had told her, is always permissible.

A was a monarch who reigned in the East
B was a Chaldee who made a great feast

C was veracious when others told lies
D was a woman heroic and wise

"The stories," crooned the woman's voice. "But that wasn't her way, was it? Now her sister. Her sister used to say on a bright sunny day, she would smile up at me and say, 'Mommy, what a good drying day!'" There had been silence. The child moved up another three steps.

V was a castoff and never restored
Z was a ruin with sorrow deplored.

"I was ironing," the woman had said, "and my cheek itched. I forgot I was holding the iron. I reached up to scratch it. How else could such a thing have happened?" The child had gone back to bed.

THE DAMAGED TILE had been replaced. There was a box of extra ones in the barn. It was brighter than the surrounding ones, but the pattern was the same. From then until the night she died, nothing of the sort had been repeated. She had stayed exclusively in the room upstairs. Nothing was done in the house except what they, the father and the child, did. Nothing was said except by them. The woman took no further interest in the household.

"We mustn't expect too much from your mother any more," the Reverend had told the child. "We mustn't tire her or question what she's doing. Think of the changes in her body, Kate. Hormones and the will of God. That's our life, Kate."

The child had played in the hallway, outside the woman's unpleasant room. She would play absorbedly for a while and then announce, "Mother, I won." And then she would say calmly, for the truth of it had never troubled her, "It doesn't mean anything because I'm the only one playing."

The woman had not replied. Her mind had long since stopped on the blank threshold of that door. Her mind no longer dealt with the child. It was over, over, in the past. But where before had been this loneliness? When the exile? Why had mere words corrupted her instinct for love?

The child had played in the hallway. An only child, amusing herself—her head full of fantastic things. When her dog plodded up the stairs and stepped across her, intent on visitation, functioning in some gentle memory of a contented time, the child had reproved him severely. "No, no, Race, don't go in there." Of course it had been just a child's frivolity, but the woman had not replied. Deep in her musing, she had carried on in her singular fashion. Her time had been divided into three parts, like a banal clover. There had been the smoothing of the bed, the idleness at the window and last and basically, the devout involvement with her burgeoning self. For daily, the child had seen her, tending to her body, cleaning it, carefully sounding and examining it. She gave her limbs brisk slaps and pinches, moved her trembling hands and mouth over her skin, scouring herself like a bird. She had become her own physician, her own lover. The child had watched the foaming tub of her belly shiver, had watched the woman's hands become delicate, swift, precise. The child had watched, unstartled. Always it had been the same. The difference was only in degree. The woman had traveled miles in that room. Centuries. Reaching her debacle, she had also attained herself.

Her face had been on the way to healing itself, in its own manner. The injured part glowed dusky under the sliding white cast of the sun. Like a map. Like the state of . . . Virginia. The child had lingered on the doorsill, tracing out astonishing creatures for play. The only thing that could kill a skoffin, she was sure she had heard her father say, was the sight of another skoffin. The woman had given little cries. Her shanks were skinny, her shoulders gaunt. Her mouth had opened into a crooked O. Her teeth lay across it like tiny fishes waiting to be hatched. The child had heard of this. Fishes born in their mothers' mouths, fleeing back there when in danger. The woman's mouth had closed with a moist sea sound. She had writhed briefly, she had straightened. Like a thick weed floating in the valley of the surf, her stomach plump and vulnerable as a seaweed's pod. The child had often thought at that point, for there had always been that point in the day at the edge of her mother's room, just before she, the child, would leave, the child had often thought that if she crept into the room, softly, so that the woman would not become aware of it, like an Indian, like a thief, clever and soundless as a hawk or a shark, that if she slipped into the room and embraced her, lightly, lightly and unbeknownst to the woman, if she encircled her waist with her own small arms as best she could and squeezed suddenly and very hard, the swollen stomach would pop like a blister of bladder wrack, it would crack like the grim Atlantic and all would be delivered and dispelled. The baby would rush to the floor in a flood. There would be a briny, shiny smell, and then the ceiling of the room and then the roof of the house would topple away leaving in the dull day, and then the winter sun, with its evaporating qualities, with its own mysteries, would drink up every drop.

But the child never entered the room. Not even cleverly. Not even in stealth. She went outside. She skated a little. She returned, she asked her father for a candy. The woman and the room were forgotten for a while. After all, what could be done? She was a prisoner in waiting, and quite mad.

THE LONG BLUE LIPS, the wave of what had been, draw back. The child is at the bottom of the stairs. There is no one in the room any more. She has no mother. She is in a house of mourners. They are all eating but someone comes out of their number and she feels her coat being taken off. She sits down and her boots are unbuckled and then they are gone too. She has loafers on, a white penny in each one. An older girl in school had approached her one recess. A penny means you're single and you're looking, the girl had said. And a white penny means you're a poor dope because they're from Canada and not worth a thing.

Kate doesn't care. How can it matter? All of her dreams are satisfied. The perils of childhood mean nothing to her. She studies her loafers, but someone guides her gently to her feet and into the kitchen. Someone ladles soup into a bowl for her. "Give the child more than that," Megan Jones orders. Kate looks up. She shudders. The room vanishes. Only the looming woman remains. An infant hangs from her hip, the tiny feet webbed like a wind-bird's, moving, making up time. Four o'clock, five o'clock, six o'clock, seven. Then six o'clock, five o'clock, four. Her mother shakes it but it goes on unperturbed through the bottom of its days. It is her mother, lovingly nourishing her, making sure she gets enough to eat. Kate's hands flail into the soup. She puts it down quickly and her mother disappears. There is simply a neighbor there, smiling and only slightly known, a dish towel bobbing at her side. "Megan!" a voice scolds, "you've filled it too high. Here you are, God love you." An arm comes out of the voice and pours out a bit of the soup into a cup with a handle. A cracker is dropped into it and bobs merrily. The child walks uncertainly into the dining room, searching for her father.

"D'you notice how much Megan Jones resembles the poor Mrs.," the civil servant, Bolt whispered.

"It happened all at once," his wife agreed. "It seems there's always one to give you a start."

Kate is looking for her father.

"*Eternity is forever the glimpse of extirpation in the eye of . . .*"

"Kate," an elderly woman grasps her arm weakly. Her

touch does not even spill the soup. It is vegetable, homemade. The thick pasta letters tack heavily through the red and green. An M floats up in three-dimension. "Kate," the old woman repeats. Her hand slips to the child's thumb and waggles it forgetfully. "We have a parakeet, you know. We wish you'd come over and see him. What a little fellow! He'll be your friend. He'll take a seed from your lips."

The thought makes Kate feel sickish. Her eyes rise from the soup, knock against the woman's smile which is peculiar, her narrow teeth seeming to alternate with another substance entirely, like grout between tile, and settles on the mirror reflecting the food-burdened table. She sees the pink jellied packing of a ham tremble as the woman who looks like her mother sets down a dish of pickles. The sound that it makes as it comes in contact with the platter comes across the room much too late. THLOK.

"Ahhhh," someone says. "It was a beautiful, beautiful service."

In the eye of what the child wondered. *Ex tir pation in the eye of who?*

"He'll cheer you up," the old woman was saying. "The best medicine. We got him after they did that operation on John. They hung those bags on him and we both thought we'd die of shame but that budgie's brought us around. He's made us smile again."

The people move in a line around the table, gathering food, choosing and chewing, eating being styptic, a check on the world. It reminded the child of the way they had filed past the coffin. The old woman selects a stumpy piece of celery and spectacularly fits the entire thing in her mouth. Kate slips away but is apprehended almost immediately by a short sad man. Perhaps he has had a little too much to drink but Kate thinks he smells very good. He smells of bread rising. He smells of the water bottled behind the peg they put in the lobster's claw. Kate has forty-one such pegs in a

leather marble bag. She has eaten forty-one lobsters in her
life. It seems impossible. Someone must have assisted her.
Nevertheless she has the pegs. She has enjoyed them all but
her enjoyment is tainted with uncertainty. They are no longer
moving through the sea.

"Eat," the man says morosely. "Eat, now." He detains her
with one hand while, with the other, he fills a plate for her.
The hand wrapped around the child's fingers is cold. It is like
a piece of gear. It is nothing personal. It belongs to his job, to
his big white boat, to the sea. Somewhere Kate has put down
her cup of soup. She sees it close beside her on the tablecloth.
She picks it up. Underneath it is a part of a fingernail.
Someone's nervousness. She puts the cup over it again. The
man forks food rapidly on a plate. Ham, meat loaf, mac-
aroni, chutney, carrots, fried tomatoes, potato chips, rolls,
orange cheese, white butter. The plate is jumbled high with
food. There is a ball of stuffing on the very top but there is
nothing visible that has been stuffed. There is no turkey. No
duck. Suddenly the child's throat aches uncontrollably. She
wants to cry. There is stuffing but no turkey. It is a ball of
dirt on top of everything.

She sees her father and hurries over to him. The ache in
her throat stops. She sits close to him, resting her head against
his arm.

"Whose eyes, Daddy? Whose eyes were you talking
about?"

"What, sweet?" His hair is an early and unearthly white.
The child had always remembered it being very white and
beautiful, folding gently back across the tops of his ears to
lie thick and low upon his neck. His fingers were long, the
nails slightly dusky, like a woman's.

"You were talking about eyes. They were very important."

"Your eyes are the only ones that are important." He kisses
the top of her head. "It's only what you see that matters to
me. . . ."

Jewel, the man who passed the plate on Sunday, said kindly. "You have beautiful eyes, Kate. Dark hair, blue eyes. You're going to be beautiful, Kate."

Embarrassed, she picks an object from her plate and vaguely puts it in her mouth. It is creamy and tastes terrible. She tries to swallow it but it lingers on her tongue. Like the communion bread, she cannot digest it. She has helped her father cut up the latter on Sunday mornings. Tiny, crustless cubes. It is simple grocery fare, slightly stale. Should it not be in the shape of a man? Should it not have the outline of defeat? The suspension of the world must be strong. The child can achieve all worlds but this one. She swallows miserably through the service. Her mother used to give her a mint. She cannot swallow fast enough. There is a limit. The pulp of the bread cube remains behind, girding her teeth, numbing her. Now, this night, she picks up her napkin and grimly excises the thing that is its artifact. It is a struggle. It resists. She knows she has not been altogether successful. She remembers her mother saying, Chew chew chew, you can't be too cautious. It is a sauced tiny onion. No one has noticed. She looks at her father. He is not eating anything. She shoves the plate quickly and disgustedly beneath her chair.

Kate's eyes. She is bewildered. *Glimpse of ex tri cation in my eyes.* "I think I'll go feed Race now," she says.

She makes her way through the mourners, wriggling past their legs. A man's voice rises thinly in the air . . . "dress up britches like a small hotel . . ." The people were bumping together and breaking apart. They swung around Kate as she walked to the kitchen. "I read in a magazine where two chinchillas will make you a wealthy man. Two of them. Can raise thousands of dollars of them right in your own bedroom." The voice was happy with an innocent greed. The child plunges through them. Once, her head is caught for a strange moment between two woolen hips. "Ahhhh, little darling." Faces lower and low. She is hugged and petted.

Kate suddenly feels like a bride. Her fingers smell of gardenias. Her mother had told her sister about blood. Kate had overheard it. She, Kate, will never bleed. This is her wedding day.

A BRIDE IN THE KITCHEN, opening a can of dog food. She picks up a knife and a sack of meal. One door of the kitchen leads outside. She opens this and tramps through the snow around the back of the house to the bulkhead that leads into the cellar. The sky rests on top of her head. Everything is still. The snowflakes falling are very tired and small. Months ago, after the first big freeze, Kate had seen the great geese flying past the moon every night. She had heard their honking, though they were miles high. Now everything is still. The ice is thick on the metal fastenings of the bulkhead doors. If she puts her tongue to them, she'll be mute forever. They have the power of witches. When the doors give, there is a pleasant thump as the snow slides to the ground and she steps into a warm darkness. She holds the sack in front of her to feel the walls. She guides herself by the beat of the dog's tail upon her legs. She turns on the light. Race writhes happily before her, picking up a ball, a shoe, a coat hanger, reeling around and around.

"You're nutty," she says, putting down the food. Then she freezes, turns slowly around, gritting her teeth and staring ferociously. Race's mouth flaps shut. He crouches, putting his muzzle between his paws, waving his haunches in the air. "Argggggghhhh," Kate growls, ponderously raising her arms, curling her fingers into claws. "Brrrrrhharrr." She stalks toward him, hung with sudden menace and ghastly intent, then shifts her direction slightly and begins to close in on him from the side. The dog's eyes hang fast to the place where she had been but his flanks tense, his tail swings back and forth with a lazy delirium.

The child inches toward him, wheezing and babbling, and

the dog's brandy eyes flickered sly and eager now as he tried to keep her in his sight. He leaps, swiveling in mid-air, facing her directly again, his head cocked to one side, his hind-quarters swinging artfully. He wraps his forepaws around her, panting and whimpering with delight, and Kate now rubs his head, digs softly at the bone above his eyes, the cartilaginous buckle of his beloved skull.

"What's your opinion, Race? What do you say?" He sits politely before the dish as she mashes the meal and the canned meat together. Then he drops his head and nudges the food, trying to eat around the meal. Kate walks to the bulkhead steps. Race has a piece of meat bulging in his cheek and when he sees her leaving, he stops chewing. "You be a good boy now." She waves. "I'll see you in the morning." He opens his mouth and the meat falls drearily into the dish. His gaze is hurt and accusing. He walks swiftly to the blanket and curls up upon it.

Kate circles the house and enters the front door. Once again, the stairwell to the second floor is before her. Her feet are wet. She has ruined her shoes. She hears someone moving about. A light goes on. It is a bare light bulb, hanging from the ceiling. It bounces a little from the pull that awakened it. Her cousin stands beneath it. She smiles up at him. While she is smiling, the bulb blows out with a slight whistle.

TWO COUSINS are sitting on a bed. The house is noisy and up-stairs it is cold. The oldest is a boy and he is fourteen. The child is a girl, seven and one-quarter years old as she says, and her mother has just been buried a few hours before. The boy has very dark blue hair like someone in a comic book and is smoking a cigarette.

"I bet you're not supposed to do that," Kate says. "I bet your daddy would give you what for if he saw that." She goes to her desk and takes out a small plastic basketball that

splits in two. She opens it and brushes the ashes out of his
hand where he has tapped them. "You're smelling up my room
but that's all right. I like it. I don't care."

"You're wet," the boy says. "You've been running around
with no coat and you're going to get pneumonia." After he
says this, he wishes that he hadn't. He does not want his little
cousin, whom he is meeting for the first time, to think she is
going to get sick and die. He is a nervous, worried boy, softly
handsome. His parents run a small drugstore in the next state.
It's all they have. The entire family works there, the boy
coming in after school. It is necessary that they like and respect their patrons, who steal lipstick and aspirin and knock
over their Coca-Cola glasses. The boy is never allowed to do
anything. He imagines himself far away, even now, in a
foreign capital, in a night club. He's read in old magazines
that there are rooms of degenerate art in Europe, houses
where evil and sexual things are displayed. He'd like to get
into one of those rooms. Just once. But they were closed
down, before he was born. He is dying to go to one of those
rooms where songs by a man named Weill are played. At the
same time, he realizes that his information is dated. He would
do anything if someone could tell him where to find a room
of degenerate art.

"I'll never get pneumonia," the girl says. "I'll probably
never ever get sick. There are some people who never get
sick and others who never get well."

The boy draws and draws on his cigarette until there is an
ash almost two inches long. He dumps it into the plastic
basketball. "Where'd you get this?"

"There was chocolate in it. Little chocolate basketballs
wrapped in foil. I ate them all."

"I'm sorry about your mother," he says quickly. "It's very
sad and I'm sorry."

The child scratches her throat and looks out the window.

"Well," she says, "you certainly didn't have anything to do with it. You don't even live around here." She wonders how long people will be talking about this. She sighs.

"No," he says, surprised.

"Your hair is beautiful. I wish I had blue hair. It's the color that a storm is, did you know that?"

"I wash it a lot," the boy says. The child is sitting on the edge of the bed, her bare legs swinging beneath her short dark dress. She swings them faster and faster. The hem of the dress is wet and wrinkled.

"Well, it's very nice. It's unusual." The child enjoys being here with her cousin. She is glad that everyone is downstairs and that no one knows where she is or is bothering her. She likes having him sit on her bed, smoking and looking around at all her things. When her father comes up, perhaps they will all have a cup of cocoa together. She wants to be a good conversationalist. "Do you ski?" she asks politely.

"I ski pretty well." The child's face is provocative and he feels harried. He feels that something is being expected of him. He lights another cigarette.

"I have a sled," the child says vaguely, "but I have never skied. Daddy doesn't ski."

The boy is perplexed. He tries to keep himself very still but it is as though he has something live and hasty buttoned up within his clothes. He wonders if he will get meningitis or cancer or become deranged because of his thoughts and his constant manipulation of himself.

"I want to show you something," the child says. "I want to show you my things." She goes to her desk and removes an entire drawer, setting it between them on the bed.

"Look. I have seventy-six wilderness cards from Shredded Wheat. All different. I have a hundred Dixie-cup tops with the pictures of movie stars. All different. I have the pictures of eight football players that can only be seen through a special red magnifying glass. Four of them are members of the Crimson Tide, a name which I think is very pretty. The Crimson Tide is all I care about. I'd give the other four cards away."

In the upper corner of one of the Wilderness cards is a deer. On the bottom is an Indian. *When one is moving through unknown country,* the card instructs, *it is wise to make small signs which will guide you back yet which will not inform possible enemies of your presence. Break the branch of a certain tree. Move a rock slightly so that moss will be visible. Make marks in streams. Beware of marked paths.*

There were flowers and dirt in an envelope, a bridle bit, a photo of his uncle, her father, as a young man, cut out precisely, like a paper doll. There was a piece of flannel shirt, a magnetic plastic lady in a bathtub. It was a new currency, giving access to a ruined land. There was a cast-iron colt, his hoof broken off.

"You can't fix them," the child sighs. "It's gone forever. It's like a real horse when he breaks his leg." She picks up a common pin. "This is supposed to be lucky. I found it honestly, on the ground. Lots of people pick up pins in department stores where they're all over the place. They go into dressing rooms where there are hundreds of pins. If you believe in pins I'll give it to you and it will probably bring you luck. It can't bring me luck because I don't believe in it. Believing in pins would mix up the whole religion."

The boy accepts the pin and sticks it in the lapel of his suit. In six more years, he will be heavy in the face and hips. It runs in the family. His mother is the dead woman's sister. In six years he will be perfectly synchronized with his life. At this moment, he does not realize this, but it will happen. Now he thinks of himself as a French gangster. He blows smoke out between his teeth in a fragile stream.

The child replaces the drawer in the desk. "There is one more thing," she whispers. "There is the greatest thing."

THE DOOR BENEATH HER BED has been there forever and only her father knows about it. Often, in the day, in a certain white and winter light, it glows like bronze, it shines for the child like the bell of an old cornet. It lies flush against the floor, the latch on that side having been removed or never existing; the latch and lock that is visible massive and cold to the touch, even on the warmest day. There's not a scratch on it. It's never been scraped with a key.

The child believes that her life is behind the door. She believes that the door will become lighter as she grows until just before she dies it will have no more weight or substance to it than a scrap of paper. She'll be able to fall right through it. She watches it every day and it never changes.

"Look," she says, and takes her cousin's hand. He kneels, pressing his cheek against the wide floor boards, his ink-black dungaree-blue, thick and damming hair spilling across the child's foot. He looks beneath the bed. He is vicious, innocent, ordinary. The child's breath sprinkles on his neck. He bats his eyelids furiously. His whole face twitches and jumps.

"What's the matter?" the child asks worriedly. Perhaps she is not supposed to show the door to anyone. Perhaps she shouldn't because it will give them fits. She takes tiny inconclusive steps to and fro and tugs on her hands. Her cousin looks like a picture she had seen once in a book about the Civil War. She begins to pat his hair.

The boy's eyes fly open and he stands up and sits on the bed again.

"I thought you were ill," the little girl says.

"There's a door under your bed," he says tentatively. The child looks at him without speaking, not knowing quite what to think of his response. "Whose door?" he asks. "Where does it belong?"

"It belongs under there. It was never any place else."

"Knock, knock," he says. The child is silent. "What's behind it? Lash La Rue? Milky Ways?"

"It's me," she says at last. "It's Katey that's behind that door." She pulls the bedspread back into place.

"Don't you think you'd better get her out?" The boy cannot imagine what he is talking about. He moves his mouth in the shape of a smile but his dry lips snag on his teeth.

The child begins to chew on her braids.

The parsonage is on the coast. On three sides is a large dead yard, empty even of the smallest bush. The front of the house faces a cliff of shining rock and purple weeds and then there is the sea. Everything is very still. Snow falls. Downstairs, the mourners mutter softly to each other. There is a clink of silverware, the sound of water running.

Outside, an engine coughs and dies. It turns over again, catches, hums, drops into gear. The tires thud softly across the snow. The boy says,

"I have something nice to show you too. It's something special. Do you want to see it?"

"Yes." The child's wrists are extraordinarily narrow, the bones huge and painful. It is as though there are two rocks jammed beneath the skin. "Sure," she says.

He leans back slightly and unzips his fly, working his penis out of his clammy shorts without yet exposing it. He takes his cousin's hand and presses it down. The child has curled her fingers and they knock uncertainly around his crotch and then open and grip. She does not look at him but instead concentrates upon her hand, sunk into his trousers, curved around something soft and feverish.

The boy rolls himself back further on the bed and draws himself out. It's raw and narrow. An eye blinks moistly. The hairs are short, lighter in color than the hair of his head.

The child shakes her head. A boy in school has a mastoid the size of a walnut behind his ear. An old woman in church has wattles like a turkey and there is a man who has no mouth. Each day he wears a fresh red white and blue handkerchief over his face. The child has seen pictures of terrible things. The Bible has told her of terrible things she cannot even picture.

"Will they be able to take it off in the hospital?" She decides that she will ask her cousin questions and see what he has to say. Then she will compare his answers with what she already knows.

"No, no, it's good. It's what men have." He moves her fingers around it. "It's for you to play with."

The child strokes it carefully. It is very warm and muscled. Like a fish fillet. There seems to be something softly crackling beneath the skin.

"Does it hurt if you fall?" She saw him becoming impaled by it with the slightest stumble, quivering like a jackknife on the floor. "Does it get in your way?"

"Yes," the boy says. "All the time. This is the way you show you love someone," he tells her.

The child does not want to hurt her cousin's feelings. She smiles.

The snow is turning to sleet. It falls like broken glass. He moves his feet up onto the bed and settles the little girl beside him. She is thinking of asking him for a hank of his beautiful hair.

On the floor is a pink and white package of Dentyne gum. The child knows an excellent trick. She can take one of the smaller wrappers inside the package and fold it two times. It spells

DIE CHUM

which she thinks is terrific. She wants to show her cousin this, but her father has disapproved of the trick and so she pretends that she has forgotten it.

Her cousin is saying something to her. His voice is slow

and turgid, the words coming out as though they are things, eating their way through milk.

She does not want to be discourteous but she is bored and she twists away from the boy's grasp.

AN IMPALPABLE SUBSTANCE, at the same time being very dense; the child unconceived. She often worried about never being born. It was idleness, she knew. For here she was. Her name was Kate.

If she had not been born, her father never would have realized that he did not have her to love. She would have known though, small gelatinous thing rotting in a womb the other side of the stars. She, floating in a cold and bloodless place, would have known that she had been the none end result of a stroke sterile and unfinished. She would have known, even though she would have been more dead than her mother was now, that her nothingness had left no absence in her father's heart.

They had been living together alone for more than a month, the little girl and her father. Her hair was carelessly braided. There was a smudge of supper still around her mouth. The house was huge but they did almost all their living in two rooms, as they had been in the habit of doing even before the wife and mother passed away. The room that they are in now is warm. There is a fire but it is a noisy one. The kindling is fir and it snaps and cracks loudly until it is wasted and the good oak logs begin to burn. Outside, the child can hear the black wreath on the door, twisting on its nail in the wind. Neither speaks. The remnants of their supper is on the hearth. Cocoa and swordfish, the last of the summer's frozen catch. Downstairs, in the cellar, behind a bench of potted sleeping chrysanthemums, behind the jars of jelly and green tomatoes, leans an oil painting, delivered just that morning by several members of the congregation.

The child had answered the door. She was barefoot, wearing a woolen bathrobe. Behind her the house was dark. The painting was wrapped in brown paper and part of the paper was dark from the falling snow. It was too large for the child to lift. They brought it inside to the kitchen. The child offered them tea. No one unwrapped the painting. The Reverend did not appear. They drank tea and looked around the bare kitchen. On the wall was a calendar but it's wildly inaccurate—a dated car journeying through a constant August, advertising a brand of tires that is no longer sold.

Before the mother died, things were more . . . under control, more up to date. The rooms had furniture, clean slipcovers, rugs. In the cupboards were candles and cans of food. The children were sent off to school with thermoses of soup. A piece of fruit. A slice of meat. Raw vegetables. Healthful, balanced meals. There were always flowers on the table. Even in the winter, there were paper arrangements. There was a smell of wax and washing and cooking. Of life being mildly but thoroughly employed.

But now . . . the house is so empty. Everything has been sold or given away. The members of the congregation comment on this without coming to any decision. There are leaves in the hallway, a box on the floor filled with summer dresses, cracks in the plaster and windowpanes. Some purpose has been forgotten. Some simple lesson and requirement of family life has been found unnecessary and not resumed. The rooms are being abandoned, their services discontinued. There's no telling how long this has been going on. It was this way before the funeral. The day of the funeral, when the women of the church arrived to fix the salads, set up the folding chairs, when the men came to remove the remains, they discovered that there was a great deal to do. They freshened things up as best as they were able. It was a house, it was clear, where someone had been sick for a very long time. And yet, of the Mrs. there was little trace. Two

rooms, right off the kitchen, there was a woman's place it seemed, a private place. The walls pale yellow, birds and fruit carved into the mantel, a canopied bed. But the comforter was flung back to expose the mattress ticking. Rust and water marks. An ant cake in the corner. A sense of departure, dismissal . . .

As for the other rooms, there seemed no plans for their use. Most are completely empty, the others almost so. One enormous sunroom on the third floor, spreading out above the sea, has a few of the child's toys in it, a record player, a stack of albums. They would look through them briefly. Classical music. Churchly music they supposed. And there was the child's room. They didn't enter that. There was a faded stencil of tiny animals on the door. The door was closed. They had a strong sense of what was right. There are three bathrooms. One has a tub filled with damp clothes and towels. Another has a tub filled to the brim with water. Cold. There is a fat creamy bar of soap in the dish. A bumpy rubber mat to keep a bather from a slip and a nasty fall. A box of powder on the commode top. Perhaps the Mrs. had drawn herself a bath, poor thing, just before she passed away. They don't blame the Reverend for wanting to keep it up, if indeed it's so. Perhaps it's just a gummy drain. They remember in Mr. Smiley's salt-box, in the dining room, the table's still set as it was on the night fifty years before when the Smileys Sr. failed to return for dinner and failed ever to return again, having been crushed when a haywagon overturned on them. It was how young Smiley showed his due to them. They can understand that.

The third bathroom seems functional enough. Shaving brush. Bubbles of toothpaste in the sink. They didn't go in. No one had the need to.

UNDER THE CIRCUMSTANCES they had examined the house as best they could. It had been a fine house. Once everyone had wanted to live in it. That wasn't so long ago. Now it was as dark and strange to them as an idea of Europe. They had to walk through it again to see what the problem was.

The child stood in the kitchen eating dry cereal from a bowl. She looked feverish and thoughtful. The oil painting was leaning against the wall. It slipped flat onto the floor without a sound. Someone picked it up and set it on the table. The child showed no interest in the painting. She was really not a very curious child, they thought. Children were supposed to be curious and shy. She ate Cheerios, picking out the perfect O's. They made themselves some more tea. Outside the kitchen window was a sparrow strangled in the end coils of the clothesline. It could have just happened or it could have happened in the last month. No one mentioned it. They didn't want to bring it to the attention of the child. She was really not a very observant child, they thought. The wind blew in from the sea but the bird didn't move. Icicles sparkled on its breast like spurs.

"I have a cold," the child said, "and won't be going to school for a week. I have all my books at home and I also have books from the library. They're overdue. I have an excellent one called *The Lore of the Horse.* One white foot, buy a horse, two white feet, try a horse, three white feet, look well about him, four white feet do without him. Daddy doesn't ride. If he did it would be wonderful. We could employ ferries and planes when necessary and ride right around the world. I know everything about horses. Horses know everything about us. You can tell the future by reading the hairs in a horse's mane. Of course you shouldn't do that."

"I'd bet you'd like to run off to the circus and be a bareback rider," Morgan, the carpenter, said. His wife looked at him and rattled her teacup. "Little girls do not run off to the circus," she said. "Only little boys do."

"Well, where do they get their girls from then," he said

loudly, not looking at her but at his neighbor, the man who sharpened blades.

"I have seen a circus only once in my time," the man who sharpened blades of all sorts said. "And it was not an astounding thing as they would like to have you believe. For example, the bareback rider, who, in this case happened to be a young man (he said this sadly to Mr. Morgan), a heavy-set fellow of another extraction, missed. He did not miss the first time or the third time, but in the middle of his act, he made a poor judgment and did not come in contact with the horse at all. Of course this is what everyone remembered. Had he done his job as he was supposed to, no one would have thought about him further."

"Isn't that the way, though," someone said.

"Why should I run off anywhere?" the child said.

"He didn't mean that, dear," Mrs. Morgan said. "You want to stay right here for now and take care of your father."

"Daddy cares for me beautifully," the child said, "and I care for him."

The house was still. There was not even the sound of a clock. Then there was a dry scrabbling at the door and the child got up and let in her dog. The hair beneath the dog's chin was gray. The child went to the refrigerator and made a sandwich which she fed to the dog. "We have everything pretty much in order now," she said. "Though we thank you very much and though they were delicious, we won't be needing any of your casseroles in the future. Those noodles and meatballs that one of you dropped off Tuesday night were really delicious. We added a little wine and we ate it all right up."

"Wine?" Bettencourt, the fisherman, said the word so angrily that it seemed to all present that he had cursed. He still wore his crude gloves, stained with grease and with a hole in each thumb. His lips were blue, even in the summer, from working on the water and his eyes were half shut.

"A full red wine is always a great help in cooking," the child said.

"I had no idea your father partook," one of the ladies said.

"I don't think wine is good for you, dear," another lady said, venturing to touch the child's shaggy bangs. Each felt giddy with a liberty they couldn't understand. The Reverend didn't seem to be home. They had almost forgotten the painting, the solemn, thoughtful reason for their visit. Hadn't the sea always seemed safer than this house? Wasn't there something about this house that was as difficult to discover as the nests of the sea birds? They glanced around it stubbornly, all but a few ignoring the child. Dirt in the potato bin; no potatoes. Up on the sill, a big seed of something, its root end hanging over a dry glass. Another relic of the mother. Nothing visible. Why were they so curious and confused? Two women left the room and softly padded up the stairs. The child heard them. She put more water on to boil. She slipped about, like an unpunished, untethered pet, across the floor boards, creaking and familiar and all her own. She watched the women go up the stairs.

"It's bad for anyone's kidneys, wine," Bettencourt said.

"That's only the very good wine," the child said, "with the stones, the silt, on the bottom. And that's only if you drink that part, the bottom of it. We haven't the means to buy very good wine, so I'm sure we're quite safe."

"Oh my dear," the lady said, still stroking the child's bangs, "where do you hear such things?"

"Well, Daddy tells me everything of course. He tells me the things I should know and the things I shouldn't know. And he tells me which is which. As God says, 'I set before you the way of life and the way of death.' That's in Jeremiah. And Daddy has done that for me."

"You're a lucky little girl," Morgan said boisterously. "And you're just a little girl certainly but soon you'll be all grown up and what will you be?" He sucked on his teacup, found it was empty, swallowed, regardless, twice. "What will you want to be then, eh?"

"The child has a cold," Mrs. Morgan said. "Don't push."

The child looked out the window, past the sparrow, along the rock ledge that plunged into the sea. Beneath the surface were the fishes and beneath them, caves, and beneath the caves were sightless, creeping creatures, wailing with a whale's song from everlasting starvation and beneath the creatures was the bottom of the earth and below that, the wealth and terror of everything. The child chewed on her hands. The seaweed on the ledges was delicate as lace, sheathed in ice and shining in the sunlight. There was dead ice and living ice, her father had told her. One was white and one was blue. Everything was living and dead together. There was always some part of you that was dead. There was always some part of you that didn't need anything and couldn't help a living soul.

"Well, I just couldn't know what you mean by that," she said. "I am what I am. Next Tuesday morning we're getting up before the sun and we'll spend the next three days singing and talking to all those people off of Marlsport, on those islands. We did the same last year, if you remember. Father and I were gone three days. It was a very rewarding experience. Everyone got together and baked Daddy a cake in the shape of a Bible open to the Psalms. It was the largest cake I'd ever seen. I don't know where they could have got the pans. It was white with red icing. It was close to Valentine's Day that year and Daddy cut me a big piece of cake and served me first and said, 'This is for my one and only Valentine.'"

They catch each other's eyes above the child. The two women who have left the kitchen can be heard as they move about through the empty rooms. Peter gets up abruptly from his stool by the stove. Peter farms a little. A luckless man, with allergies, but vain. He gives the child a little pat and then goes to a closet, opens it. Turns away. Pushes on a light. Then walks with a quick step through the house. Some present murmur. They feel like a mob. They feel slightly dangerous to themselves. The women think of a vast sale, the sale of the century, where fantastic bargains are offered. The men are ruttish, warm. They think how long the nights are, how cold; how little warmth familiarity brings. They are in this house at last. Though they have been guests here before, it was not the same. They would like to take something from here. What? They want to steal something from this place, anything, something trivial. Who knows? They want to push this child away, put her in her place, this silly simple child who makes them feel so rancorous. Nothing is here for their taking. This makes Bettencourt nervous, almost sick. He has always had this problem.

BETTENCOURT HAS TO THIEVE A LITTLE, otherwise he feels that he himself has been robbed. Each year, late in the spring, he and his wife drive down to Boston for two days. It is their anniversary. Each year they stay at the Parker House. He steals dinner rolls, glasses. The last time he took $1.85 from the pay radio in their room. Once, on the trip home, on the new highway snaking around the city, a station wagon in front of them lost a suitcase from its luggage rack. The rope securing it to the roof broke and a dimity-covered suitcase sailed across the highway. It landed in Bettencourt's lane, exploding on contact into a bright flower of ladies' weaknesses, clothes, hats, little purses and boxes and bottles. Bettencourt was a slow driver. He witnessed this slowly. He braked to a stop beside the broken suitcase. The station wagon backed up. Bettencourt's ready help was much appreciated. The occupants of the station wagon were a man and two shiny blond women just off the ferry at Woods Hole. Bettencourt was fearless and shambling quick. His wife screamed for his safety as the cars whistled past. Everything was snatched from the asphalt and thrown in the back seat of the wagon amidst many regrets and wild thanks from the women. The rest of the trip was without incident for Bettencourt. His wife sat in the back seat. When they crossed the border into Maine, she sang all the verses of the Maine Stein Song. She had been doing this all her life, every time they came back from Boston, even though she had never gone to the university. Bettencourt never sang along. In this particular case, he drove with a pair of panties in his pocket. They were the color of peaches. On the left hip of them was *Tuesday* in pretty scroll-sewn letters. The thought that all the days of the week were represented in such a way made him gloomy and dissatisfied. The panties, he thought, were of silk. There wasn't enough to them to cover his wife's elbow. He had them still, and he enjoyed having them, even though he didn't look at them very often.

Now Bettencourt is in the Reverend's house. It is all he can do to keep from scowling at the child. She seems both burden and obstruction. She seems to block something in his mind. Like the black water, he works every day, setting and pulling his traps and nets, there is something into which he cannot look. She stands by the window, regarding them all absently, patting her dog. She is tightly cinched into her bathrobe. The cord of it belonged to some other garment and was too long. She had wrapped it around herself twice.

Bettencourt's hands had been toying with a paper envelope of pills that were lying on the table. He slides them in his glove. They are pills for the dog, obtained from a veterinarian. The dog has ulcers in his ears and the howling of the wind here bothers him. They are for the dog's pain. Bettencourt does not know this. He would not plan to swallow the pills anyway. He wants merely to remove something from this house. Now he has done so. But he knows that he has been duped. The child sees the pills disappear. Life is so artless, is it not? There is so much that meets the eye?

The child said, "On Saturday nights Daddy and I dance
upstairs. It's always chilly in that room. Our breath stays in
that room as long as we do. The snow can fall right into
that room when the wind is right. On Fridays we sometimes
dance too. And those nights he gives me my bath. We're not
in need of anything that I can think of." She looked at the
painting all wrapped up. "You really shouldn't have," she
said, "and I hope this isn't perishable, for we haven't the
room for it. Perhaps you could take it back until another
time . . ."

The men and women are scattered throughout the house,
walking, rattling doorknobs. They still wear their heavy out-
door coats. Their boots make wallowing tracks in the floor's
dust. They look through the windows at the bright, starved
landscape. The house seems abandoned; it simply cannot be
lived in. Whatever they are searching for has already been
taken.

And behind them is the child's voice. She had not followed
them but she has such a pervasive, inhibiting quality that
they feel she is at their backs. They have seen her everywhere. Grocery, graveyard, boat basin, tumbled duck-blind.
She is that part of their days that they cannot come to terms
with. She is that part of themselves that they cannot recognize. In springs past, they have watched her, trotting a horse
through the crumbling frost-heaved streets of the town and
into the sea. She wore gray jodhpurs crusted with sea water
and the animal's sweat. She wore a small stern blouse, buttoned tightly at the throat and wrists. They heard her high
clear voice at dawn and dusk and holidays, bringing the
horse to a gallop. Now the horse is dead too. A big clay-
colored horse with a black mane and no name. Its legs
got thick as railroad ties and it cried blood-stained tears
before it died. The child cries herself, even now, when she
speaks of the horse. They remember the day the carcass
was burned, behind the owner's barn. It smoked and smoked,

a hopeless blue. They remember her walking through the town, fumbling at the wide hips of her jodhpurs, trembling, the tears springing from her eyes. The breeches were second hand, brittle, about to tear. They remember her as she walked stiffly past their houses, her hair white with dusty grain, and then began to trot, to canter, changing leads, loping miserably in her shined boots beneath the smoking sky.

GALLOPING HORSELESS TOWARD HER LIFE, which is up past the hill, in the parsonage, in the winding halls, in the rooms gone to storage, in this silence, this requirement, this breeding place of dreams . . .

They hear the child's voice.

"I thank you for dropping by, but I'm afraid if you stay much longer, you'll all be sure to come down with my cold."

"Yes, we must be going," someone said. "It's almost lunch-time. What do you have for lunch, dear?" They found it so tedious speaking with a child.

"Daddy and I often don't have lunch," the child said. "We try to use that time more constructively. We speak of things and such."

Everyone straggled back into the kitchen. They didn't consider that they had actually left it. What right would they have to do so? What reason would they have given? And yet they were tired and troubled as though they had returned from a long and fruitless journey.

"Well now," Mrs. Morgan began, coughing slightly, un-necessarily. Her words had been chosen and approved by the group. It was disappointing to her that it was merely the child she must address, but it seemed apparent that the Reverend was not home. And yet, had he not been present in one of the rooms they passed by? Had he not simply ignored them, making no attempt to restrain them? Had he not been there, oblivious to their petty acts of trespass?

And was not this child, trapped in her awkward childhood, feeding in his cold gaze even at the moment?

"I'm sure we would all like your father to be present for this," Mrs. Morgan began. The child was doing an odd and formal dance, touching her heel with her toe. She was not paying attention. And the men were in the hallway, eager to be off, their stomachs growling.

Mrs. Morgan said, "It's for both of you, of course, but we would like your father to be here for the moment of its unveiling."

"But he's not here now," the child said sensibly. "He's resting and thinking. I can understand that perfectly, can't you? I understand everything he thinks. Later today, the two of us will open this together. I wouldn't care to see it by myself. Father and I will look at it together, at the same time. I know that would be best. I hope this isn't valuable. I mean, I hope you didn't spend a lot of money on this. True value lies in self-knowledge. All else is rust and rot. You must excuse me now. When you leave, please don't slam the door because then it won't catch. I have a fever. When you have a fever you should get ten or twelve hours of sleep a day. I haven't begun any of them yet."

She pirouetted around the corner. Mrs. Morgan pursued her appointed course doggedly. "You're a little young now, dear, but we're sure as you grow older, you'll see the pricelessness of this portrait. And we were so happy to be able to do it. Though the price was considerable, for we dealt with no sign painter, we dealt with a real artist, an artistic, creative person. And how could the price be too great in this case? For in its way, this will live right along with you. We're sure you will dwell on this portrait often. And may your hearts be glad! Do not sorrow any more!"

And here she dropped her voice for there had been disagreement among the congregation whether this should be said. "Who knows the joys of heaven? I wouldn't dream of saying anything out of place, but who knows the arrangements the Lord has made for our everlasting peace? For Time is only here on this sad earth, isn't it? Another example of man's ignorance? For in God's Love there is no Time! There is no East or West!" The lilt of the hymn caught her up. Once her future had been bright, so bright. Beside her photograph in the high-school yearbook so long ago they had said *a girl with her eye on the stars who will go far.* And what had happened? Where had she made her errors? "For in heaven," and she smiled bravely, her voice rose again, "beyond the limitations of our poor lives, will not all promises be kept, will not all our dreams become real? And will we not all sit at the Lord's table and rejoice, with all our lost loved ones restored to us, with the moments that were and the moments that could have been at last One, Triumphant and Complete!"

She stopped. Mrs. Morgan felt that she had never been so eloquent in her life. She had tapped a new and wealthy source within herself. She moved her hand up to her breast and the fluttering of her heart. He eyes descended onto her husband. There he was, quite fat; Mr. Morgan, with a look of wonder on his dumb and dumpy face.

The child danced around the corner again. The robe had slipped down over one shoulder, exposing her thin flat chest. "I hate to say it," she muttered sadly, "but I think I know just what you've got in there." She tipped her head far to the left and then far to the right as though she were shaking water from her ears. She left them all again, and this time did not return.

Those present agreed that they should unwrap it. They carried it into the room that seemed most lived in and hung it on the wall, on a conveniently placed nail.

"It certainly does become the focal point of the room,"

said the wife of the man who sharpened blades, as the painting was going up.

High above them, in the sunroom, the child was dancing with her father. They moved with measured slowness across the wide pine boards of the long room. They danced to Bach's Toccata and Fugue in D Minor as played by Albert Schweitzer. The music is inventive and bold. It is known that Bach composed most of his religious music as he played it in the little and large churches of his youth. The music was created as it went along. As is the dance in this cold and endless room. As are the dancers.

THE PAINTING was, as is to be expected, of a family grouping. It is done in oranges and yellows, shrimp and sun colors. Most of it was copied from an old photograph, taken a year and a half ago, in the garden. The garden, at the time, was quite spoiled and brown. It was not the season for a garden. The mother and the girls, Kate and her sister, are seated on a little wrought-iron bench. The bench is too small for them all. The child, Kate, is turned sideways and it appears that she is giving more room to the others. The Reverend stands behind them, wearing a white coat which is also out of season. Somewhere, beyond the picture, there must be a stiff wind blowing, for the mother is holding her skirt down across her knees and laughing while the sister seems to have just returned from a motion of brushing back her hair. Kate is wearing a pullover sweater and shorts. She is not smiling, for she has lost her front tooth. She fears that she will never get another one. There is a great deal of foreground. The sky is not even visible.

The man who took the picture was the sexton. He had not taken many pictures but he had recently bought a camera at a pawn shop and he was trying it out on everyone. He also bought a lie detector and four metal ornaments that

had once been fitted to a Japanese sword hilt. His wife
said he'd gone soft as a sneaker. The sexton thought the
lie detector would be a nice way to pass an evening with
people if his wife ever had anyone over for coffee and cake.
His wife was not a hostess. The lie detector went its way.
Little Kate wanted it, but it passed into other hands.

So the sexton took the picture and in time it was developed
and printed. And it was this picture that was brought to
the lady painter on the mainland with the artistic personality.
She could not be reached on the phone or in person. She
had to be dealt with by correspondence.

The painting was large. The likenesses were not excellent
but they were good enough. That is, no one would mistake
those who were being represented for others, who were
not being represented at all. License was taken with the
land. It is covered with flowers. A dress has been put on
Kate and she has been turned around to face the others.
Everyone's hand seems vaguely on top of everyone else's
hand, as though there was a mallet between them and they
were determining who should be first at croquet. And before
them all, his own little hands resting on his mother's knee, is
a standing infant. His back is to the viewer. He wears a
charming, common smock and his head is covered with tight
blond curls. His head is tipped slightly toward his mother's
lap. And everyone's head seems slightly tipped toward him.
The expressions on the faces of the mother and her oldest
daughter are marked by a tight-lipped calm, as would befit
those, we might suppose, who have passed on. Entwined in
the lower windings of the iron bench is an empty nest.

The father has told the child that those who have loved
become a single angel in heaven or a sole beast in hell.

They sit in front of the fire, the father and the child. The
wall is empty, as it has always been, except for a little while
that morning. The child says, "I think that that thing should

have a name, like graves have words. What do you think, Daddy? Of course it's a foolish thing, it almost makes me want to laugh, Daddy."

"Some things don't have names," he says. "Many things."

"I think that maybe if it had been done another way I couldn't stand it. But nothing was right, was it, Daddy? The eyes or anything. It won't be like that, will it? We won't be all together again? It would make Mother so unhappy. You know, sometimes she comes back to me just before I fall asleep and her face is like a movie star's, but I know it's her because that's the way dreams are. She's sad and pretty, Daddy, like once you said she was, and she holds my hand like she used to, Daddy, remember she was always interrupting me and holding my hand and I would be busy but she would hold my hand and hold me back and say, I just want to know that you're here beside me for a moment, Katey. I just want to know that I'm here with my little girl. And I would say, Yes, Mummy, but we never could give her what she really wanted, could we, Daddy? And now when she comes to me at night, she's sad but not crying and she doesn't say those terrible things any more. She doesn't say anything for a long long while, but then she always says, please don't ever bring me back again. That's what she says. That's all she ever says."

The Reverend is silent and the child shyly drops her eyes. GOD IS IN HEAVEN AND THOU UPON EARTH THEREFORE LET THY WORDS BE FEW. Ecclesiastes 5:2 or 2:5, she thinks and begins to chew nervously on her nails. She keeps forgetting things. Sometimes she trembles because she can never seem to keep things straight in her head.

"Don't do that, sweet. You'll spoil your pretty hands."

Her hands are freckled and yellowish. They were always being scratched or bumped or squeezed. She puts them away.

"I think a nice title for that thing, that painting, if it ever sees the light of day again would be *Mortals prepare for you must come and join the long retreat*," the child says.

He looks at her gently. "Where did you see that?"

"I heard it one day, from you."

He has a cold blister at the corner of his mouth. He touches it with his tongue. "There is no retreat," he says. "Words are often a presumption and a sin."

The child knows all about words. And sin. She knows that even a baby is polluted in the eyes of the Lord. She knows that every person who has ever been born had been born bad. Everybody living is sinful and everybody dead and everybody quick. The baby that had died in her mother's stomach, that had killed her mother, had nothing on any of them just because it had never been born. It was only twice gone, that's what it was.

The child knows all about faith too. She knows that punishment doesn't have the slightest relationship with what you do or don't do.

They go into the kitchen for dessert but there is nothing sweet in the house. They settle for a wedge of cheese.

"This is very sophisticated," the child says, not enjoying it much.

The two of them sit side by side at the table in the position they had always held.

FOUR OF THEM had been at the table not so long ago. It is the Fourth of July. The Reverend Jason Jackson is at the head, a handsome man, wearing his hair a little long, a little out of style. There is one eye, his left, that he cannot close. The nerves are severed in the lid. An old injury. He is thirty-one. No one is aware that his eye is curious. It can only be noticed when he is sleeping.

To his right sits Katey. She hums and stares past the worn window sill toward the sea. She has thick dark braids, tightly knotted. Her hair troubles her. She feels it is a vanity and is afraid that some day when she is riding the neighbor's great bay horse, she will catch it in an oak tree like Absalom and die.

Opposite her is her sister, a round and freckled girl of eleven. From her schoolmates, she has acquired a flat New England accent that no one else in the family has. She is energetic and affectionate and studies her mother shamelessly, trying to detect how to be a lady.

Kate has no desire of becoming a lady. She wants to be sexless, like an angel.

It is the Fourth of July and they are eating salmon and peas. The mother insists that they adhere to the tradition of each holiday. Shrove Tuesday there are pancakes, every Easter a ham. Each Christmas there's a pudding with the beef.

The mother does favors for them all. She likes nice things. She has learned of nice things in the state of New York where she tells the girls she was born. New York seems to Kate as distant and as cheerless as the desert. She tells the girls about New York. She tells them that Dewey was not elected President because of his mustache. She tells them how to eat an artichoke should they ever be offered an artichoke. She instructs them in the writing of thank-you notes. Kate receives this information mutely as though she were accepting punishment.

The day is incredibly white. Sailboats with striped spinnakers rim the island. A blueberry pie bakes in the oven. It is taken out too quickly. The bottom crust is thick and underdone. The mother cuts huge wedges for everyone and puts them on old pewter plates. She pours out glasses of milk for the girls. On the bottom of Kate's glass is a picture of Charlie McCarthy. She is a child and this is her glass. Each time that she lags in drinking her milk, her mother urges her on with the promise that there is a surprise at the bottom. Kate has seen the picture a hundred times and loathes Charlie

McCarthy who even in real life is only made of wood. She thinks her mother is simple-minded.

The mother and sister are talking to one another. The girl is speaking of a friend's dachshund on the mainland. It's slipped a disc and is in a pet hospital.

"They're not made properly." The mother laughs. They chuckle and chat.

Surely this is not what is actually being discussed. Kate is so little, beautiful and glum. She is constantly trying to hear. She can hear perfectly but she doesn't believe any of it. Her mother has expressed concern over her vocabulary which is rigid and obscure. Sometimes the mother wants to hug her or slap her because Kate turns eyes upon her that are totally passionless and without mercy.

Kate takes the filling out of the pie and spreads it across her plate in an unpleasant paste. She is thinking about a little book that she has in her room on the Ten Commandments. It is a Golden Book of crummy construction. Each commandment is accompanied by a picture depicting what is going on. Opposite THOU SHALT NOT COMMIT ADULTERY there is a drawing of two little children running away from a house with a broken window. Kate can't understand this and she asks her father to explain it to her. He does, the mother believes, a little too explicitly. He does not comment on the picture which is so subtle that it suggests the workings of a truly erotic mind, but he speaks of everything else. Kate sits with her mouth ajar. Her sister starts to cry. The mother is furious and the meal is a shambles, the pie forgotten by everyone except the Reverend. He finishes his portion, oblivious to the commotion around him. He wipes his mouth with a napkin and then makes a steeple of his hands. He looks at them.

Kate begins to giggle. "You are a rascal," the Reverend says. She smiles, her tongue raised over her missing tooth. She feels obdurate and lighter than air.

"I won't have that," her mother hisses. "I won't have that." She takes the older girl by the arm and pulls her into another room. There are mutterings as they gather up their purses and sweaters. Kate draws in her cheeks. She thinks this makes her look tubercular which is the way she sometimes likes to look. Her mother stands between the two rooms, still gripping the older girl by the arm.

"Everything's funny, isn't it! Everything's a nasty little joke. Well, I want you two to clean everything up here," she says. "Washed, dried and put away. We're going." She tugs her daughter's arm for emphasis. Kate's sister holds herself carefully in a starched white dress. Her face above the collar is like a strawberry cream. "We're going and we'll have a nice time." Her mother looks drawn, even frightened. "You two do what you want, but you needn't follow us. You needn't bother us."

They turn on their heels, the mother and her more tractable daughter and rush away. The door slams. Other doors open and shut. An old engine turns over, backfires, wails out of gear, stalls. A door opens again, the hood is raised, banging on the bound linkage ensues. The hood slams shut. The door slams shut. The car is backed up and driven off.

Kate puffs out her cheeks.

"You still want to go, don't you?" the Reverend asks her.

"It doesn't matter, Daddy." Some people in a boat are shooting off fireworks into the daytime sky. It excites her. The idea of candles burning while it's still light.

"You had been looking forward to it."

"Yes," she admits. "I'd like to see the donkey again. I'd like to go down in the mines in a donkey cart. I'd like maybe to go on the merry-go-round once."

"Then we're going, of course. It's a big park. Your mother doesn't have to see us there if she doesn't want to."

"We give her fits, don't we, Daddy?"

"Are you ready to go?" he says.

"Oh yes, Daddy." Kate slides out of her chair and skips outside to where the family's other car is parked. Sometimes it doesn't even start. There is no guarantee that a journey will result simply by turning the key in the ignition. Kate and her father get into the car. It is an old white Hudson. Someone has painted it by hand. Hairs from the brush are fossilized beneath the paint. The interior is beige. Kate bounces several times on the seat. She pretends she is aloft in a marshmallow.

The engine rumbles spiritedly. "Good-by, Race." She waves to her dog graciously. He takes a few steps toward them, ramming his paw into his water dish. Kate and the Reverend drive onto the ferry and are taken across the sound to the Independence Day celebrations and the amusement park.

HER MOTHER LOST HER MIND. Kate saw it. It was not after her sister was killed but before. Kate witnessed it. It flew out of her mother like the black puff of a devil's breath, and enmeshed itself in the workings of the merry-go-round, entwined itself in its cheerless and monotonous music.

The riders were quaintly solemn, thumbing rings from a chute. All looked desperate and disappointed. The horses were welded into place.

Kate stood with her sister. Her sister was fretting over a spot on her white pleated skirt. They had been sharing a hamburger. Grease had dripped down from the bun. It had ruined her skirt, she wailed. Everything was ruined. Kate looked listlessly on while her sister rubbed at the stain. A woman holding a styrofoam cup had come down from one of the concession stands and she said, "It's all right, honey, this will take it right up. You just watch this, honey." The woman had a star cut out of one of her teeth and the star was gold. "Watch this now," she said, but Kate was watching her mother and father standing on a little scrap of darkness shed by a faded purple awning. Her mother's face was white and distorted. She looked ancient, inhuman. Before them, fat sea gulls waddled about, for the park was on the coast. They looked like toys. One shuttled around Kate in a stumbling circle, making a poor sound, a long piece of string trailing from its open beak.

Kate heard her sister. "Oh!" she said. Her voice was pained, incredulous. "Oh, what's happened, what's happened! Why did she do it? Why did she want to do such a mean thing for? Oh, Katey, look what she's done!" Kate turned reluctantly. Above them, the woman from the stand was alternately shaking her head with a frown and grinning encouragingly, the star in her mouth sparkling and wet. She was drawing off thick pink milk into a glass for a customer. Kate looked at her sister's skirt. It was now corrupted by a much worse mark. The woman had daubed cold coffee on the grease and the stain seemed darker and twice as large. The sister wadded the cloth into a brown bunch like a wilted bouquet and little Kate looked at her wryly. She was not interested in this—in clothes, in outward appearances. Besides, it had looked hopeless. She shrugged.

Later that day when her sister was dead, lying between the green oak and the wheels of the mother's car, Kate wished that she had said something nice, something reassuring. She wished that she had said, Why that dress will be white as ice, white as it was before in just a little while. She wished that she would have known that that was the way it was going to be so she could have said that. For, a few hours later when her sister was lying dead on the road, that skirt looked brand-new. It hadn't even been mussed or dirtied by the fall from the door. And neither had her sister. She had flown soft as a butterfly into that giant tree and the sound, when she struck, was not loud, as one might expect but a low, poor, redeemless sound, like that of the dying gull. Nevertheless they heard it, Kate and her father, for they were not far behind and their windows were down and the air was still. And it was true as well that they saw it, what there was of it to see. For the moment passed so swiftly and then the girl was dead even though it was only her hand that seemed damaged at first glance. The mother, in her confusion, had backed the car over it. It lay bloodlessly hidden beneath the patched tire. It was the fact that she had crushed her daughter's hand that seemed to affect the mother most. And it was the sight of the spotless skirt that Kate would remember. And it was the Reverend who took the gum from the young girl's mouth and smoothed the collar of her blouse. Death brings order, does it not? There is nothing too small to rest in peace?

Kate was brought back to the car to wait. There was a bag of pretzels there and she began to eat them. She wanted never to eat another pretzel again in her life, so she ate them all, to finish them up. Once her mother came to her and she seemed to have a calm, almost studious expression, an aesthetic air, but beyond suffering any more and without light. And she looked at the child, her daughter, the last, left. It couldn't have been long, no more than a moment, for there was so much confusion around them, noise, unfamiliar voices and the more generous sounds of a summer holiday, the humming of birds and insects unseen and the bright whistling of the car ferry as it moved out of the bay. They had missed it. The four of them had missed going back forever. And all these sounds and strangers were imposing upon them, insisting that something be done or said, so it could have been no more than a moment that the mother was able to look at her living child with such hatred and such intimacy.

Kate's sunburnt lips smarted with the crude salt. Her fingers continued to rummage dreamily through the empty bag of pretzels and her mother stayed her hand before it could rise once again, spasmodically, to her lips. "I wish it had been you," her mother said softly, almost musically. "You listen to me now. I've said this to the others and they pretend they

haven't heard. I wish with all my heart that it had been you."
She moved her face closer to Kate's. The child noticed the
extraordinary thickness of her mother's lashes. They were
tangled and some were turned inward, brushing the balls of
the eyes.

Why doesn't it hurt? Kate thought. Where is Daddy?
When will he drive us to the boat? Her mother was stroking
her limp hand. Kate's face was expressionless. She knew what
the woman said could have no bearing on her life because the
woman was mad. She had lost her mind while Kate was
watching. Her mother's mind had lodged itself in the obscure
mechanisms at the core of the Wooden Horses. Kate had seen
it all except for that which had brought about the exorcism.
She had turned away only for an instant and when she looked
again, everything had been accomplished. She had looked
again and her father was walking toward her, looking ar-
rogant and exasperated, and the mother was walking toward
her too but slowly, so slowly, her hands pressed to her temples, and from her head, Kate saw the black, corrupt and
weightless blossom of her knowledge fall.

"Evil suckled you," her mother said. "You'd never take my
milk. He would never let me touch you really. I wanted to,
you were my baby. But he took you the moment you
were born. The doctor couldn't stop him. He took you and
cradled you and wiped the blood from your eyes. He was
covered with you. I was disgusted, embarrassed. He was
covered with the wetness and the slime of you. No one could
stop him. He bathed himself in you. You were seconds old
and a terrible chill came over me, a premonition. Such cold! I
knew that a terror had been delivered of me. And you remain
still, don't you? Nothing touches you." She did not move
away from Kate, intimating by neither gesture nor pause,
the crowd, the tree and the old car she'd been driving and
would never drive again, her life from that moment on until

the end of it, being tractless and impassable. She stroked Kate's hand gently, at odds with the words, a mother still, "that innocent and loving child over there is gone. He told me, 'You'll only destroy yourself.' He told me, 'We'll go our own way.' And he was right, wasn't he! I've destroyed the only person who ever loved me." She shook Kate's arm. Her lips were almost resting on Kate's own. "I know all about him, little girl, though you'd like to think I don't. And I know you too, and your sly cute ways. Daddy daddy *daddy*, it's made me sick for years!" She lowered her voice, though she had never actually been shouting. "I won't scream. I'm not going to do anything that will make me seem to be the guilty party. I'm not the guilty party, I never have been."

The phrase had swum up in little Kate's head. She had heard almost nothing of what had been said but now she thought of a dreary hall, riddled with black and brown crepe, tables of disgusting food, broken toys, cowering chicks and kittens and rabbits in fetid boxes, and everyone there, all the children, weeping, blindfolded and in chains.

"YOU'RE SICK," she said to Kate. "You must be helped." She stopped, breathing shallowly, drawing back a little. She examined Kate who sat mutely, looking through the windshield. Whose child was this now? Where had all this time taken her? Why had it taken so many years to arrive? And the other child, lost now. Had she ever truly been beside her, all that time before this time, present beside her all those years and chattering dearly, her death existing before her life had begun?

Confused. She felt herself becoming confused, lightheaded. Shock, she thought. I'm going into shock. I am aware of that, she thought.

"Sick," she repeated with effort. "Don't you think I know what's going on? And yet it was only today that I found the strength to act. It was as though at last I had roused myself from a drug. His drug. I had at last shaken it off but too late. Hours too late after years! But today I had a plan. It was so simple, so right. We were just going to leave. I was going to take her away, my poor dear little lost . . ." Her fingers fluttered feebly and momentarily at her lips. "She didn't know about any of this. She never saw—I shielded her from it as best I could but today I faced it at last. I knew I couldn't go on. It was up to me to save her, to get her away. We were going to run away and you would have been dead to her. There would be nothing in her life to remind her that she had a father or a sister. I tried to make it sound like fun to her, an adventure. 'Just the clothes on our back,' I'd said. 'We'll live in the mountains. Like Heidi,' I'd said. She was worried about friends. Oh, she would always have friends. She was like that. She never lacked for friends or happy times."

She looked at Kate as though she were making some final plea to a cool and inquisitional power. Two policemen reluctantly approached. "Yes." She waved to them with an uncertain gesture. "Yes, yes." Kate looked through the windshield. "There's no reason for me to go now," her mother said. "My reason is gone so I'll stay. I've never been strong but I'll stay and take whatever Jason's God is preparing for me." Kate gave a start. Her father's name was so seldom mentioned. She stirred in the dusty seat.

"It's a personal God, Jason has, belonging just to him. That's always been clear. Viciously clear. I'm not strong but I'll stay now. I'll stay and I'll fight. I'll fight you," she said. "Yes," she said to the policemen and walked back with them to the ambulance.

Kate thought of her sister. Once her sister had given her a pin with Kayo on it. Once she had given her a tiny book of drawings of Woody Woodpecker. The pages were stapled together at the top. You thumbed them rapidly and they became a little movie—Woody Woodpecker rescuing a kitten from a tree. She had lost the pin. She had lost the little book. The thought of that made her grievously sorrowful.

BUT THAT TO THOSE WHOM HE GIVES UP TO CONDEMNATION THE GATE OF LIFE IS CLOSED BY A JUST AND IRREPREHENSIBLE JUDGMENT.

At the first allusion to the baby, months later, Kate had been sick. She hadn't said anything but she had thrown up. She is not so old now but someday she will be older. Surely there is something frightful in this.

The fact that she can be no younger than she is now is one that we don't have to accept.

When she was first told about the baby, Kate tried to fix the hint, the sign, the foreboding of the disaster and disloyalty that was so complete. It was as though her father had struck her. He seemed more and more like the fanciful fearsome God he had taught her to know.

Kate remembers. She and her mother are in the amusement park once more. It is fall, a few days after school had opened. Her mother had been waiting for her in the schoolyard. They had taken a bus. Her mother had insisted that they go on some of the rides. The air was raw. No one but themselves were in the plywood pit of the mines. Even so, when one donkey was hired, all the others would go with him, pulling their wooden carts. They were all strung together. They wouldn't be un-harnessed until night.

The child remembers . . . there is a head hanging in a splinter of light until with a shriek it slides along a wire into a basket. Glued to the empty cart rocking before them is a pink sticker, *Don't Follow Me I'm Lost*. There is a roar of rocks, of a cave-in, and a stone wall coming toward them at furious speed through the donkey's ears. A stuffed bear dances round and around in a wire cage, one ear gone, holding a violent bouquet to his plastic snout.

In the daylight, her mother had put her hand on her stomach.

"He's living right here. He's being made here."

The calliope played. The donkey, with a sigh, shuffled in his traces and freed a wide sparkling stream. Kate pulled her fingers away from her mother's stomach and rubbed them over the donkey's warm burred head. There was the smell of the tide and of clams and of tomatoes baking on dough. Everywhere there were sputum and paper blowing, religious pictures and the faces of movie stars sliding out of machines.

They walked down to the beach and sat on a bench, watching the green calm sea and the lace curtains blowing in the windows of the old hotels. The child remembers . . . her mother's face is extraordinary. A brown vein throbs in her temple. The child cannot look at her mother. She never looked at her, unless she forgot. She never looks at herself either, in mirrors or photographs. She has no interest in it. An old man walked in front of them. He wore a tight brief bathing suit. His limbs and chest were brown and oily. He was very old. Kate watched him and he in turn looked at them curiously. The teeth in his mouth were like kernels of corn.

She remembers . . . wishing that the old man would take her mother's hand and walk away with her, into one of the decaying hotels. The man looks as though he might do something like that, if requested. In one ear, he has a ball of cotton.

"He loves me," her mother said. "He wanted this. He comes to me every night. He won't leave me alone." Her hair was wet on her brow. Her mouth was wet.

THOUGH THOU BE SOUGHT FOR YET SHALT THOU NEVER BE FOUND AGAIN. Her father had taught her everything. Ezekiel that was. Words were more important than the things they represented. That was why using some of them was a sin. Kate's throat was bitter. She swallowed.

"It has to be a boy," her mother said. "A boy would kill

him for what he is. He wanted me to be the one to tell you. As though it weren't any of his doing."

A drop of saliva dropped on Kate's bare knee. The damning wish rose serenely and without hate. Without hate. *I hope it rots and molds and dies inside her. And then maybe she will leave us be. They had to shoot the horse because he was sick. He didn't know how to be a horse any more. Then they had to set him on fire. I just want her to leave us be.* Dismally, she was sick. It was as though she had spoken aloud and the words had come into the clear air, darkening and putrefying everything. She vomited onto the sand.

Her mother did not move right away. Then she took a handkerchief out of her pocketbook and walked down to the water. Kate raised her head. The old man was still passing by. He seemed to have a grapefruit in his crotch. He had tiny dugs wreathed with long white hairs. And he was still passing by with a look of disgust and impatience.

And then Kate saw it. Propped between her and the place where her mother had been was a faint bundle, wrapped in a white blanket. It was bubbling, amorphous and horrendous, a clear liquid restrained by the blanket folds. When she touched it, her fingers fell through to the amnion slickness beyond. *There it is and it's never going to be any different. It's never going to get beyond that. She might as well take it out of her stomach now and sell it to the traveling circus. Daddy and I will not discuss this, how it got inside her stomach, we will not mention this.*

Her faith had taken on a terrible reality. Her faith had taken on the substance of things hoped for and the evidence of things not seen. Kate stood and tottered from the bench. The old man was passing by. And her mother came and reamed her mouth with the dainty cloth soaked in the cold sea water. She pushed back her braids and wiped them clean.

The child remembers . . . She tastes, she thinks, the fish that have swum in the water. She sees the form and future of the world in the shabby exotic skyline of the amusement park. Almost everything has already happened in her life. What can remain?

"I want to help you," her mother said. "How can I turn my back on you?"

WHAT CAN SICKNESS NOT DO? Now the child is a woman. She is in the woods with her young man. The woods are far, far away from the place where she was born.

The land is owned by a paper company and can be bought for $150 an acre. They are not beautiful woods but they will do. They are still scarred from the logging operations of ten years ago. The loggers cleared and burned. Later, they planted seeds but the resulting growth is ramshackle, delicate. The larger animals never returned. The land is shocked, stilled. Everything is wet and tapping from a rainstorm in the night. In the leaves, fearful rustlings are heard, but only tiny finches emerge. The woods offer no enlightenment. They are a huge barred door before God.

The boy points to a square of soft earth. "A fox," he says. He has slow pale eyes and thick hair, lying like a cap on his head. All the buttons are missing from his shirt and his thin hard chest is exposed. Above his navel, a blond furrow of hair begins. It is soft as seal would be, the girl thinks. She loves it. His jeans are faded. Around the pockets and the fly, the fabric is almost white.

The girl kneels beside him. She is tall and a little awkward. She has a wide sad mouth and two dark moles near her left eye which give her a convalescent look. To the boy, she seems different each day. It is nothing that he can explain. Her face seems to change. He is not yet used to her. It is as though her life has lacked the continuing experience that will make her what she will become.

She cannot make out the paw's imprint. She searches for it on the damp ground, ashamed. She reaches for his hand and presses it to her cheek. At last she finds it—a very faint impression, more a memory than a mark. "In China," she begins, "if you give a fox a home of his own, and incense and food, he'll bring you luck."

"Incense." The boy smiles carefully. He has strong nice teeth, white as bone.

"Of course." She nods. "In China, a family is very fortunate to be adopted by a supernatural fox."

The boy rises. "Do you wish that you had been adopted?"

"Oh," she says, stunned. "Of course." This land depresses her. The red ground sucks at her feet and the pines are tall and empty of life.

"Perhaps we could go to China," she says. "Or we could live in Mexico. Some country where there is a magic and mystery and luck."

"All that's right here." He spreads his arms wide, taking in the trees, the swamp and distant bay and sky, the roll and ruin of the land.

She shakes her head.

"Why not Canada?" he says. "Why not Alaska?"

"No, it's too cold."

He tells her a joke about Eskimo children. The last line is *don't eat the yellow snow.* She laughs. It is so innocent, so harmless. He touches her face with his.

The girl knows that they will never go anyplace. Before she met him he had a job. Earnest ambitions. He had a car and a few nice possessions. But now he has stopped working and sold everything except the car. He spends all his time with her. They live on his savings. He is self-made, clever, charming and shy. He owes nothing to anyone. But now he seems to owe a great price to her. They are students but seldom go to classes. Sometimes he does not touch her for days. It's like a game. Being in love is not what he had expected it to be. She has taken away his energy and replaced it with premonition. He had imagined a different woman.

Often he had imagined no woman at all for this was not necessary to him. He could make his way on nothing. Now he is involved with the nothingness within her.

The girl knows that other countries are not open to them.

The woods are sunny and then dark. The sky is full of square, swift clouds moving across the sun. Shadows flow down the trees like water and then evaporate. The boy walks several feet in front of the girl, leading them back home. Suddenly he stops and grasps her arm. He points to the left, to a hollow beneath a runty cypress.

There is a dog lying there, a big red hound. His big eyes gallop toward them, but he is scarcely breathing. He lies on his side. They can see the cracklings and mash of his dinner lying in the scummy pool around his head. He is torn open from his balls to a point a few inches before his front leg joints. The rent is straight and neat as any zipper opening and the guts hover still within the belly in bluish globes.

The hound's eyes run toward them and the boy moves forward and crouches by the dog's head, stroking it. The folds of flesh on the dog's neck and shoulders are soft, crumpled like velvet. The hound doesn't move. Two ants crawl across his nose.

"A boar must of got him," the boy says. "He got caught up by a big mean boar." The girl nods. She doesn't know what to do. Her hands hang ponderously useless at her sides.

"Is he dying?" She can't hear herself speak. The dog's eyes are incredible.

The boy stands and walks away. He picks up a short thick branch, hefts it, pushing it against a tree to check its strength. The girl slowly opens her mouth. Deep in the limbs, the trees crack. The air shimmers in the morning heat. She doesn't know this boy. They met stupidly, at a dull movie. He had been sitting in the aisle behind her and had bent over her shoulder, saying something, thinking she was someone else. It's all a misunderstanding. A case of mistaken identity. He is going to brain the dog, dispatch him, club him expertly as he does the fish he catches.

The boy is taking off his shirt. "What is it? What's the matter?" He hands her the shirt. "Tear it up in strips."

The girl looks at him closely. He is still a stranger. She doesn't really know what he should mean to her. She can't remember anything about him. She feels as though she has wandered into a painting. The dog smells like straw. The sun burns her neck.

She rips the shirt in four pieces and the boy takes them and ties the dog's legs to the branch. The dog makes a hissing sound but doesn't show his teeth. The pads of his paws are torn and there are large ticks buried in the fur around his mouth. The exposed guts tremble fretfully with the movement and something oozes out and onto the ground like batter.

THE YOUNG COUPLE walk through the woods, the hound between them, swaying upside down on the pole. Sometimes, the boy holds the pole with only one hand and uses the other to slap at the flies which hover across his back. The girl uses both hands always and pants with the weight. She tries not to look down at the dog but it is all that she can see. The open belly swings and shines below her. The tail droops down, exposing the brown bud of the anus. A pellet of turd appears and slips to the ground. The hound has great dignity. His great eyes unblinkingly study the sky.

They are almost two miles from the trailer where they live and they walk without speaking. The woods slowly change. They become thicker, primal, cooler. The boundaries of the paper company are left behind. The girl is lost but the boy knows the way back. He has always paid so much attention to these woods that he no longer has to be familiar with every part of them. They reach the river and follow its course until they come to the trailer. It's very old. Battleship gray and shaped like an egg. Tiny windows like machine-gun slits in a bunker.

The boy wedges the pole in the crotches of two young pines and runs to the trailer for fishing line and needles. The dog's tongue hangs out of his mouth. It seems to run for yards. The boy sews skillfully—tight short stitches. The girl does what she must without questioning him. His presence, his essence is beginning to return to her. She suspected his gestures and now she feels terrible. Of course he would not kill the dog. He is to be trusted more than herself. Everything she does is unfaithful to him.

She is unreliable, she says.

"Oh no." He looks at her briefly and then down again to his work. Her face is clear and shiny as though she has just awakened. She holds the belly together as he sews, pinching it together with the tips of her fingers. "You're fine. You're doing everything you have to do."

His hands are greasy and spotted with blood. He wipes them distractedly across his chest. He knows that this is not what she means but he does not want to talk about it.

"I'm sorry," she says.

He finishes stitching up the dog and knots the line. He lowers the animal to the ground and unties the legs from the pole, carrying him, then, into the trailer. The hound looks huge yet shrunken, like an empty gourd. The girl throws a pile of blankets and towels on the floor and the boy arranges the dog upon them.

"I've got to wash," the boy says. He looks like a butcher. She watches him run through the woods and dive into the river. In a few minutes, he throws his jeans and shoes upon the dock. He swims to the far bank and returns, again and again, a blunt chopping stroke. It seems that hours have passed. The girl moves an ice cube around the dog's jaws and the dog sighs and closes his eyes.

She walks to the river and takes off her clothes. The dock

is made of six planks, set half a foot apart, floating on oil drums. She lies on her stomach and the boy drifts on his back beneath her. He flows down the length of her. A breast falls slimly through the planking, a long strip of rib, waist, hip, thigh. He sees one fourth of her precisely, no more. She can see nothing of him, her face is turned aside, one cheek resting on the wood, her eyes somewhere in the scenery. At some point she falls asleep. The boy floats beneath her. It gives him an odd and hurtful feeling to be there in his tarred and barnacled cage. Above him, the girl becomes nothing—a piece of hanging bait. She is a pastime for him like the stars. He cannot believe that always there will be this love which consumes him yet which changes nothing. He cannot believe his need. Or why when gratifying it, he is not satisfied. What can be beyond love? He wants to get there. With the girl. Together, they could arrive at this point. But he feels that she does not know the way. She merely represents the way, and they are lost, somehow, with each other.

When he gets back to the trailer, the boy lies down on the couch. In a corner, the hound is breathing lightly in a heroic whisper. The air of the room hangs in dusty layers. Lizards skid across the glass. Everything smells unused. It is something he cannot understand. Everything here seems to be used slightly for the wrong purpose, although, he would admit, the results seem to be the same.

The walls of the trailer are cardboard. They buckle out like sails. The girl has taped up colored pictures torn from magazines. None of her selections are original, but she has insisted upon explaining them to him. There's a picture of a sculpture of James Joyce beside his new grave in Zurich. There are recipes for rich desserts, ads for movies, clothes, hardware. Her favorite, she told him, is the photograph of a tropical bird. She loves it, she says, and describes it to him. It requires high temperatures and is gregarious. Its massive soft bill is a puzzle, as is its long bristled tongue, as it only eats fruit and has no need for such equipment. The bird is actually seven different colors. Mauve, she says, one, blueberry, rose, purple, four, she tells him, emerald green and smoldering orange. That's only six she realizes, but the other is merely white. Flaming and liturgical colors but the photograph is black and white and fading. It wasn't dipped in the proper solution. It's almost gone but will probably not disintegrate further. She insists that the bird is truly as depicted. It possesses the requirements of another creature.

The boy despises metaphor. He grows irritable. To think of her is maddening. He wants to reach some point of reference, something marvelous about them as lovers, but his mind dwells only on the commonplace.

He wakes once. It is dark but close to morning. The night has passed and he is making love to her. It is so good; she is smiling and her body is cool. He feels cured, rediscovered. He turns on the light and the hound blinks at them, feebly raising its tail and letting it fall, and everything seems beautiful, full of hope and lucky chance and love. He tells the girl this and she agrees. The animal closes his eyes once more and sleeps. Together they watch him mend. No man has ever died beside a sleeping dog.

THE UNIMAGINABLE PRETENDED TO BE INEVITABLE. Inevitable it was. Unimaginable it was not. Kate has a young man. They may or may not be married. If so, it is a secret. Married girls, past, present or future, are not allowed to reside in sorority houses. Uxorial vagaries are not permitted. How archaic the idea of a sorority house, how truly peculiar! All the references made within can be construed as sexual ones. When in doubt, snicker. *Nihil est sine spermate* they shriek over their tuna fish.

Kate is living with the girls at Omega Omega Omega. Not just yet, but in a little while. They do not know there that she has a young man. When she returns, they will recognize her as the girl who had been with them before, scrubbing herself with a bar of tar soap in the shower stall. Tar soap—the funniest thing they'd ever seen. She was queer as the girl from Massachusetts. Things that Northerners did seldom caught on. Things either caught on or they didn't. Your boy friend had either a Porsche or a Pinto. You either knew how to do all your Christmas shopping in Goodwill stores or you did not. They will know Kate when she returns. In her absence, the girl from Massachusetts had left for good. The peachy complexion of the girl from Massachusetts had gone all to bumps in the South. She attributed it to the fact that she couldn't rinse her face in her baby brother's pee any more. Diluted. Five to one. Among themselves, the others agreed that Northerners were the oddest things and fast and filthy in their ways.

In college, Kate studied French. She studied French and she had lovers, usually men that she picked up in the afternoon or evening. Kate never made an acquaintance before one o'clock. Men can't think strange in the morning. Men in the morning think of ham and hotcakes and money. They want order and the familiar.

She was never disappointed with her lovers, even the dreadful ones, because they gave her life the feeling of great transparence and they made her feel restful and inconsequential.

Her first dreadful lover in town was the first one she took, shortly after she arrived. It was the day of the evening she met her friend Corinthian Brown. Her first lover was not very pleasant. He was a cab driver. He told her one thing right away.

"I used to be a deep-sea diver," he said. "For seven years they could count on me to go down after anything. Anything. Jewels, boats, bombs, bodies. No matter what it was, the last twenty feet I'd be sinking through silt. That's no kind of a job," he said.

She hailed him as she came out of a used book shop. She

had just been given as many books as she could take away if she took them away right away and so she had called for a cab. Kate had taken to walking through the town in the dead part of the afternoon. Nothing ever came of it. Her back would get wet from the terrible sun. She would wait until three o'clock before she'd have a cooling drink. It was the least she could do. It was the most she could do to wait until three. On the day that she took shelter in the book shop, it was not yet three. She went in there to get out of the rain. The sun was shining and the rain was pouring through the streets like smoke.

"I'm not in business any more," a woman hollered to her. "I'm not keeping things going for that crummy bastard any more." Kate looked glumly at the rain. "Take what you want. I'm Lady Bountiful. Clean the place out," the woman screamed. "He never gave me a thing I didn't end up paying on. Forty-nine years with him," she yelled, "and not one happy moment."

She wore a hairpiece that rose and fell on her head. She wore a dress that had a print of flowers and their scientific names and she smoked a Silva-Thin.

"I suppose you came in here to get out of the rain," she snapped. "Well, it's all past mattering. I'll tell him if he ever has the nerve to ask. I gave them all away, I'll tell him, all your crummy books, to a chippie who at least had the crummy sense to come in out of the rain. Well, come on," she said. "COME ON, goddamnit!" Kate had never met a retiree before. She was not astounded. Nevertheless, she was careful not to move too quickly.

Kate helped her throw the books in boxes. There were dry bug shells on the shelves.

"Over there was where I saw the rat," she said, pointing into a little alcove. A sign said hopefully, THE ROOM OF KNOWLEDGE. "He didn't do a thing about it naturally. I got it myself. Peanut butter."

"What?" Kate said, speaking her once and only.

"Peanut butter," the woman said irritably. "IN THE TRAP!"

Kate hauled several cartons of books onto the street. The rain had stopped and the air was steamy. She waved to the old woman. The old woman was eating yogurt and she waved her spoon at Kate. Then Kate called the cab. They put everything in the back seat and she sat up front with the driver. His hair was combed back flat and wet and severely from his forehead in a '20's fashion and he reeked of Juicy Fruit.

"Yeah?" the driver said, raising his eyebrows.

"Omega Omega Omega," Kate said. Her sunglasses were steamed up. "Do you have a Kleenex?" she said.

The driver looked at her sideways. There was something about her, he decided. To get women these days, a man had to have good instincts, accurate judgment. He fancied his mind as being swift as a steel trap. He fancied his body as being hard and cruel as a steel trap. He saw himself, it's true, as one mean old knowledgeable boy. And this fare was showing off her underwear. When he was putting the books in the cab for her, he saw her bra. Not the wide, white kind that his wife wore, which was big enough to strangle a hog, but a tiny colored one, a tiny blue polka-dot piece of nothing.

"I'll stop and get some," he said. He pulled into a gas station and bought a box of Kleenex. He pulled out several for her and then put the box in a glove compartment. "You're my last fare of the day, isn't that coincidental," he said. "I mean it's been a long day but it's still early. Too early to start in reading all them books." Beneath the Juicy Fruit there was a smell of spicy tomatoes. "You don't look like a bookworm to me."

Kate wiped off her sunglasses. She put them back on.

"How about joining me for a drink?" he said.

"Why not," Kate said. Her reply did not surprise her although it was not at all what she would have imagined herself saying.

"I know a nice little place. It's a bar on the water and they give you free lasagne roll-ups with your drinks until six." He took a series of hard rights and turned onto the highway. The books slid across the seat. In less than a mile he turned off and down a partially paved road that led to a point on the bay. The land was bulldozed flat. Models for condominiums were scattered around and little flags and pennants were strung between concrete electricity poles. Then the land became wild and overgrown again and then there was the bay.

The bar was a shingled house on pilings. Nailed on the walls were sharks' tail fins.

"Two of those mothers is mine," the cab driver said. There was no one in the place but them and the bartender. The bartender was sneezing. "Two Mai-Tais," the driver ordered. Kate turned on her stool and looked out the window. BRYANT'S BEASTS, a sign said over a crooked building on the other side of the road. BRYANT'S BOATS BRYANT'S BUNGALOWS. "Here's to you," the driver said. She took a swallow of her drink. It was all rum with a plastic orchid and a canned pineapple chunk in it. Her throat constricted and her eyes began to water. The driver coughed. "Them sharks will go for your hoses every time," he said. "That's no kind of a job." He coughed. "What's going on?" he asked the bartender.

"Algae," the bartender said morosely. "Two days now. It's not red tide but it's some lousy algae rotting out there."

"Goddamn," the driver said. He got up. "You wait here," he told Kate. He went outside and walked over to the bungalows. Kate thought of Uncle Wiggly. He was always so snug and clean. She swallowed her drink until it was gone. She saw something change hands between the driver and another man. He came back to the bar, coughing. "Two more Mai-Tais," he said.

The bartender turned away. "Why don't we drink these

over in that little cottage over there," the driver said to Kate, smiling firmly. "We can't hardly breathe here. They got fans in those cottages." The bartender set down two fresh drinks. "Where are those free noodles today?" the driver asked him querulously, looking up and down the counter.

"Nobody's been here all day. I didn't make them today. It wouldn't have been economic."

"Goddamn," the driver said.

"I don't kiss," Kate said.

"I couldn't care less," the driver muttered. She followed him to the first little cabin.

"Look at that," he said before they went inside. "Ain't that cute. Little window boxes and a weather vane." Inside, the room was cool. Her throat and eyes stopped troubling her.

"Bryant's the biggest flit I've ever seen," the driver said.

When they came out later it was almost dark. The wind had changed and the air was clear. The bar was lighted and Kate could see people moving around inside.

"I gotta get back," the driver said tensely. "I got obligations."

"I think I'll stay," Kate said. "I think I'll have another drink."

"I couldn't care less," the driver said. She went back into the bar and played the juke box. The patrons were mostly parents and their children drinking ginger ale.

"That was the song!" a child shouted. "That woman played just exactly the song I was going to play. Now I won't have to play it."

Kate went into the ladies' room. GULLS it said. She washed her hands and went back through the bar and outside. Between the bungalows and BRYANT'S BEASTS were stacked the boxes of her books. Her sunglasses were steamed up again and she still didn't have a Kleenex. She took them off. She could hardly see any better even then, it being night. She went over to the crooked building that held the animals.

There was a bleak smell of droppings. She tried to look in the dark windows.

"What are you doing around here?" a voice hissed. "You been sent out here by somebody to drop a match?"

"Oh no," Kate said sadly.

"They probably said 'You just go on out there and move around and smoke a little,'" Corinthian Brown's voice said.

"I came over to see the animals," she said. "I just wanted to look at them."

"Jest?" the voice rose. "Jest! That's something which ain't easy at all!" But the door opened up and she went in.

CORINTHIAN BROWN'S DADDY shot down robins in the winter and baked them in delicious flaky pies. His daddy always would say that he could never understand how a bird so full of shit as the robin, dumping all his mean bug and berry shit over the clean clothes on the clothesline, could taste so good cut up in little pieces with a few peas and a little flour and water. His daddy shot up robins so neat you would have thought they weren't dead at all.

One morning as Little Corinthian was turning out of the yard to get to school, a police cruiser came screaming up the street and turned into their yard, shaking up the mud and almost knocking down the porch. The Audubon Society had complained, the Chamber of Commerce, the League of Women Voters and the Surfside Bank who always had their ear to the ground for the rumble of possible trends. The tourists were horrified, the paper indignant and Brown became an object of rage and the chosen warning to the Negro community that the sick practice would no longer be tolerated. In Night Court four months later, he was sentenced to two years in the County Jail. The only voice raised in his behalf was that of an ugly smart-assed little dribble of a man who was later found to be not wanting to pay his federal income tax and who said that the shooting of songbirds in the neighborhood would not be necessary were there better housing and more jobs. Everyone agreed that if they heard that song one more time they'd throw up.

Corinthian's daddy didn't say anything, not even to his boys. After one year in the jailhouse, he showed enough potential and good intentions to be considered for the position of dog-boy on the work crews sent out daily. He was a good dog-boy because he was strong and had an easy way with them and because he had good lungs and legs and could run with them through the sloughs and across the fields and weeds when the sheriff's people were after fugitives. Brown no longer had anything to do with the police who were a loutish bunch of questionable authority. For running with the dogs he got a lot of fresh air and 1,500 extra calories worth of food a day. Two days before he was to be released, he wound the leashes of his dogs around a light pole and stepped down the road for a can of beer. He was rearrested and sentenced to an additional six months. After that was up it was springtime and he took a bus up to New Jersey where, after writing a note to his boy Corinthian on the back of a postcard which depicted the colorful Howard Johnson's on Exit Seven of the Turnpike, he disappeared forever.

The writing on the postcard said:

"I'm sorry about doing this but I am worn out and got nothing to give you anyways. I hope that by now you have stopped pulling on yourself and have found yourself a woman and cleared up your face. I had a Fisherman's Platter here and I hope you and Amos will be able to get one of those some day."

Corinthian could see that most of the message was for him but the part about the woman must refer to his brother as Corinthian was only seven years old.

CORINTHIAN BROWN'S BROTHER shot up mayonnaise and peanut butter as well as anything else he could pop. He had blue eyes which are always very bad luck for a black man. Corinthian loved his brother and worried about him incessantly. When Amos wasn't messing himself up in the shed, he would be very sweet to Corinthian and make as much of a meal that was possible for him when he came home from school. Most usually, it was a lard and sugar sandwich and a pitcher of Kool-Aid. In the months of May and June it was a strawberry and sugar sandwich. Amos always asked Corinthian what he learned from his books and would always find his replies hilarious.

One evening just before suppertime, Corinthian heard a scuffling in the shed and opened it to find Amos writhing on the floor, his blood, for the most part, filled with liquid Sterno. It seemed the police were always driving through the neighborhood and this evening just before suppertime was no exception. They saw the little boy howling and crying and taking dizzy steps into and out of the shed. By the time they carried Amos into the back of the squad car he was already dead.

"Lookit that," one policeman said to the other, "it's pissing all over the seat," and they made Corinthian clean everything up before they moved on.

Amos was buried in a place that was difficult to get to. Corinthian couldn't remember if they had told him where. Corinthian had a series of jobs for the next few years which didn't work out. He had an unpleasant skin condition which people were fearful they'd contract. They thought it was catchy, like ping-pong flu. All the doctors Corinthian had seen had told him that the disorder was psychosomatic and caused neither by heredity or dermatophytes. How could it be catching? It had caught him and that seemed to be the end of it.

"Are you often afraid?" Corinthian asked Kate that night.

The ostrich was following the darkness falling off her silver earrings as she moved her head.

"They like shiny things," Corinthian said, interrupting himself. "They like to play with spoons."

"Yes," Kate said.

"Are you afraid all the time?"

"No," she said.

"I'm afraid all the time," Corinthian told her bravely.

TERRY BARFIELD'S PRETTY PIEBALD was the reason he was in the sheriff's posse. That horse represented the life he loved and couldn't get enough of—the gear and the parades and the good camaraderie and the dragging for criminals or fishermen who drowned off the keys or in the swamp. He knew it was all ornamentative and an anachronism but it was easily the most significant part of his life. He had four daughters who gave him nothing but back talk and one frail son who spent every moment messing with numbers, adding, multiplying, subtracting, dividing like a fancy computer. "There's never enough paper around here," the boy would scream and beat his head on the table until it bled. Terry Barfield had nothing but trial and misery and his beautiful piebald horse. He was a cracker and his poppa had been a cracker but a real one, an expert with his whip, and foot-loose and fancy in his leisure after driving cattle all day, and Terry Barfield wished that he had been him, born him or even born before him. That was the time to have been a man. He would have shown them what for then. He would have been cock of the rock.

Now he was just trying desperately to hold onto his horse which his wife wanted to sell so she could get a gas barbecue. He was working too much and suffering too much, he said. He had a bellyache all the time. Sometimes it hurt him to piss. His wife told him that was from the horse. He'd liked to have strangled her.

He worked all day driving the cab and then he drove his truck for the county all spring and summer through the mosquito and tourist season. He drove it in the three hours before dawn. He drove it now. It was five o'clock in the morning. He was in the college compound, smoking a black cigar and pulling on the lever he'd installed that released the malathion. His headlights picked up a raccoon hustling across the winding road in front of him. He tromped on the accelerator but the engine just grunted. "Oh Christ," he said, grinding his teeth. He shot out a cloud of chemicals and spit out the cigar.

The truck moved along. It had been made from a car, the back lopped off, pine planking wedged on the chassis where the cylinders were mounted. A green and benignant truck, one headlight kicked in, something winglike fluttering against the exposed radiator grid. "Oh Christ, Christ," Barfield roared. He turned the wheel so hard that for one awesome moment he thought he'd broken it off, and moved the wheels up over the sidewalk curb for a hundred yards or so, bouncing and weaving toward the nigger boy who ambled along there like a fool, his hands fanned out as though he were holding a plate of hors d'oeuvres. Barfield had worked this route for weeks, licensed by the county, being paid by the county and using their gasoline and equipment but wearing out his own truck and wearing down his balls and his own, what he considered to be, innate good nature for nothing more than he could see than another piece of crap his wife would buy and set up in the house. He owed 673 dollars to the finance company and his old lady was having the change. He was so sick of it all he'd liked to have spit and the final indignity had become the first for each morning before the sun came up as he was doing his honest work he would come across this loitering nigger doing his party time right before his eyes.

He was afraid of making too much of a racket. He didn't

want any complaints. But every day he wanted to make a mulched stump of Corinthian Brown.

AL GLICK'S SIGN on the edge of his junk-yard says

> Anyone caught beyond this point without my per-
> mission had better have settled for his soul to go to
> God because his ass belongs to me

The sign troubles Corinthian Brown even though it is his job to be daily beyond the point that Glick refers to. Al Glick killed his first and last wife by pushing her face too hard into a hot pan of her cooking that he didn't care for. He broke a waitress' hand in an argument over the price of a slice of pizza and he put a boy's eye out in a fight about pinball bowling. So each early morning that Corinthian enters the cars' graveyard, which is still as any graveyard, he can feel himself getting shot. He can feel it and he can see his head popping off and rolling into the morning wet weeds where they'd shovel it up like a rabid squirrel's, put it in a box and send it up to the laboratory in Tallahassee. Each morning he moves past the sign, coming or going away again, he knows it's his last moment. They are going to dismember him. He's going to hear a snap behind him and they're going to be on him like white on rice, turning him every which way but loose.

But nothing of the sort happens. Corinthian stands intact within Glick's boundaries. The dogs trot up and sniff him thoroughly for he has the smell on him of all of Bryant's Beasts. Corinthian works continually. He is a wakeful watchful boy. He seldom sleeps. He has probably slept only one hundred hours in his whole life. He moves through the dogs which wind themselves around his legs. Each morning, the dogs suffer the same indignation, hysteria and delight as they glut themselves on the scents of the Beasts. Corinthian reeks of feed and droppings, fish and mice, hair, hide, scaled backs and feathers. Corinthian is truly a phenomenon, a representation of the natural world trapped, an example of the basic made bizarre by cages. But those who speak are not aware of his existence.

Now it is not that Corinthian is himself caged. It is not that he does not move out into the world. He has places where he goes. He has his routes. He uses the movie theatre, the County Book-Mobile, Super-M Drugs, where he buys lotions for his skin's disease, and a café where he eats supper and breakfast in the morning. He leaves Bryant's Beasts while it is still dark, for Bryant begins each day early and eagerly. Bryant believes that each day is the one that will *turn the tide*, that will make him a *man of means*. He is a big bouncing man with fine pale hair and big teeth. He has many frustrations but he remains hopeful. He loves jujubes. He chews on them all day long. One thing that annoys Bryant is that he can buy jujubes only in very tiny boxes that seem to be only one-sixth full. He would like to have hundreds of them available at all times but the fulfillment of this small desire does not seem to be in the near future. Another thing he wants is to be allowed to become a member of the Chamber of Commerce. This is remote. The thought of Bryant becoming one of their own makes the members drink too much and speak unseemly. Bryant's Beasts is just within the city's limits, a maverick on the Gulf's backwash, a tin and broken blemish which drives the mayor and commissioners mad. "Jest let that pissant make one mistake and I'll close him up," the mayor says several times a week. But Bryant is a modest citizen, obeying the laws. All of his toilets function. His animals make no noise. No one has ever gotten sick on his snacks. The only thing that the commissioners and the Chamber of Commerce can do is hope that the place will burn down. Then they can forbid him to build it up again because of the zoning.

In the meanwhile, Bryant comes to his establishment early, rakes up the beach and sets up for his patrons. He sells mementos, nut logs and jellies. He rents beach umbrellas, rubber rafts, and three bungalows, day, week or season. Bryant would naturally like his Beasts to become a *tourist must* but visitors are uninterested in anything which is not indigenous. After all, they might as well have stayed at home if they're not to see something indigenous. The Beasts are the weak link in Bryant's business. His driving range is patronized as is his chili-dog and soft ice-cream stand. His paddle boats are popular. It is the Beasts that no one wants to pay to see even though the price is only seventy-five cents. He has a black bear, a llama, a leopard, a buffalo, a coyote, three deer and two egg-eating snakes. He has two dusky sharks, a bull shark, a tank of turtles and cow-nose skates and two walking catfish, which should alone guarantee half a hundred visitors a day. He has parrots, an ostrich, a kestrel and a vulture. Almost no one comes to see them. Days go by without anyone having observed the Beasts, but nightly, Corinthian, their caretaker, watches them and leaves with his watching pure and unbothered. For no one watches Corinthian. Or would give a penny for what he saw.

Corinthian knows that no one watching or listening is one of dying's little tricks on life. No one's yet come up with any tricks life might have on dying. The Beasts fill Corinthian up. Each night he comes to them empty. He's been sitting in the daylight, thinking and reading and dreaming and trying to fill himself up. He's read about the animals. He knows everything they're supposed to do naturally. Their games and pridefulnesses, their diets and habits, their methods of mating and fighting and hiding. He knows the ostrich, for example, with its tiny wings and heavy legs has adapted itself to running and not to flight. Now in its tiny arena, with its straw and washtubs of soft vegetables, it seems to have adapted itself only to dying. Corinthian reads and studies. None of the rules given apply to the Beasts. He has even read Darwin who says *all animals feel a sense of wonder and curiosity*. But the Beasts' mouths spill open with their own fur and feathers. They bite themselves mortally and without pain. Corinthian sees very clearly that they've begun to gnaw on themselves, even the vulture. They are trying to eat themselves up. Corinthian knows what this terrible hunger is like and tries to apologize to them for it, pushing out his hands to touch them. They do not respond. Sometimes a creature moves its muzzle slowly across the floor. Sometimes a bird moves a talon just an inch farther up the bar. Nothing more happens. Corinthian's medicine of conscientious regard fails. It grieves him to think that his watching the animals doesn't make any difference, that his eye seeing is worse than no eye at all because it has nowhere to turn but inward where the beasts, now twice bereft, vanish. They are suffering creatures, suffering his intrusion. And they go on. The continuing is all that remains to them. They have achieved what people think they themselves hope for. They cannot perish any more.

AN ANNAL OF CRIME, the girl begins. The woods are hushed, waiting for the night. Light comes late here and leaves early. From where she and Grady are sitting, only a scrap of sky can be seen, a tear in the crown of the trees. A buzzard circles high in the tear as though it were his inescapable arena. Of course he owns the sky but to the boy and girl, he seems pinned to this small pocket.

"The tidy housewife," Grady says, "mopping up the world."

The girl lies back and studies the bird gratefully. Interruptions shape our hours. How else can our time here be measured? "It is a very peculiar thing about buzzards," she says. "People do not care for them. No one tells their children charming stories about the Little Vulture that Could.

No pretty myths have sprung up around them. And yet they are just as good as a unicorn."

He laughs. "Better than a unicorn any day." He loves her, he loves her. Where is the danger?

"Despite their great size," she says, "they never kill and will not touch food that shows any sign of life. That was one of the most pleasant attributes of the unicorn."

"The buzzard is more wonderful also because he exists."

"That is always true," the girl agrees. "The unicorn was so gentle he would not even step on live grass for fear of injuring it."

"That is not even a consideration of the buzzard, he is so pure." He kisses the girl softly. The bird floats out of view. There seems a small black dot where he had been.

"Would you like a little something to drink?" the girl asks miserably. She goes into the trailer. The boy ambles down to the dock. There's a logjam of branches and leaves a little offshore. Tiny fish sprinkle off it like stars at his approach and drop off into deep water. In the trailer the girl fills two glasses with ice from the cooler and spills in a little gin. She fills another glass with raw gin and drinks it. She washes out the glass and goes down to the boy.

"You didn't care for that truck full of mirrors, did you?" he says.

"It made me dizzy. I was afraid we'd get confused and run off the road."

"No way," he says in the light lilt of the country.

"They seemed to be mocking us," the girl says haltingly. Her throat pulses, hoarse with the gin. "The way they were arranged. That closed tepee. It seemed they had taken us out of the world. There was just ourselves riding. Anywhere you looked, that was all that was left."

"There's a carnival in Torrent's Landing, that's probably where it was going."

"On to the fun house," she says unhappily.

They sit on the dock. A turtle climbs up on the logjam. The gin is so cold and clear. The girl hangs suspended in it.

"I'm sorry we didn't get to the beach today," he says. "We'll go tomorrow if you'd like."

"Yes, another time."

He holds her face between his hands. "What is it, blueness? Too much alcohol in the blood surrogate?"

She shakes off their joke from the brave new world. "You never ask me any questions," she says stubbornly. She knows how stupid this sounds. His body so close to her is unnerving. She rises without moving as though for love. Her throat is a glacier, melting.

"Ah, blueness," he says wearily. He rubs his chin. The sound is staggering. It seems to resound inside her head. Like axles grinding.

"I want to tell you a little story. It's just a little story I read." She sips her drink. "It would seem to have a bearing on our situation."

"Our situation is fine," he says.

She tosses her head. "This is how I would like to begin," she says. "With this little story." He sighs. She hears it like a sound that hasn't happened yet, like the first cry her baby will make. "An annal of crime," she announces. "In the French countryside in 15 say 14, an eleven-year-old girl was married to a boy her own age. The wedding was not consummated for several years, but soon they were old enough to live together in a portion of the fine house that would be theirs upon the death of the boy's father. The father was a cruel man. Once, he had struck his only son with such force that he broke the boy's jaw and knocked out four of his rear teeth. No one felt the old man's passing to be an unfortunate event. The young couple moved into the house they were heir to and began their instruction in the management of the rich estate. The girl was taught her uxorial duties. They were soon parents of a baby boy although they were

hardly more than children themselves. The girl was faithful
and mild and obedient. She grew to love her husband although he offered her little reason to. The child had become
a handsome but harsh and passionless man, besides being a
casual father, quick to anger and slow to please. Yet they
had another child, the seasons changed, the harvest came and
went and so on."

"A regular saga," Grady says politely and without interest.

"It was not that they did not get along. The girl had
many fine memories of their life together. She couldn't
imagine being happier or anything being other than it was.
Then one spring morning, he came to her and told her that
it was necessary for him to go to another town. A three days'
ride away. He was going there to buy the land that was
adjacent to their own. The owner lived there and it was
necessary that he meet with him. He said he would be gone a
week. She kissed him dutifully and saw him off. Of course
he was not gone for a week. Years went by. It seemed that
he had vanished forever."

"The scoundrel!" Grady interjects. "Of course we must
remember he had been married since he was twelve."

"She never lost hope that he would return. She raised her
children and tried to keep their father living in their minds.
She kept the farm flourishing and themselves rich. And of
course she was true. Everyone was in 15 say 28."

The girl finishes her drink. A dragonfly is on the rim of
her glass. He stays on it as she raises it to her lips. He
remains while she puts it down again.

"Then he came back. Lean from the wars for that was
where he had gone. The same fellow certainly. All the old
servants rejoiced, all the old friends. The children were de-
lighted and the young wife found life worth living once
more. She also found her prayers for his return had been
answered double strength for he was a much more loving
and kind man than he had ever been before. He was tender,

honorable and exemplary to an extreme. She had never felt such pleasure; she had never known such joy. Then she began to worry. She bore another son and her worries increased. A terrible doubt had taken hold of her. She did not think that this man was, her love, her true husband. He certainly looked like him. He was even missing the four teeth that her husband had lost as a boy. He seemed to recall and even extrapolate on all the incidents of their life together before his long absence. Neither his children nor his servants nor his own sister and mother who still lived on the farm had ever entertained such a bizarre notion that he was anyone other than who he appeared to be. Nevertheless, the young wife's suspicion became her belief, strong as her awareness of the strong love she felt for the man. She confided in her husband's sister. The sister was understandably dismayed. She felt that the girl was losing her mind. Quickly, the household became aware of the astonishing nature of her thoughts. She would have nothing more to do with her husband, refusing to share his bed, refusing to even discuss the matter with him. He tried to be understanding although, daily, his wife became more hysterical and committed to the notion that he was an impostor. Eventually, despite the opposition and incredulity of everyone, she managed to bring him to court. There was no witness against him but herself, holding her nursing baby in her arms. The charges were dismissed as preposterous, yet how could this reassure her? Shortly after this, several shabby fellows from the battlefield, on hearing of the strange case, came to her and claimed that they had actual knowledge that indeed this man was a fraud, that her true husband had sold the facts of life together to this lookalike for a considerable amount of money and was still living, a professional adventurer. The wife, relieved but heartbroken, went to court again. This time the man she had so steadfastly accused, the father of her youngest child, was led before the judge in chains. She wept to see him so, for, as I've mentioned, before her doubts, she had never known such happiness or love. It still seemed, however, that the charges would be dismissed once again and forever for the court was losing its patience and there was no additional proof other than the statements of these very unsavory and unpleasant soldiers. But . . ."

"But . . . ," Grady repeats distantly.

"Suddenly in the last moments of the trial, the door opened and another soldier, as unappealing as the others, strode into the room. He bore a striking and uncanny resemblance to the prisoner in the dock. The real husband had returned at last and all present sadly recognized him for he had lost none of his cruel and dour bearing. The prisoner admitted to the deception and was duly guilty of imposture, falsehood, substitution of name and person, adultery, rape, plagiary and larceny."

Grady stirs beside her. "Imagine that," he says. "1500. Things like that wouldn't happen today. People aren't as . . ." He laughs. "Women aren't as thoughtful."

"He was put to death," the girl says. "She murdered him. The father of her son. And she had loved him, but only in thinking that he was another. Touch, word, act, daily passion and affection meant nothing you see. It wasn't even a matter of fidelity."

"What became of her?"

The girl shrugs. "Stories stop," she says.

"But I must draw a conclusion from this?" he says slowly, puzzled. "There is something that applies? There is you and me and the third who always walks beside us?"

The girl rattles the ice cubes in her empty glass. Unseen, the hounds are baying again in the woods. They are famous hounds. She can feel them. They race across the tightening band that grips her head. They are eternal and usually sleeping, but they have always awakened to seize the souls of the dead if one happens to lament them too loudly or too soon.

"Who is to be accused of imposture in our trinity?" Grady asks playfully.

The hounds are hurting her head. They run and run. She rubs her head with an ice cube. "I don't know," she says. "I want to tell you about Daddy."

THERE ARE NO HOUNDS in the vicinity of the sorority house. The housemother has a dog but it is a cocker spaniel. It lacks both voice and genitalia. The housemother had the veterinarian remove its bark and compromising organs. It hardly seems a dog. It is more of an experiment that is still going on.

The housemother lives in the sorority house. Her significance is unknown. She seems useless and unpleasant. She is so lame and arthritic that she cannot walk up to the third floor where the girls sleep in their bunk beds. She cannot climb to the second floor where the girls' desks and record players are, where their bright new clothes hang in the closets. She cannot see well, she lacks any real authority. Nonetheless, everyone hates her. In the dining room where she shows her fine upbringing by eating very tiny quantities of everything, she moves her fork in and out of the food many times before she brings it coyly to her lips. Her stomach is round. She is full of fluids, gases and tumors. Burps and bubblings come from her corner of the room. She likes to say cruel and pointed things to the girls, things that will embarrass them, but it takes hours to think of the words, sometimes days. The proper moment never comes.

Once this woman was married but her husband expired a long time ago. She looks upon those years without much interest. She has never been in love. The girls have boys to love them, sometimes several in a single year. Despite this difference, the housemother is similar to the girls in many ways. She cherishes Kahlil Gibran, just like them. When bathing, she soaps her breasts carefully, as though they could still be useful to her.

If she were younger or if someone had ever loved her, she would be able to do more harm.

One evening at dinner, she finds herself seated beside a girl she has not seen for quite some time. She has never liked this girl and in the midst of spooning Dream Whip on her pudding, she realizes, quite strongly, that the girl has been up to something rotten in her absence. The house-mother has never feared her intuitive powers. On the contrary, she has always welcomed and used them. She takes a bite of pudding and says,

"I know your background and I am sure that those who love you would be very ashamed at your recent behavior."

That, she is sure, will cover it for the time being.

BOOK III

Oh, this is the animal that never was . . .
Of their love they made it, this pure
creature. And they left a space always,
till in this clear uncluttered place,
lightly he raised his head and scarcely
needed to be.

Rainer Maria Rilke

20

Sweet Grady gave me a feeler gauge. I've had it with me all this night in the pocket of my hip-hugger pants. The pants are tight. It's left a mark on my leg, like a burn, where it's been chafing. I take it out and hold it safely. If Grady were here, I would laugh with him, I would say, "The answer is 1-5-3-6-2-4 and what is the question?" And he would know. He would say that it is the firing order of the cylinders. Such a game would delight him. Crazily, he would think that by knowing things he would know himself better. He would be so happy, proud of his hands and his quick bright head.

There's blood on my hand. I don't mean to appear overly dramatic but there is blood on the palm of my hand, the one I grasped the fence with on my wedding day. I've always favored it. I disconnect the radio and go into the bathroom. A sister has just left it. The toilet is still running. Burnt matches float unflushed. They think that sulphur masks it. They're always thinking here. For example, they've planted lemon trees over the septic tank and grease traps.

Still, one can't help but sniff. Childlike absorption with the barnyard.

I go to the faucets. My hand drips a little. I drop the gauge to suck on it and of course the worst happens—the gauge falls down the drain and disappears.

21

On the balcony, Cords and Doreen sit, sometimes hugging. There is a fountain beside them, two feet tall of marble, a lion's head with a sealed tube for a tongue, the tile basin all fuzzy green from the rains. They're there each dawning. This is what they were doing the dawning of the day I began the baby, the day the train bore Daddy down, the day that brought the night my Grady held me for the first time. I turned away. I'd seen it before. Cords dropping her hand down Doreen's spine. Dropping her hand in a rubber glove so tight that you could see the smashed cuticles all bunched behind it. They're doing it now. All those months gone by. The hand pats Doreen's bottom. The hand travels up again. I try not to listen to them. They're saying the same thing. Corinthian Brown is walking down the street outside on his circuit to Glick's and Cords is calling him Pellicle Pete. This is what I heard once. This is what I hear today.

"Pellicle Pete," she sings softly, "you wanna come up and help the girls make brownies?"

I turn away and try to listen to Grady instead but everything gets in the way. All that's happened. The words. The Jaguar planing through the woods. *Do you understand?* I enjoyed it thinking I was dead. But I tried to hold his hand.

Not to hold him back. To let him know . . . I was with him. But my touch. It seems my touch got in the way. It tampered with the angle.

I listen but he is not saying anything to me any more. He has stopped. There is just the sound of his breath sprinkling from his sides. His face is so fragile. It is as though they have strung small pale bulbs beneath his skin. The color blue, the wattage fifteen. His sex is raised and swollen beneath the sheets, pulsating beneath the sheets. It's cool. I could wrap my hand, my lips, around it. A glass of water . . .

I wish I were not so thirsty and famished all the time. I would like to starve to death. If only more foodstuffs were like bananas I would be on my way. I'll tell you I've never been able to eat a banana. The thought that a male banana tree and a female banana tree are necessary to produce little bananas has always upset me. I never eat anything that has been born or pollinated. If this were only so! It's true I've tried it off and on. *I only lie when I am very tired.* I want to starve to death but the hunger, the hunger . . . Ninety pounds. Then less. A child weighing no more than an empty trash can. Then to barely toddle. Then six pounds at birth. I would be present at my birth . . .

Oh, the dreariness of it all. I already was on hand once and I'll tell you, the demands start immediately. Mucus in their throats, the cord still dangling from their tummies and baby girls are ovulating. Within a day there's blood in the swaddling. And it isn't nature's first mistake, this premature menstruation. The egg drifts down. Five hundred to go or so. Is there nothing that has not been going on forever?

22

"Pellicle Pete," Cords sings from the balcony. She raises her arm from Doreen's back and waves. I imagine Corinthian going by below, windmilling his arms because he thinks the moving air is good for his skin and sometimes running and sometimes reading while he walks in the thin and eager light of dawning. I can see him now, all of a pattern. Even in full sunlight his form is rakishly checkerboard; even in total blackness, it's full of shade and innuendo. Sometimes he looks at the girls on the balcony. Most often he doesn't.

"She thinks she's so smart, that girl," he told me, "well I knew what it meant the first time she said it and I bet she had to look it up before she started to use it."

"Whyn't you come up?" Cords calls.

And in that part of the morning that was so long ago and in the part that is now, Doreen is clamping a pink hand over her mouth and dropping it to Cords' knee and saying,

"Why we dasn't do that. We dasn't let him into the house, he's a cullud boy."

"Gracious," Cords says, "it's so."

"I thought that ee-u-nuchs were always fa-et," Doreen drawls.

"He's not a eunuch," Cords says. "The flesh means nothing to him."

"And that's why he's losing it," Doreen crows. "Jest like an ol' snake."

Cords' hand floats back to Doreen's shoulders. Her voice is solemn.

"Have you been dreaming about snakes again?"

STATE OF GRACE   197

"Oh no," Doreen says, aghast, "I couldn't do that after what you said. It was just so awful what you said, it scared me out of dreams altogether."

"Dream of snakes one more time and you'll wake up deaf and dumb. Dream of swimming and you'll lose that which was dishonestly gained."

"I never got anything that wasn't gotten proper," Doreen says.

"Dream of machines and you'll be rendered Pellicle-like." Cords sighs, snapping her arm away. "No more human intercourse. No more salvation through the flesh."

Doreen shuffles her eyes from one part of Cords' face to the other and then down to the street where Corinthian had been walking. Cords was always telling her things she couldn't make head or tail of. Nevertheless, she felt that she had an instinctive appreciation for just about everything that was offered. "Ha," she breathed.

"Po' pure Doreen," Cords smiles. "You'll be sacred to us all. It'll be you the sisters will activate to and not that lady of the rolling eyes in the warped picture frame. Pearls will cascade from your armpits thick as dusting powder and semi-precious stones will rim your box. Catherine," she twitters, "Cathy baby, we've found us a true dee-ciple."

"Ha," Doreen says.

"But there's no reason for you to be down on Corinthian Brown, insulting him and what not." Doreen blinks but doesn't object. *Thoughts are acts,* Cords has told her. *Attitude is all.* "Because Corinthian Brown is going to help us," Cords goes on. "He's got the cat that's going to make you Queen. You've got to be nice to folks, Doreen. You've got to treat them right."

"Oh, I know!" Doreen says, heartfelt.

"Without that leopard, my presentation of you will not be as effective. But Corinthian will come through because our Kate will convince him that he should. Kate will help us out."

"Never in my life," I hear myself saying as I lie in my bunk bed, "have I ever been a help to anybody."

"She'll do this for us," Cords says. "It's such a small thing. She needn't even consider it a favor."

"I've seen myself sometimes walking in Hollywood," Doreen exclaims. "I'm wearing those terrific sunglasses that terrific women wear out there, you know those huge sunglasses tinted pale blue? And I've got a leopard on a leash. Wouldn't that be something? I'd bring him everywhere and even when I entertained, like, you know, he'd be in the room."

"You've seen that, have you?" Cord says.

23

I lie on my bed, fully clothed. Alarm clocks are popping off all around me. The girls are getting up, sniffing themselves, squeezing out the hairs that have incredibly grown out overnight in this loamy clime. Cords and Doreen step in off the balcony. I am not listening to any of them. *Is it over?* Grady said. The floor empties. Now the girls are all in the kitchen. They eat standing up. I can see them in my head. Splashing water on the instant. There is Beth with bruises on her legs and a short flat haircut. She smells like a chlorinated swimming pool. She applies her nails to her scalp and scratches. Then she nibbles on the scratchings. There is Debbie eating a piece of bread, jogging carefully around the edges with her teeth. It is a perfect circle, becoming smaller and smaller. It is as though she is eating on the moon.

I can see it all, it being what it was I saw before. On the highway, the tourists are stroking through the technicolor morning. They are travelers traveling, making time. One little

family in a station wagon sit beneath a cloth deodorizer in
the shape of a skunk.

Cute.

It hangs by the neck, absorbing the odors of thighs and
caramel corn. The skunk is working like mad, doing everything it was created for, but like the power of evil, it can only
last for seven days. *The power of good is everlasting.* Then it
must be replaced. Everyone is stuffed with ham, quaint grits
and papaya juice. They are heading for the *Last Supper*,
which is being enacted somewhere in the middle of the state.

See, the little girl is counting Mercedes automobiles. One
two, three, a diesel, a 190-SL and an error for it is actually a
Rolls-Royce. The small boy has soiled his pants and is changed
at seventy miles an hour. It looks funny. Greenish. Curdly
whey. The mother is distressed. Before she had children she
had never thought about it, but now it seems that she is
always examining shit. Is it pasty and odorless or cheesy and
foul or slippery and shiny or fat and dull? It seems . . . to
fall into certain patterns. It seems to have a tale to tell. She
has found that shit will often supply the answer when all else
fails. She even has the suspicion that shit is the *lane-end into
heaven* and so on, *the lost key opening* and so forth.

She peers at it, slides it around in the diaper. She is alarmed
and expectant. In the past, everything has reverted to normal
before she can apply the remedy. She joggles the diaper up
and down. Her gay young womanhood passes before her
eyes. She shows it to her husband. . . .

Now here is something I really am an observer of because
I have arisen myself now and am standing on the balcony. A
hint of Doreen's perfume is there with me. Now I am not
supposed to be here, observing on the balcony. One is supposed to do nothing on the third floor except get in and out
of bed. For this purpose, there are fourteen bunks arranged
against the walls. On the top are the smaller girls and on the
bottom, I've found, are the ones with problems. In the center

of the room is tastefully empty space covered discreetly with a Persian rug. Above each bunk is a window. The girls on the bottom see the sky when they look out and the girls on top see strangler figs. Some of the windows are painted shut and around them the smell is terrific.

I am on the balcony, looking at the morning through the strangler fig and stinking cedar, and watching the highway over them.

They were all tourists, Father said, *excluding myself*. There is a caravan of Airstream trailers, heading north. They have been in town for their annual powwow. Each year they meet in a field just outside of town and for three days they cook hamburgers and play volleyball. Then they drive off. *Freddie and Gussie from Stillwater*. On the road, making soup of turtles and small warm things, grinding up pollen and seeds. They identify themselves to everyone. *Jack and Cherry Lane from Portland, Maine*. To all the relicts sickly eating straw in the roadside zoos, to the babies playing on the fallen privy door, to the waitresses biting ketchup off their hands in Dew Drop Inns . . . *The Fergusons, Donald and Shirley*.

Hullo, hullo.

24

I believe that our modest home, Grady's and mine, was an Airstream. It wasn't in Grady's style but there it was, and it was his. We spent the days of our married life therein, his sperm warping the floor boards and my cooking blackening the walls. It was perfectly concealed in the woods. I can't understand how it ever came to be in there and it was obvious that in order to get it out, several large trees would have to be chopped. It would be most reasonable to assume that the trailer was there before the woods were, which is absurd. Just another mystery like the boat in the bottle or the *one* in Revelation sitting on a throne and looking like a jasper and a sardine stone. So much mystery but no surprises. I can't understand it.

I have to get back to the trailer. Grady would expect me to. All my things are there, my picnic basket and wine glass, my card

> Hi! I'm Rh negative
> What are you?

But Grady is not there. It is difficult for me to keep this in the front of my mind. He is in Room 17, Section C. *The exploded view*, that's what I saw, just as he used to show me in the Jaguar manual. *The servo unit, exploded view, the wormshaft end float adjustment and bearing pre-load exploded view.* Just as it was in the diagram, the car flew into all its parts. And it was I who was running. It was Grady who was sitting still. One of us was running. Relativity is not reasonable! Part of the car was driven into Grady's side. A pin or a bolt. Part of the Jaguar is missing in my Grady's side, beside the lung. And there are slivers of metal in his head and jaw. Shavings peppered shining in his blond head. They've excised all that was visible; now only the missing remains and they won't touch it. *It is over*, Grady's breathing said as I ran and I had to say *not yet*.

I will not go back to the trailer. If I had been taken there immediately by Ruttkin . . . but it would have been difficult. It was night then. Never had I left the woods except with Grady. Never had I come back to them except with him. I don't think I could have found the trailer by myself. It was his life there, you see, that he took for a time with me. Only the stupor was mine.

And Sweet Tit Sue may be there now. That is a very real consideration and one I could not face. She may have repossessed it. She may have left her own little cabin recently hacked out of the woods, introduced out of nowhere by five pastel concrete squares and taken the trailer again, found our bill of sale in the Rimbaud, you know the part, it went we-wandered impatienttofindtheplaceandtheformula, that was where it was when we drove away last night, found the bill of sale and held it under moving water and taken the trailer again. Wherever she will be, I could not face her again, having done so once. My manner excites disgust, I know. . . .

I did not have the smallest difficulty in finding Sue's cabin. In relationship to the trailer, its location was clear. I knew where it was and I found it. Five decorative steps leading up from nothing and dogs lying beneath the porch but not barking and chickens pecking in the brush. I found it myself. I never got lost. A little less than two miles down that river but with no view.

I set out one morning the instant Grady left. If Sue started right away, I felt that I could be back at the trailer before he returned. *I took a fall*, I would have told him. *I think I've hurt myself*. I didn't care if she did it well. Badly, I would have preferred. I ran through the woods. The cedars were dropping their sweet berries. Grady was on the highway. Until recently, suicides were always buried on the highways. They were not allowed respectable graves. This was not my thought as I ran through the woods, but the fact remained. Until recently.

Please, I had said to her. Sue had a child of her own, a boy eating rice and cookies as I talked. I don't know what you're wanting, she'd said clearly, each word a soft explosion. They told me she wouldn't do it in her own place. They had told me that you had to name the place and she would come there and do it. They had told me that she took it away. We don't know where, they told me but you should just see how green her garden grows. I ran through the woods. EVERY SECRET THING SHALL GOD HAVE JUDGED.

I was told you could help me, I had said. How green her garden grew. The boy finished eating and went into the little cleared yard, picking up the eggs the hens had laid. Sue was making a brine, throwing salt into the water. I was still running with the momentum of reaching the cabin. I had had a plan and the plan seemed perfect but I could not think on it for long. If I could lose the baby, would there still be something in me that would tell, that would talk on and on in punishment?

You are nothing but trouble, she had said. I could see the first time you were nothing but hard times.

Then give me something I had said.

Suicides were buried on the highways and nothing stopped for them.

You can just take a lot of anything that's handy, she had said. It probably won't make no difference but you just keep eating on a quantity of something and get sick and keep eating a quantity more. She shrugged. Sugar, she called to the boy, You bring Momma an egg here for her brine. You got it all wrong from somewheres, she had told me, I ain't never done it, not even once. I haven't never stopped a baby.

Her boy came in, holding an egg gracefully in each hand, between thumb and forefinger. She took one and eased it into the pan. She added more salt until the egg floated up. The boy was holding the remaining egg carefully enough but he somehow stuck his thumbnail into the shell. Blood swelled up over his finger as though he'd been sliced and he dropped it, the thing spreading dismally outward on the floor all broken up and scattered, all its colored jellies and beads trembling in a small and violet pool.

Ahhh, Sugar, Sue had said. One of the dogs came in to lap it up. I stepped off the last orangey steppingstone back into the woods and was back in the trailer by eleven o'clock. Hours still, before Grady would return. I had several drinks but nothing in excess. Whenever I closed my eyes, I could see the baby floundering out of the womb. I didn't close my eyes for several days that I can recall and when I did at last, I could see the curve in the road flaunting my Grady. It was not my thought that it was a curve at the time. It was just the shape my dreams took thereafter until now.

25

Here, it is quarter past noon. All the clocks say this, more or less, on the third floor. The sisters have eaten lunch and are all coming back up here for song practice. I hear their babble as they tramp up the stairs. I realize quite clearly that I am, at present, in the sorority, in my bunk bed. Soon, I will get up and go to Grady who is in Room 17, Section C. I realize this, nevertheless, something untoward happens, my head whirrs and it is Grady touching my shoulder, waking me up. I am so happy. I shudder with relief. It is Grady, saying, "Miss, the movie's over."

And it is. Everything's shut off. Kinugasa's *Crossways*, I think it was, or more likely, something with Tom Mix. There was a chase and an open air setting. Something was resolved. I see the screen for the first time and am annoyed to note that things I believed to have been imperfections in the film were, in fact, freckles and streaks upon the screen.

"They're closing up."

He says. It's true. They're locking all the doors. Someone has pulled a sheet over the concessions. I'm sore all over. I have a cramp. And he must help me up the aisle for I'm hobbling. My leg is still asleep. They won't be showing another picture for hours and there's nothing to do except go off with Grady. He's barefoot but his feet are remarkably clean. He takes me to his car which is moored directly beyond the door shimmering like a yacht in the heat. We drive to a liquor store. It's almost night but everything is still hot to the touch. Grady takes off his sunglasses and exposes to me two dim rims around his eyes.

He leaves but returns immediately with a bottle of gin, a bag of ice cubes and two paper cups. We sit in the liquor store parking lot and drink. I request some bubbly water. It's filling up. Men and women, single women, men and men. We're all sitting in our allotted slots, watching each other and drinking. It's very pleasant. Four carpenters drink pints of peppermint schnapps. A tanned lady, very pretty, an older lady, refined, drinks brandy. Potato chips fall out of her mouth. Someone kisses me. It's an awkward moment, but we have another glass of gin. I can remember it all. Every detail. It gets dark. The sky was a patched-up tent. The lot is lit indirectly from the liquor store on one side and a nursery on the other. A green growing thing for everyone and something for every place, for sand, muck, marl and rocky soil. A sprinkler works its whippety way across the plants and dribbles water across the hood of our car. Beside us, a few children in the back of a truck protect their candy bars from the spray.

Yes, it's very nice. There were three children. Three candy bars. I could tell by the wrappers that they were Zeros.

The last time my very best friend saw me, she said.

I'm fine I'm fine but where is the grapefruit you promised to send.

?, and this was in a dream. Things that I have loved have vanished into acts I can only accept. Someone lays his tongue between my breasts. I am falling, falling, and kiss the belted hip of the man I love, but everything is controlled for I know how it goes. *We are not to rely on what we can do to insure our acceptance with God. We are to accept God's acceptance of us.* There are boundaries within which the worst can work. And I'm working. Yes, I was made to work, if nothing else.

I'm in a controlled fall for how far can an orgasm take you? My chum on the airwaves said only to me,

"An orgasm and seventy-five cents will get you into the silent pictures. . . ."

We return to the movies. The gin is all gone. Upon going back, we pass a pimpled boy, running. And then a gentleman in a white smock and elevator shoes. We piece it together, Grady and I. The gent's a druggist, making a prescription. Everyone is yelling. The boy skids around a corner and a bar of soap falls out of his sock. The pursuers seem satisfied with this and turn back, although no one picks up the soap.

As Grady parks the car, I slip behind the pneumatic door of the movie theatre. Everything is holy and works upon the principle of exhaustion. In and out. Open and close. Win or lose. *No one can gain from this experience.* The door closes behind Grady too. We can't see; the floor slopes. Once again I'm guided to my seat. I feel smug but nervous for I didn't have to pay. I came in after the show had started. The cashier had turned her head. I never paid for anything.

And there on the screen is an empty beach. Blurred. High green water. Puddle of dark pine trees on the sand. There may even be some snow, strings of ice in the grasses. A crib is set up beneath one of the pines. Solidly constructed. Fine craftsmanship. Brahm's First Piano Concerto is playing. The part that goes

da taa taatee ta

What a foundation that crib has! The legs are set in concrete that lies buried but may very well run the entire length of the coast. This was made to last! It's very cold. Of course you cannot feel this, but you can tell simply by observing the elderly Dürer hare at the lower left, in the wind slough behind a dune. His eyes are frozen shut. There's no one there. Everything is white, brown and green—indigestible colors. There's nothing in the crib but surely with a little imagination, a baby could be placed there.

The film has been terribly preserved. It's Delluc's *The Silence*. And something's wrong with the projector. At this rate it will be tomorrow before we get out of here. And how do we get out of here? Ingress or egress. Who's to give permission? Ahhh, what I thought was the cause is instead the consequence. Here.

The sisters assemble themselves in the middle of the room, obliterating the Persian rug. I stay in my bunk even though I will be fined for this. Fifty cents for the first absence, one dollar thereafter. I owe the sisterhood a fortune. The girls would like to send this money to the Indians in the Everglades but they don't. They bought a Waring blender. Before that it was a fake brass fixture for the jane. Sweet God, the "jane." Some things I refuse to bear.

The girls link arms and start to chant

"Lean Mean Doreen
Our Jungle Queen"

It's all a lie of course. Doreen's a dish and brainless as a cracker box. She comes leaping out in a rattan bikini and does a few bumps and grinds. The skit is very flashy, very complex. Cords created every detail. It involves extensive props, including a rented leopard and a burning bush. Ha. Pardon. A gyneco-holy term. A smutty synergism. Rather it's a burning hoop or something through which Doreen will emerge while the sisters wail

> "She'll eat up your heart
> And that's just the start
> Doreen will make you burrrnn."

I slip out of bed unnoticed and go down to the kitchen. The room is cool and empty. The floor's waxed. The day's recipes are taped to the butcher block table. There are some fresh greens there with dirt still on them. Very nice. And some red and green peppers. And a bull's tongue, all black with trauma at the tip.

I go outside and ask directions to the hospital from a passer-by. As the days go on, I am able to find shorter routes. Good-by, good-by.

26

OH THAT MINE HEAD WERE WATERS AND MINE EYES A FOUNTAIN OF TEARS THAT MIGHT WEEP DAY AND NIGHT . . . But the stupor was all that was mine. Only the stupor. Now Daddy . . . always . . . told me that my ruinous life was quickly and immediately determined. He did not elaborate. Now I wouldn't say that I agreed. I was a simple child! Daddy used to say, *Beware the wrath of the Lamb* but daddys say that, you know. It was just a little joke. But I was a simple child. I was always straightening my drawers, for instance. I

was always arranging, arranging . . . Now it's true I suffered
from lack of sleep. I dreamed but did not sleep. Daddy was
mistaken there. He saw me pretending, I suppose. They say
all children maintain this, but I want to tell you, I never
slept. I would be the last to say I saw it all, but never was I
sleeping.

It's true I often had fevers. Daddy told me I had fevers
but he always brought me back to health. It was the house
that did it. The house was always cold and I was chilled. The
elements were always falling in the rooms. Or some of the
rooms. The rooms I liked to play in. Snow, and in the summer
it was rain that fell on me.

But I was a simple child. One incident is very clear. I was
swimming with Daddy, splashing in the shallows while he
watched, and little fish swam into my hair and caught there,
you know, in my tangled hair, for Father did not always brush
my hair, and the little fish had died by the time that we discovered them. It's very clear. It seems I was unconsolable.

But I was tired, so tired. It seems I could hardly keep my
eyes open. All night, I would walk through the rooms. And
I would hear the sounds of living, those unmistakable sounds
of growing, you know, as all things do, toward their death.
Obscure, obscene sounds. None of it ever spoke to me. They
told me I would walk through the rooms the way that Mother
used to. It surprises me now. What did we think was possible?
What chance of finding anything that was ours? I'd never do it
now, I'll tell you. I wasn't much of a child, to be truthful,
even then.

There was nothing in the house then as I walked. Daddy
had taken it all away. They tell me Daddy wanted to encourage no bad memories. But isn't that the hope of the
smallest of us . . . to become another's memory? But, regardless, everything was nothing in those rooms. So much
broken and so little repaired . . . The snow, as I've said,

would fall in on us while we danced, melting on our
faces . . .

And things were always out of my hands. I have always
been grateful for that.

27

The dream is always the same.

A woman is riding sidesaddle. There is no space involved,
no scenery. Just a woman in a long black gown and sweet
old-fashioned beribboned hat riding a galloping horse. She
is holding a baby in one arm and there is a dog running beside them. It is quite apparent that the dog is going to leap
upon the child and eat it. I always imagine that if I could
successfully preclude this intimation, I could alter everything.
The dog jumps upon the infant and eats it. Or rather, he
rests on the woman's lap and tears busily at the blanket in
which the infant is held. Everyone seems calm about this.
That is, the woman seems calm and I, who dream the woman.

It never varies. If I were not so knowledgeable about what
was going to happen, the next scene would not result. It is
obviously Dream Number Fifty-Eight with its natural sequel
Forty. A hand extends a bunch of balloons to a figure whose
face is turned away from me. The figure reaches for the bright
balloons but fails to grasp them. They float up and out of the
dream's framework. No one dares to follow them with their
eyes, least of all me.

It is obviously my non-viable dream. Although it always
wakes me up, it brings me calm. Not any satisfaction and
not my approbation but a calm. Certainly a calm of sorts.

I turn on the radio. Someone has changed the station.

". . . a good man
Preaching in the bottom-land"

I garrote the song with a twist, but cannot find my chum, my crush, my sweetness, my answer action man. I twiddle with the dial for hours. I cannot pick him up. At last I hear an old man's voice. A very old man. He is polishing stones in his rock tumbler. He refuses to turn it off while speaking. That is why the transmission is so bad.

"Yes," "Action Line" says. "In answer to your question. The differences between rising every morning at 6 and at 8 in the course of 40 years amounts to 29,200 hours or 3 years, 121 days and 16 hours which are equal to 8 hours a day for 10 years. So that rising at 6 will be the equivalent to adding 10 years to your life."

He seems a little repulsed at the thought.

28

I am lying on my bed. They've taken away the sheets to be washed. It doesn't bother me. They expect me to become excited about that! They're welcome to everything. It's just my little radio I care to retain . . . it is looped ingeniously among the bedsprings. It's all I have now. I was never much for having things. I was never very good at it.

Sometimes my answer action man comes to me after signing off. He is a dwarf with a vast soft head. Quite horrible.

I can't make love now, I tell him.

Yes, he says.

I'm going to have a baby.

I understand, he says.

Now I know this is bad, his coming to see me like that, perching at the foot of my bed. He, and the fellows off the bottles, all the smiling men . . . It's bad but it could be worse. They could stay longer. I could really insist that I had seen them. It's bad all right, their being there, but it could be worse.

The sleeping room is empty except for Doreen and Cords who are lying on a bottom bunk several rows away from me. They are not doing much, just lying there, talking low. All the other sisters are down in the cellar, in the activation room, imparting the secrets of Catherine, our virgin patron lady, to nine pledges. They are all sitting on board and block benches in that stinking windowless hole, grasping hands, waist to waist, sculpted toe to pumiced heel, all in white and unadorned, listening to a sister who has an undisclosed, undiagnosed *fungus* and is not at her best this evening. Her runny voice swims up the fresh air ducts to me.

". . . Catherine is said of *catha*, that is All, and *ruina*, that is falling, for all the edifice of the devil fell all from her. For the edifice of pride fell from her by the humility that she had and the edifice of fleshly desire fell from her by her virginity, and worldly desire fell from her by her despising of all worldly things. Or Catherine might be said to be like *a little chain*, for she made a chain of good works by which she mounted into heaven, and that chain or ladder had four steps which are *innocence of work, cleanness of body, despising of vanity* and *saying of truth*. . . ."

"Yeh, yeh, yeh," says Cords.

"Ha," says Doreen. She is rubbing Tanfastic on her aureolas.

"Why aren't you down in the activation room?" Cords says to me.

"You should be there too," I retort wittily.

Sometimes my Answer Action man comes to me before

signing on. He is never still. He has the high metabolism and temperature of a bird.

I can't do it now, I tell him.

You needn't make excuses to *me*, he says.

I'm seven months, twelve days along.

I understand, he says.

Two fat bronze palmetto bugs waddle across the mattress and over my ankles.

Your group should pledge hedgehogs instead of girls, he says. They love cockroaches and can be taught to answer to their names.

Whatever their names might be, I say.

Cords is speaking to me. "You look terrible. You're nothing but skin and bones."

"What you should do," Doreen murmurs, "is make yourself a nice milk shake and put some yeast into it."

"I'm fine," I say.

"You're terrific," Cords says. "We're going to have to call someone in to pour you off that bed and into a Mason jar."

"I'm fine."

"You're wasting away," Cords insists. "You're getting to be all conscience. Isn't she just one skinny conscience, Doreen?"

"Uh-huh," Doreen says.

"You'd really better put some weight on. Go down and spoon some jelly or something."

"Ha," Doreen says. She tosses her beautiful hair. It falls across Cords' arm.

I lie on the bed and watch them. The sister's voice rises up through the duct. The fungus is rising in her throat like blood, I would imagine.

"We here tonight have a responsibility to our womanhood," she is saying.

Forty or so milky southern bosoms swell with pride and purpose, I would imagine.

"When is she going to get to the part about the wheel?" I say to no one in particular.

"She's never going to get to the part about the wheel," Cords replies. "It's been dropped."

"Wheel?" Doreen says. She is still dipping into the Tanfastic. "The wheel of love?"

"Four wheels of iron, all covered with razors which detrenched our poor Catherine over and over again and cut her up horribly in torment," Cords elaborates helpfully.

"Ichh," Doreen says.

"You like that part do you, Kate?"

"Oh certainly," I say.

"Personally," Doreen says, "I've never seen myself passing on."

I look at them. They've both taken off all their clothes and are lying there, not moving much.

"You're jammed in neutral gear," I say pleasantly.

"You should get out more," Cords says just as kindly. "Loosen up. Circulate."

I get up all the time. I eat and drink out. I go to the hospital. I see my friend Corinthian. At this very moment, I am getting out of bed.

"When you see 'Pellicle Pete,' tell him seventy-five dollars. Seventy-five dollars for ten minutes."

"Better than a model in New York City," Doreen says reverently.

"I'm not going to be speaking with Corinthian," I say. "You're crazy to want a leopard. That's out of hand. Why don't you settle for a great Dane or something?"

"I've seen myself walking sometimes, you know on one of those fantastic beaches in Mexico? And I'm wearing a silver lamé tunic like and silver earrings, and I'm barefoot in the shining surf." Doreen is talking quickly as though she's on to something.

"Doreen's an eclectic," Cords acknowledges.

"And I'm walking with two great Danes," Doreen finishes breathlessly.

"No leopard." I am walking downstairs.

"Oh, it has to be a leopard," Cords calls after me.

Down in the kitchen, I open the refrigerator. There is nothing there but the prize steer of the county fair, rearranged in neat and mysterious packages. Daily, the cook pushes her hand into the cold. The result is uncertain. A gristly Ouija. It could be pot roast or brisket, eye of the round or sirloin tip. The steer has invaded their lives. He is everywhere. There is no room for the sisters' diet-cola or for their underwear on sizzling mornings. They have been eating him for weeks.

From the cellar, the voice drones on. Someone whistles. The secret whistle, for god sakes. Such cheery girls. I had high hopes of becoming one of the bunch. And of course I am. One cannot deactivate. It's not in the rules. Every girl remembers her activation day. Excuse me. There was sun. Later it set.

29

Corinthian is standing on a stepladder, changing the fly strips at Bryant's Beasts.

"I have never seen a car like that one must of been," Corinthian says.

I left the Jaguar on the curve. I have not paid the towing fee. I have not gone to Al Glick's where it has been taken. The highway does not pass Glick's. Only the railroad tracks.

My head hurts now from the crashing. It didn't hurt then but it does now. Glass is still breaking inside my head and my Grady is saying, *no mistake.*

"Never," Corinthian says. The night is warm and there is juke-box music coming from the bar. All the windows are open in the menagerie and I can see people dancing in the bar. smooth.

I am sitting beside the shark pen. The water is oily and smooth.

"I can't understand how you know if they are still alive or not," I say, looking at the water. It shines off the cages, dappling the bars.

Corinthian shrugs. "I don't even know how many are in there any more. Bryant puts new ones in that the fishermen give him and then he takes some out as well, so there's no way of telling. I've stopped feeding them because the fish were all floating back up." He climbs down the ladder and comes over to the pen. "I don't believe there's anything in there at all," he says.

I look at the water. The South is full of things like this, I suddenly realize. Rotted and broken-down handmade cages and hutches and wire-wrapped boxes and tanks. Perched or suspended or shored up. Outside filling stations or drive-in restaurants or boatyards or vegetable stands.

And empty. Maybe a pan in it or a stick. And the quality of the disquietude is very complete and precise and centuries old.

"Never will touch a man's head," Corinthian mutters. "Will bite off the rest of him save for his head."

"What are you talking about?"

"Sharks," he says mildly.

"Don't be a ghoul," I say.

"It's not me being ghoulish," he says. "It's the facts that are. Things are out to get a body, that's the truth. There are some who've got just one thing waiting for them and there are

others who've got ten, twenty things waiting for them.
That's just the truth."

I don't say anything.

"Once there were a lot of things I wanted to do, but
lately I can't remember any of them," Corinthian says. He is
drinking from a warm bottle of Coca-Cola.

I look at the animals fitfully. The cages are all occupied
and the alarm one feels at this is accurate and ancient too.
There is a kestrel here. The windhover. I cannot look at him.
It is his eye that will not allow it. Not my own. The windhover. How free he must have been.

"Look here," Corinthian says, "that box of books you
brought here that time. Were they all yours?"

"Yes," I say. My obstreperous retiree. My deep-sea diver
with the butterfly stroke . . .

"Look here," Corinthian says listlessly. He has gone into
another room, a room where Bryant keeps the feed and
hoses and brooms, and he comes back and hands me a book.
It is *Heart of Darkness*. It falls open to a marked-up page.
EXTERMINATE ALL THE BRUTES, someone has circled deeply in
ink.

I don't understand. I look at Corinthian and then at the
book.

"It wasn't me," I say finally. "I didn't do that."

"Doesn't matter."

"Corinthian," I say as clearly as I can. "You know very
well it was not me."

"It doesn't matter that it wasn't you." He takes the book
away and puts it back where he got it. He drinks his warm
Coca-Cola. We sit and watch the animals. They are portents,
like cards or constellations. The juke-box music stops. The
lights go out in the bar. The only sound left is that of the
aerator and the water slapping against the sides of the tanks.

Corinthian gets up and unlocks the leopard's cage. After
a while, the leopard walks out.

"How long have you been doing this?" I ask.

"Two weeks," he says. "I did it for two months before he would come out. Now he takes water from my hands. You've been here when the cage was open and you didn't even know it because he wasn't coming out."

The aerator seems to be assisting me with my breathing. Everything is effortless. Everything is simple and whole. The words are easy as I say them.

"Would that leopard walk beside somebody for a minute or so?" The animal is close enough for me to touch him. I rest my hand on his calm judicatory skull. He does not move away. His eyes are like suns.

I tell Corinthian about the Queen Serenade. He is reluctant. But the words are easy. I convince him. I am impressed how his concern and gentleness are changing the beasts. Is it not true that they are changing? Have they not responded to his love? I become very animated. I reassure him. It is all arranged. Corinthian's mood lightens. We talk cheerfully until morning. We are friends.

30

I go to the hospital daily, to the smallest wing in the hospital, the old wing. Everyone seems to shun it, being more interested in the recent additions. Small men move about, pushing floor polishers down the hall. It is not sanitary here. For example, only the corridors, where the patients never are, have been tiled. Tiny tiles in a random design of fake slate. The rooms have brown rugs which absorb oxygen and which, a helpful candy striper told me, could be fatal if brought in contact with vinegar. Vinegar thrown on these rugs would produce copper acetate which is poisonous. This, she told me, is true in any hospital whether it be a Memorial one or not. I'm telling you this because you can't be too aware.

The candy striper was very tiny although not young. She had a tiny pocket in her apron from which she took a miniature snapshot, the type that is responsible, if you ask me, for all the cataracts going around. It was a photo of her cat which had since been smashed flat. She also offered me a tiny piece of gum. It was not the real thing. Lewis Carrol, who as you well know, was as well not the real thing, once invented a substitute for gum. I believe that this was that.

This place is not at all favorable to health. The pitcher beside my Grady's tape-wrapped hand is only one half full with gray water. Their excuse is that the water table is down. There is a bureau in which there is a mirror (this discourages me, but when I make inquiries, I am told that it's for the patients' primping), three wash rags, a pencil upon which is stamped VOTE FOR PARIS SHAY LEVER 2, a half-gone sponge cake and a bedpan. All these things belong to the hospital. Nothing here belongs to Grady but me.

He is so tiny. Everything here is so small. The white bed made of skinny noodles of iron. The sheets with their tiny mends folded just so across his chest. On the window ledge are tiny rods which one uses to open the windows. One inserts them in a tiny hole and cranks. The protozoans in this room! The energy! It is difficult to remain calm. Around my Grady's eyes are hundreds of bruises. And tiny lines, all across his lips, his pale cheeks, visible for the first time. In the hall there is a little cart laden with tiny plates of food. Tiny Foo-Yung. Tiny breaded veals. And for the less able, cups of broth, 1- by 1-inch squares of Jell-O. Let me tell you about Jell-O. Any new mother (of one or two days) could but you do not have any new mother. You have me. I will tell you about Jell-O. The secret of it. The Cult. Its importance to healing and the rhythm of life. In remote communities, families often worship Jell-O in lieu of anything else. There has even been buggering of Jell-O. It is a protean item. Its true importance, however, lies in its presence at our hour of birth. For you are aware, I'm sure, of the passages in literature and in films when the woman is in labor and the order goes, bring clean towels and heat a pot of water. The water is for Jell-O.

The wheels of a hospital are greased with Jell-O. It mends a man. It comforts the nurses who administer it for they feel that they are truly doing their part. No one gives my Grady Jell-O. They bring his lunch in a soft plastic pouch which resembles the bags of fresh livers you buy in groceries. It takes a little over an hour and a half for him to eat. I wait. Down the hall, someone is playing the greyhound scores on a radio. A nurse comes in and looks at me, sitting on the floor by the molding. There is no room for chairs in this ward and thus no need for visitors. Nevertheless, I am one and, crouched by the molding, am trying to be careful. The nurse can't help but see me, I am so gigantic. She goes to the bed and moves it out a bit from the wall. Behind it is a nickel and a few hairpins. She picks up the nickel and leaves. Grady has finished eating. I am trying so hard to be still. I am making such an effort to not be disruptive in here. Everything is so small. I could hold the whole place in my hand, even on the tip of my finger. There is a light which has been on ever since I arrived even though the room is naturally bright with noon. I get up and lean over Grady. The floor creaks. The tubes and hoses swing in my wake. I crawl into bed beside him. There is sweat on his temples. There is a hole beneath his jaw. It is covered with bandages but the hole's presence remains. Nothing fills it properly. It glows through the most professional and cleverly wrought wrappings. I place my lips lightly on his pillow which is clean, crisply ironed but blotchy, with small colorless spots. I pull the sheet up over us. I can hear the radio. It announces the Big Perfecta. Through the wall a woman's voice is coming.

". . . thought the roast would be good for ten . . ."
and close by, maybe directly over us, someone says,

"That poor young man. Doesn't he have anyone?"

"I guess not. No mail either."

"That poor young man."

Beneath the sheets, I whisper to my Grady. His hair moves with my breath. "I'm sorry," I say. "Don't die, Grady. I love you and I'm sorry."

No one answers.

"He'd be about the age of my Randy, I should think," the woman says.

"Who could tell?"

"My rat Randy, my own son. Isn't it nasty the way life turns on you?"

"Just be grateful he has all his faculties, not like this poor devil here."

"He's his faculties all right and uses them for nothing but tearing around and breaking his mother's heart."

I whisper to my Grady, "Don't go, Grady."

No one answers. The women leave. Beneath the sheet it is blue and rocking like the sea. "I could go with you," I say. He is growing smaller still. I am so clumsy. My neck bangs against the ceiling. My kneecaps shoulder the door shut. This will alert them, I know. Doors are only shut after you here. "If we're lucky we could be like radiolaria," I say, "and become something really beautiful. They're plankton and when they die, the cells disintegrate and they form pretty shells which almost always become fossils. Wouldn't that be something nice to happen after we're dead?"

No one answers. "Oh, Grady," I say, "I don't mean that. You musn't believe what I mean. We don't want anything to do with that oceanic ooze. Listen, Grady," I say brightly. "Remember the river fog, the way it would come in the

middle of the day and make things so bright and sharp, not at
all like New England fog which hushes everything up. Remember how pretty everything was?"

I never cared for it myself but I am host to Grady's loves.
It is his world that is lacking in this ward, not mine. You've
done the same I'm sure. For love. For the lingering. "You
always loved me up so well, Grady," I say.

No one says anything. My words are cumbersome as my
sprawling body. I try to pull myself away from him but I am
so monstrous now, I am so vast, and my words lie with us
beneath the sheets, resting on Grady, pushing my Grady
down. Between the bandages he is naked. In his prick is a long
plastic rod, flat on the end like a golf tee. I kiss him. So lightly.
And yet . . . a crust of flesh returns on my lips. I embrace
him. So slightly. And yet my arms return coated with something like natural shinola. His hair is cold as though he had
come out of the snow.

"Oh, love," I say, "let's begin again. Let's be good to each
other and careful with each other."

Grady is deciding what to do . . . "if left my mind, I've
life in a way; it would be worth the pain" . . . that's the bun
they try to peddle here. Baking in their brain pans daily.
"Nothing's too hard to endure but Death," they shout over
the racket of the machine shop as they discreate a hand, a foot,
a nostril or perhaps a neck even though who knows it was
just a mole that itched a bit, nothing that couldn't have been
helped by scratching. But Life's the dish served here. As for
drama, there's not much. After all, if you won't have that,
there's not a soul, licensed or what, who can help you. They
wheel it in and drop it off. There it is. You regard it slowly.
Oh, of course take your time, they say (and there's little else
to take at that point, they've got you at that point). And you
say, May I take it into my privacies and look it over? May I
have it and return it if displeased with no loss to me? Well,
there's a charge for that, they say. Well.

But my Grady will decide what to do. Watching him, my breasts ache as though I was in the days of weaning all my children. Even though I have none. Even though I am swollen with waiting. My head and stomach are tight as a drum and pounding with the waiting.

Grady turns his head a bit. Something black runs erratically out from someplace in his head. At first it doesn't matter. It comes and goes. I can't even remember it beginning, that's how slight it was at first. In less than a minute, however, it overwhelms everything here, even though it is hardly anything, a trickle, very tiny, and a dull black. In less than a minute again it becomes a lake, very miniature, but enough to flood this room, and although I am here (or rather, although my stomach is here, my mountainous stomach spraddling this tiny bed), I dare not move for to do so would be to crush thousands of weeping invisible things, for the air is full of them. For this shrinking room where my Grady lies, into which an assault of personnel are coming to take me away, is crowded with things infinitesimal. Things annihilable and yet without end. Like the pain the evil suffered in Daddy's pulpit hell, there is no limit to their reduction. And the very least of their reductions has a weight that the mind can't bear—

It all stops. Three nurses come in. They are actually a little larger than I. The room becomes quite ordinary. White. Airy. I see the lacing of one of Grady's boots trailing out of the closet locker. There's a breeze and it shakes the shade. The nurses are very angry. Two I've seen before. One depilates her arms, but only to the elbows. The other is the novice who gave me the substitute gum. The third does all the talking.

"How did you get in here! It's quite apparent that there's to be no one here. You have to get a pass at the desk and the pass must be punched. It's only good for the other floors. There are no passes accepted on this floor."

"Oh please," I say, crawling from the bed. "There's something there on the pillow. Something that's come from his head. Please."

"That's our concern," she says.

"You'd better straighten up and start breathing deeper," the shaved girl says, "or that baby of yours is going to come out harder than a watermelon."

"That's right," the talking one says, "you've got to think of those who haven't had their living yet. Put the other affairs behind you. Last summer I worked in the birthing ward and each night I'd go home, I'd like to tell you, with a song in my heart."

31

I try to think of the baby once and for all but things keep getting in the way. I know this is my only chance, to think about him now, before he comes. I try to think of his needs. Things that I can buy that will define him.

I forced myself to go into a store. But I was stymied by a bib. A tiny drooling bib. And then a small washcloth. No bigger than a saucer. I stared and stared. I couldn't think. Women came and went with casual assurance. Salespeople asked me again and again what I wanted. At last I was asked to leave.

It was not a success. Except for one thing. I learned one thing. Hidden beneath its blouse, each Raggedy Ann doll has I LOVE YOU printed in a heart upon its chest. I think that is one thing that more people should know.

32

It's June third. Where has the time gone? Sometimes you can hear it overtaking you, making, while passing, small crunches, like owls breaking the backbones of mice. There's certainly nothing subtle about it.

I've always disliked this date. It's an anniversary of course, everything is. And every day brings back to mind something mean or blue. The man on the radio reminds one of this continually. Just before daybreak, the last caller calls in. Yes. The lady caller says,

"The parakeets nest each night in my punk trees and are driving me crazy and what can I do?"

"Action Line" is a little annoyed. After all, he's answered this before, but he gives the proper reply as always and then it's sign-off time, preceded by one minute of "On This Date."

"Eleven years ago today," he says, "a nurse shark in the Durban Aquarium threw up a human arm before the distressed eyes of visiting schoolchildren."

On this date, the Japanese beetle was introduced to this country.

And 135 people simultaneously went mad in Sverdlovsk U.S.S.R. after eating rolls from a dirty bakery.

Then they stop transmitting. The man goes home, I suppose.

Well, I want to tell you something.

On June 3, 1844, on the island of Eldey, off Iceland's southwestern coast, a nesting pair of auks were killed by Jon Brandsson and Sigourour Isleffson. Their single egg was

*smashed by Ketil Ketilsson and the great auk was forever lost
to the world.*

A CRIME AGAINST NATURE. At last, the proper use of the
term. No one speaks any more about crimes against God.
Perhaps they never did. And the auks were good creatures.
Not wicked, like the types that attempt to defend themselves.
As for the men, I imagine they had good teeth, warm clothing
and sweethearts. Now where has all the time gone with them
safe in their graves? I have heard that others wanted to claim
the distinction. But were not accepted. Turned down by dili-
gent research. Like the Hiroshima pilot, everyone wants a
piece of the pie.

It's seven o'clock and the sun has come up as usual like a
picture postcard. It's June third, come around again for the
first time. With just a slight dislocation, I feel that things
could be better. A small act of substitution could make up our
life. But the variance never comes. Each day has only enough
difference in it to make what you've already learned unnecessary. We're all left out of the years that might make the difference. Not scheduled. Scratched. We're all just pieces of
marbly meat, with great margins of white to our lives, not
off to the sides where they belong, but running right through
our best days.

Grady's sleeping. They say it's only sometimes that he
sleeps. Other moments he's doing something else. It takes a
conscientious eye, however. It takes a practiced witness to tell
the difference and I am neither. His lips rest on my face. His
breathing whispers to me but it is almost impossible to understand. It rises in despaired intensity. I try to calm him by plac-
ing his hand inside my blouse. My nipples are shiny and like
glass. His fingers fumble and slip off them. They are so bright.
Like hard little spoons. Once I looked intently at them myself and found reflected there a child, baking obscene cupcakes. It's only a toy oven but, nonetheless, everything works.

I kiss him. My mouth is tired. My lips swollen, my gums

faintly metallic. I practiced my cornet for two hours one evening but that was more than nine years ago and surely my lip would not be exhausted still. I was a child then and now I am of course a married pregnant lady, waiting for deliverance and stinking dimly of milk. For weeks now I have been awakened by the cold wet sheet of my bed and the sight of my poor wilted breast, the left, squashed as a tube of tooth-paste carelessly employed.

Deftly, I unbutton my blouse further and slip out a breast. I feed it to his cheek, hoping he'll root for it, not that it would give him any nourishment certainly but it might mean some-thing. But the gesture's dry as my tit once was and someone comes in and interrupts the moment. I can tell they're not going to like me in this place. They don't like my attitude and they despise my circumstances. As Father said (of course about himself), *easy to calumniate but difficult to imitate.* And I'm my father's daughter, born and bred in his love.

Father, of course, was the one who alerted me to this date, albeit in another season. He mentioned it at Mother's service and drove the congregation wild. He said, FOR THAT WHICH BEFALLETH THE SONS OF MEN BEFALLETH BEASTS AS THE ONE DIES SO DIES THE OTHER THEY HAVE ALL ONE BREATH SO THAT A MAN HAS NO PRE-EMINENCE ABOVE A BEAST FOR ALL IS VANITY.

The people protested but it was difficult to disagree. Father quotes everything more or less, and is impeccable in his sources. The souls on that island were simple, good-hearted, ordinarily vicious. All they ever had were boats to catch fish from and a pot to cook the catch and a ballroom in the center of town where a five-piece band played monthly. They knew that all was worthless and that they were lost but they didn't want to be as lost as the animals they shot. That was asking too much. Because they knew how they died. And they knew that their hides whipped from car antennaes and rotted on mud-room floors. They didn't want any part of that.

But they honored Father in spite of what he said. Father was *God's instrument* and we were all the instruments of Father. They respected him enormously, because in that land of silence, he managed to be more silent than them all. It was known that no one ever had a conversation with Father. The words he made had . . . great silences between them. Their lives depended upon the interpretation of the absence around them. And my life depended upon the interpretation of Father.

The people valued me too, of course. Our family was highly thought of. For eleven years we were the only ones on that island who were ever born or died. Sister and I were born and then sister and Mother and baby died. Nothing was going on all that while except my childhood, if you know what I mean. Everything else remained the same. Summer brought no rebirth there—just the same blighted berries and the same dry wind from the sea. The island swung in the Atlantic, out of time and out of season, and the only things that happened were to me. Of course all that has changed and the people there are dying now. Everything I ever wished for has come true. It all came out the only way it could and hustled me right along with it. No, I'm never left behind.

33

They are always driving me out of here. Grady's awake now, I am told, although nothing has changed. There are two glass jugs, one leading in and one leading out, with the clear liquid lessening in one and gaining in the other. Not a drop is lost. It doesn't seem proper that the stuff's all the same.

Healing should be different, don't you think? The processes of life should be distinguishable from those of death. Wouldn't you say?

Some woman leads me roughly to the door. Face pretty as a cardboard crate. They don't even want to give me my post-partum pack although it's required. They'd like to see me bleed to death. Problems like me can all be attributed to *a great laxity of morals and a promiscuous admission* to the Lord's table. Father said that this has always been so.

34

I'm at the Siesta Pig, which is a convenience store, selecting a cup sundae when the bag of waters breaks. It's not unlike the bottom of a bottle falling out and I can almost feel the color draining from my lobes, my lips, both inside and out. I push up closer to the freezer, at a loss.

A woman with a hearing aid pushes past from sherries. I drip discreetly. It's pure water, I have nothing to be ashamed of and if it were bottled it would probably be a cure for something, God knows. Acne perhaps or gout or glos-sitis. "Thank yew," the woman hollers.

It's nothing nasty but I hustle out, alert to the manager's possible distaste. I feel nothing except that my pants and skirt are soaking wet. I walk across the street to a gas station. I have to get the key to the rest room from the attendant. It's hang-ing over his head on a plasic ring six inches wide.

"I'm sick of people like this," he says, handing me the key. "They ain't got no cars, they ain't got nothing but full blad-ders." There is no one in the place but me. I feel that he speaks to me at the expense of others in deference to my condition. I walk to the cubicle with my incredible key. It is not very clean but there is paper everywhere. In the holders and stacked against the walls. I try to blot myself dry but the water pours out and can't be checked. I sit on the bowl and wait. I put my head on my knees. I may even doze a little. I can't tell, I don't feel anything. I know I am supposed to be lying down with my feet elevated. Moving around may injure the baby's head. I don't know. Nothing seems to apply. I am spurious and specious to the moment. The moment does not seem to be significant. I work my skirt off over my head and attach it as best I can to a chrome nozzle on the wall that dispenses warm air. Where is the deception and the shame? The water's pure as tears. I saw Grady cry this morning. They disagreed but I wiped away the tear. They say the signs he shows can no longer be interpreted in the same manner as those exhibited by a living person. But he wept. It was only for an instant. I wiped away the tear.

That seems to lack significance as well. Nothing seems to bear. At times, all things seem to center on those parts of Grady's arms where the tanning stops. Each afternoon I look first at his arms and I see the demarcation of the sun and then I sit and hold his arms. But that promises nothing one way or the other. It is suggestive of nothing. I enter Grady's limbo when I hold his sunny arms.

The water stops at last. I put on my warm skirt and open the door. Half a dozen women are there in a ragged line and three little girls with their legs crossed. Waiting to enter. Vacationers all. Polite as refugees. I return to the Siesta Pig and complete my transaction with the sundae. It tastes greasy as though it were revolutionarily fried and frozen.

"Big doings at your place tonight, huh?" the manager says to me.

"Pardon," I say. I can't feel the baby any more. It as though

I've misplaced him. I look around a little uneasily. I do not want him crawling around and knocking jars off the shelves and cutting himself.

"Those shows you girls put on at the school. They're tonight, aren't they?

The Serenades. I had forgotten. I was supposed to borrow a car and help Corinthian bring the leopard down.

"I always make a point of attending for good relations," the manager is saying. "Besides that, it's a nice break in the routine. In addition as well, some of those favors those groups give out are pretty nice. Last year I got four of those insulated mugs to keep your beverage cold for nothing. If I sold them in here I know I'd have to charge at the least two twenty-nine. And one of those sororities was just giving them away and another one of those sororities smarter yet was pouring free beer into them."

I have to borrow a car. It is a small leopard but with wild, judgment eyes.

"What's your group going to be giving?" the manager says.

"Thrills and chills," I say.

"Nothing, huh? Well that's probably not too smart."

I buy a box of cereal from him and start walking toward the college. Several times before I arrive there I tell myself that the baby is going to be born soon. It doesn't seem relevant. It is not that it seems impossible, it is just that it does not seem indicative of change.

At the hospital they are cutting Grady's hair. I beg them not to, but they do it every week. They are always cutting his hair.

35

The girls are all on the top floor of the sorority house getting into their bikinis, and Corinthian and the leopard have been brought here by someone else and are in an old garage behind the house. The leopard is sitting on its haunches in a cluttered corner and is still as a statue. The garage is hanging with cobwebs and there are cobwebs spanning the leopard's ears. Corinthian rubs them off with his fingers.

Just outside the bolted door of the garage, the housemother is straightening the garbage cans. She is wheezing and red.

"It disturbs me," she says, "it disturbs me so. These men never put the containers back in the same place twice. Sometimes I can't find the lids and sometimes I can't find one of the cans. Sometimes there's still garbage in the bottom. They won't scrape it out and all they need is a stick. There are plenty of sticks around here. They wouldn't take yard trimmings away if you begged them. Well, today I told them. If you don't tell them, they think you're not noticing and all the easier for them. Well, I spoke to them. I was up early this morning and I came out as they were banging around and raving at each other and I said, 'I give to the NAACP, I send out their stickers on the backs of all my envelopes and I just want you to know that I am a member of that organization and I would think that a great many of the girls in this house are members too.' So we'll see. We'll see what happens now. Miss Jenson down at Sigma Kappa says she puts a quarter on the cans each collection day and she never has a bit of a problem but I told her, I said, 'That sounds to me like someone has bullied someone proper.' I don't know what kind of a budget some of those women have to work with but our budget here certainly doesn't allow me to throw quarters away like that and I don't think you girls would approve of me throwing away your quarters like that."

She looks at me and realizes that I'm the one she does not care for. "Aren't you going to get dressed and sing in the Serenade with the others?" she asks sharply.

"No," I say.

"I suppose I should say, 'Aren't you going to get undressed and sing in the Serenade.'" Her head shakes heavily.

"No. I have a cramp."

"You always have a cramp," she says, chuckling. "You always look as though you have a cramp. You haven't ever understood the idea behind sisterhood. Generosity of time and talent. Co-operation."

She climbs the back steps into the house and just before she opens the screen door she says, inspired, and without turning around, "You *are* a cramp!"

I go over to the garage and look through the dirty panes at Corinthian. He sees me and raises his chin. I unbolt the door and go inside. I latch the door from within. Just a little hook and eye. The leopard is much smaller than he appears in Bryant's. His paws, however, are the size of buckets. His flanks rise and drop imperceptibly. Around his neck is a light strong rope that's been wound with purple velvet that the girls bought.

"I'm sorry I didn't come out to get you," I say to Corinthian.

He rubs softly at a bloom of scale on his jaw. He is so slim and peeling down to nothing. A suffering novitiate. "Did you forget?" he asks.

"I remembered when you were almost here, I guess." It is not so bad that I forgot to get him. He is here and isn't that the point? I sit beside him on the floor and open the box of cereal.

Count Chocula. Some gruesome kiddy fare. The leopard shuts his eyes, deep in an animal music.

"That girl Cords came out in a van for us. She is a menace on the roadway. She doesn't know her left from her right."

"That's Cords," I say. "It's a persistent mannerism."

"It's just in the last few minutes that he's calmed down."

Curiously, the leopard does not seem out of place here. He has made a jungle of the close air. A terror grips me.

"I'm sorry!" I say, panic-stricken. "I'm sorry!"

Corinthian stares at me wonderingly.

"I am a very easy driver," I say more quietly. "I am very sorry that I didn't come out to get you." The terror fades. None of this is out of place. I have arranged this for Corinthian so that he can earn seventy-five dollars. He has brought the leopard down here and that is half the money and bringing the animal back is the other half and in the middle is just one minute and a half where Doreen holds onto the purple rope and walks the leopard between the singing sisters and the crowd.

None of this is the point. There is nothing in Father's house any more. There is nothing to reconcile any more. We are all somewhere. Even the baby and Grady are not nowhere and that is not the point.

I have arranged this for Corinthian so that he can make seventy-five dollars. I have tried to be a friend and I have tried to be a lover and I have disobeyed Father who always had the point.

"I will take you back as soon as it's over," I say.

"I am never going to do the likes of this again," he says. "I have taken away any little bit of peace this animal has made for himself and I feel bad. I can see that this all is beneath him when it wasn't at all beneath me and I feel bad."

"I'll take you back as soon as it's over," I repeat helplessly.

"I certainly would appreciate that as we are not about to get into any mode of transportation at all with that girl again."

The light has stopped struggling through the windowpanes. It's dusk. The leopard's eyes are open in the darkening garage, glittering and isolated. His eyes are furnished by the coming night. With the night, he opens his huge floating eyes.

Corinthian and I sit and chew Count Chocula. I know I am not supposed to be eating anything. I am supposed to be lying down with my feet elevated and not eating anything. If I wish I may fill my head with numbers or conundrums. If I wish I may keep my mind occupied that way. There is a twinge deep between my thighs. Not of pain. It is nothing. Just a ripple. It stops. Corinthian doesn't eat any more than a handful but I eat and eat. I weigh one hundred and seven pounds. That is not enough. I have been feeding something outside myself all this time. Some famished object took its form outside me long ago. I look at my arm. It's a stick. My legs are sticks. I do not look at my stomach. I am so forgetful. I want to starve to death. I remember between swallows.

Corinthian's hands tap the rope nervously. He shrugs his shoulders sorrowfully, thinking to himself.

"If he were free," he says aloud, nodding toward the leopard, "he'd be hunting incessantly." He says the word with astonishment. "Incessantly."

The animal's eyes are fixed and emphatic, watching the fading light.

36

I tell Corinthian to put the leopard in the van as soon as Doreen has finished her walk with it. I will get the keys from Cords and meet Corinthian there and drive him and the leopard back. We will be there before Bryant returns from

Miami where he has gone to buy a monkey. Bryant would not know that Corinthian had taken away the leopard until after he returned and everything was over and successful.

"I certainly hope that it is not a mandrill that he brings back," Corinthian says.

"I certainly hope not," I say.

"He wants to bring back something curious and ferocious so that people will feel it would be dull of them to stay away."

I feel the twinge again. It is hardly anything. A hesitation is all, like the skipping of a heartbeat. Think of riddles, they'll tell you. Think of the curiosities of numbers, of ellipses and enigmas. A concern with riddles, Father told me, is permissible. The oldest riddle on record is in the Bible.

Yes, Daddy. Judges 14:14.

That's right, darling. It is summer. I am on his shoulders. He walks along the beach and into the frigid water. I am squealing with the cold. My hands beat upon his neck. I slip off. I start to drown.

"Perhaps we can take the long way back there," Corinthian is saying. "I haven't seen much of this town by car. Actually I haven't seen a bit of it by car. All the time I spend sitting in those automobiles . . . Now if only they'd been moving, what places I'd have been."

I agree to his suggestion greedily. I am an easy driver and will drive till the gas runs out.

"I can't stay away too long," Corinthian says, "but I thought a slightly roundabout route back would be nice."

I tell him the long way back doesn't take much longer.

The baby is coming soon. It will be here soon. It's not a matter of much time. But if I am not there? Not present? If I have other promises to keep?

> Father, wait for me
> Father, wait for me

The little wombless
Who is it that has forgotton my mother?
The little wombless . . .
How swollen are those eyes!
Wait till the little wombless comes.

I think of Father telling me a story once. It seemed just odd imagination. I am talking to Corinthian but I am thinking of Father. I see him sitting at the open window, watching the late spring sky. The house is empty of its past. There is nothing there, but Father has bought a cradle. It has been delivered and is on the dock. He walks through the streets, holding it. The wood is light and gracefully woven. He carries it in one hand. He enters the house and chooses a room. He puts the cradle in the middle of it, where the light falls. He buys a chair, a blanket, a picture for the wall. He attaches a string of Christmas tree lights around the window frame. They cast a soft and sourceless glow such as a child might find comfort in, waking in the night.

"What's the matter?" Corinthian is saying.

"Isn't it about time?" I say. I hear the distant sounds of crowds and music.

"Someone is supposed to come out and tell me." He gets up and moves over to the leopard. He rubs his knuckles down the animal's backbone. The leopard is impassive, indifferent. "How is that man of yours doing?" Corinthian asks me.

I feel leaden. Dust motes dance around the leopard's perilous head. Grady's boots are in the locker but they had to cut his clothes away. The laces are caught beneath the locker door, knotted and muddy and forceful. I try to think of Grady before he was so still.

I don't answer.

"I am going to watch the Serenade from the porch," I say. "I'll see you in a little while." I leave the garage. I walk through an arc of bougainvillaea. The sky is bloody with flowers. The petals on the ground are as delicate as rice paper. I try not to step on them. I make every effort to avoid the sound of breakage.

37

I pass Cords. She looks at me indulgently but doesn't speak. She has such curious, brittle ways—distasteful yet effective ways, for I had done what she requested. I had asked Corinthian for the leopard. They are here. I have stopped, I tell myself. I have stopped long before now, but the decisions I cannot make continue, subtle and unslaked.

In the bathroom, one of the girls is shaving off some of her pubic hair. She puts the bottoms of her bikini on, frowns and shaves off a little more.

I sit on the porch swing beside the housemother. She smiles at me gassily. Her lipstick bounces disembodied. The crowd mills about wooden and impatient, waiting for action. On the lawn is a deputy sheriff. It is Ruttkin. I lean forward.

"Ruttkin," I whisper, "hello."

He looks at me with a friendly lack of recognition.

"How is Ronald?" I persist shrilly.

This time he does not look at me.

"Do you know that young fellow?" the housemother says.

"I guess they all look alike in the dark," I say. It seems the punch line to some joke. The jokes themselves are hardly necessary any more. The endings will suffice. I feel so heavy. My legs feel buttoned up in mattresses. Think of quizzes of all sorts, they'll tell you. Keep your mind off the pain.

The answer is *the time taken for the fall of the dashpot to clear the piston is four seconds* and what is the question? The answer is *when the end of the pin is approximately ⁵⁄₁₆ inches below the face of the block* and what is the question?

Grady, Grady.

"These young fellows are the salt of the earth," the housemother is saying. "My husband was an auxiliary highway patrolman and he knew them well. He always told me they were the salt of the earth. It was his life being in the Auxiliary. He was in the Legion too but that meant nothing to him. He only stayed in the Legion so he could be a member of the Auxiliary. Every Monday night and every Thursday night for fourteen years. They had uniforms just like the deputies but a little lighter, just a bit of a different shade. And that's how I like to recall him best. Going out of the house in the dignity and responsibility of that uniform every Monday and every Thursday night."

Her dog is between us, trying to bark at the crowd. The housemother swings forward and raps him on the head. He sits down and then lies down, resembling a rag.

All along the street, the girls from the various sorority houses are dancing and singing. Rented spotlights play across them, slide up the rococo buildings and empty themselves in the stars. In the South, there are men that rent these spotlights, big ones and little ones, surplus from wars and airstrips and stadiums. They carry them on flatbed trailers attached to '62 white Cadillacs. These men can always be reached. In the South, there are always men available in white Volkswagen buses who will give you a blood pressure reading for twenty-five cents. These men are always present, though not obviously so, soliciting your desires.

The housemother and I sit on opposite ends of the swing. She is a tub and I am a stick, yet I hold my own end of the swing down. It is the baby that is accomplishing that. I imagine the baby inside me feeling long and tight and smooth as an ear of corn although actually I feel no such thing. I am detached, unanxious. I watch the men on the back of their white Cadillacs pan the spotlights past the sly faces of the crowd and rest inquisitionally on Corinthian Brown.

"They're showmen those people," the housemother says irritably. "They've always got to get into the act. There's not a bit of reason for him to get into the act."

Corinthian stands implacably in his T-shirt and work pants. The light picks up the hectic disorder of the hollows of his face and his face seems to be galloping toward some terrible realization that his body hasn't reacted to yet, but he is motionless in the light. And the leopard beside him, as always, is motionless, although its tail is flickering in the air, showy as flame, but that movement does not alleviate the stillness as much as it reinforces it.

"Once I went on a tour of Beautiful Homes," the housemother says. "I can't imagine now why I ever bothered. I'll never do it again. The silliness of those people with beautiful homes! Two of them had big china animals just the size of that one there sitting on the lanais. Strictly ornamental. You couldn't use them for a single blessed thing. Never in my life have I ever had anything strictly ornamental."

The sisters are singing. They are in a semicircle, facing the street, their backs to the porch, in rows of two, the fatter girls in the rear, a tier of flesh mostly, sparkling like fryers in a skillet. The crowd increases. There are a few whistles, an inflexionless yapping sound of children. The spotlight fades and is put out. I can hear, it seems, its rattle as it cools.

"There's too much money and waste," the housemother says. "Do you know what I do? I put a little pan under the air conditioner outside my room and it catches the condensation from the machine and I use that water to water my ivy. It takes a little thought but I think anything like that makes one a better person."

With the spotlight out, the torches are visible, tall inventions of bamboo, and palm fronds and jars of gasoline. There are

smatterings of fire and light everywhere now and the crowd
is silent because they are impressed. They are impressed because this is all free and yet stagey and professional. Better
than New Orleans they think. They are in the darkness and
they are so silent, it's as though the street is empty. They are
being courted and they are being entertained. Their opinion
is being sought. And it is better than New Orleans and it is
better than Miami. They feel their presence here tonight
strongly. They are speechless with their worth.

And then Doreen becomes visible in her scant outfit of fake
tatters, her long hair swimming to her thighs, and there is
still no sound from the crowd. She is bony and beautiful and
a little foolish. Her face in the cast from the torches changes
from being pretty to not being at all pretty to being clown-
ish. It changes so rapidly. She starts to walk, very pale and ab-
sorbed and ephemeral, and the effect is winsome and lustful
and lost on us. The crowd, me. The housemother says,

"I don't believe anyone's at their best when they're nine-
tenth's naked."

Doreen walks, her face, out of the light, aged and predis-
posed. The leopard beside her has its muzzle almost on the
ground. The motion is fluid with a hasty hesitancy. Doreen
walks. She looks gorgeous and sulky. Her legs rise up pure
white and impossible to her manufactured little loin rag. She
turns. She starts back to Corinthian. The sisters bleat,

> "Doreen's the Queen
> Who'll make you scream
> With wantin' to get to know her."

The cramp begins again and I shift myself on the swing.
The housemother gives me a sharp look. The cramp moves
up and encircles each breast, like a lover might, like Grady
might with his warm hands. Think of mind teasers, they'll
tell you. Think of the ingenuities of language and rhyme.

Cords has made everything rhyme. Her song is a fortune cookie, a penny horoscope. Think of a rhyme, they'll tell you, for step or mouth or silver or window. Think of things that are diversive or exceptions to the rule.

The cramp is gone and I feel nothing. I see Father. It is summer. He brings a baby down to the sea. He sprinkles water across its sleeping eyes. The sea is opalescent with its fathomless order and law. They watch it, the baby, blind and cautious and still, and Father. Little flowers grow between the higher rocks. The littlest flowers I've ever seen.

Doreen has almost reached Corinthian. A small spot comes on again and floods her prematurely. She is handing the rope to Corinthian. We all observe the *deus ex machina*. The error is corrected. The light goes out. Doreen is in shadow and suggestive once more. The crowd's breathing becomes obvious. They are aroused on all the levels of their loneliness. And now the leopard rises, moves leisurely in a tall and searing spiral and attaches himself to Doreen's shoulder. It is as though the animal is whispering some absolute secret in her ear and the beautiful girl is receptive to it. It is as though the beautiful girl bends a little to hear it, sagging against that singular coat.

Doreen screams. It seems frivolous. She screams and screams. The leopard leaps away into the darkness. The chaos is fixed and rigid. Ruttkin unholsters his gun but there is nothing to shoot at. Everyone is moving and shouting now. Doreen's thin scream is the current beneath it all. I sit on the swing and raise my hand to my throat. I don't feel anything. The night offered nothing to my eyes. It took nothing from me.

38

They put me in a white room in a white bed with high sides on it so that I cannot climb out. Nonetheless, when the nurse leaves, I climb out. There is a curtain in the room and a toilet behind it and I sit on that. I think that if only I can go to the bathroom that will be the end of the terrible seizure in my bowels and then I can get on with having the baby. I cannot do anything. Nevertheless, I feel much better. I climb back into the bed.

An adult female consumes seven hundred pounds of dry food in one year. No one ever tells you that there comes a moment when you have to pass it all.

I am in a seersucker nightshirt with little blue flowers on it. A prerogative of the ward. I have another contraction. Another moment gone. Something I could reflect upon now if I cared to. I think about it in a way. I think that they do not put nightshirts with blue flowers on patients who are critically ill. Once she cut her lip while shaving her legs. Once she fell while getting out of her underwear. Now how can a girl like Doreen be all cut up and better off dead?

The nurse comes back into the room. She has white hair and a white uniform and she puts her white face very close to my own as she puts her fingers up my vagina. She steps back, wiping her hand on a tissue. "Cervix has dilated this far," she says, holding up three fingers.

"How wide does it have to be?" I ask, though having her dawdle there is the last thing I want. I want only for her to leave quickly so that I can sit on the toilet again.

"Seven wide," she says. "One hour."

It was said that one of my cousins was born in a chamber

pot. It didn't seem to matter. It was one of the few stories that Father ever told me and therefore I cannot comment on its meaning. I would say, however, that it was just a story that didn't matter much.

39

I am a funambulist, the act, at last, proceeding without interval. They've placed an enormous clock on the wall for encouragement of a sort, the only kind there is. *Time passes.* And they have nothing else to offer, no matter what they claim.

"I can see the head now," the nurse says. "Half an hour."

My eyes are open and I am thinking of Little Red Riding Hood. Or rather not of *her*, that postiche pudendum, but of the wolf. They snipped his stomach open to get her out and then they filled him with stones and sewed him back up again. And when he got up, he died. Now that is very Freudian and shows the limitations and protractions of life.

"That was a good pain," the nurse tells me.

"I only want the bad ones," I say.

40

There are a great many lights in the delivery room but they are not doing much to dispel the darkness. Everyone here is masked against it, protected and shielded in beautiful popsicle green. I am left to see nothing but am urged to breathe freely. The smells here are unsuitable but quite obvious—erasures, mimeograph ink, chalk shavings. There is loss, there is banishment. The world in this room is skewered with a crumbling stick. The world in this room holds no promise or danger and the only hope of my own is for expungement. At last I may be punished. . . .

The nurse bends over me, smelling like a pressing board and pushes away the spots that rise and fall before my eyes.

"No, I still can't play tennis," the doctor says. "I haven't been able to play for about two months. I have spurs on both heels and it's just about wrecked our marriage. Air conditioning and concrete floors is what does it. Murder on your feet."

A few minutes later, the nurse says, "Isn't it wonderful to work with Teflon? I mean for those arterial repairs? I just love it."

The doctor says, "They served cold duck with dinner. Would you imagine that, please? Cold duck?"

A few minutes later, the doctor puts the baby on my belly while he cuts the cord. The child has navy-blue eyes like a foal but does not look at us, having no interest in anyone here.

The doctor's mask does not move. I cannot see his mouth making the words but I can hear the words,

"It's a girl," he says.

She is a success.

41

I want to tell you something. It's not much. The fight for consummation isn't much.

The girl in the bed beside me says, "I lost my baby."

"I'm sorry," I say.

"I think this is a heck of a place to put me, seeing that I lost my baby. In the maternity ward. I would say that was one heck of a place."

"There was probably a mistake," I say. I am sorry but I do not want to hear about it. Nevertheless, I continue to look in her direction, a gesture that connotes interest. I do not exist. I have had a child. It is the seal set on my own nullity.

The girl looks at me bleakly. "They said I had lost him yesterday night."

"I mean it was probably a mistake that they put you in here." The pads in this ward are double size. There are four gross of them in a box beneath my bed. They expect me to bleed a great deal.

"They make mistakes in this hospital all the time," the girl says animatedly. "I had a friend and he came into Emergency with a broken leg and they set the wrong one."

"I've heard that," I say. You always hear that.

"I had a friend and he had one good eye and one bad eye and he had to have an operation to have the bad one removed and they removed the other one instead."

"Which one?" I say.

She raises her bed until she is almost perpendicular. "What's your baby's name?"

"I don't know yet." I am aware that I don't bleed much.

"Well, now that's a funny thing because we couldn't decide on a name for our baby either. Nothing goes with Apple. I mean my name is Jane Apple and my husband's name is Wendall Apple and neither of those seemed to fit and nothing seems to fit. So we never did come up with a name. So it doesn't seem as bad, although it is of course."

"What?" I say. Outside, there is a laurel tree which they have pruned devastatingly so that its branches will not rub against the window.

"Just as bad."

"The babies are coming!" a nurse cries vigorously. "The babies are coming!"

I rise dumbly from my bed and go to the sink to wash my hands. I return, dumbly. The girl pulls the curtain between the two beds and lights a cigarette.

They wheel the train of babies down. They distribute them. Later they are collected and returned to the nursery. Then there is dinner. Then it is night. At some time in the following hours, a figure invariably appears at the doors and says, "Anything for discomfort?" No one, to my knowledge, has ever replied one way or the other.

42

The baby is brought to me shortly before midnight. She is bitter, outraged. A core of willful heat. Her head is damp. She cries without moving, without hope of satisfaction.

"Why is her hair wet?" I ask.

"It's not wet. She's just been crying, that's all."

The baby and I lie and watch the butchered laurel tree. The baby nurses, frets, sighs. We hear ambulances arriving, doors slamming shut. Once, I think we can hear a nighthawk. It is probably not a nighthawk, but the sound of a part of the air folding shut resembles one. The baby is a strange companion in the night, fixed and exciting and untroubled.

There's always the danger of falling asleep, they'll tell you. In nursing, one should always assume a slightly uncomfortable position, they'll say.

We lie and watch the laurel. Figures try to rise up between the branches but I drive them away. Somewhere in this town now, there is an animal that hunts incessantly. I tell the baby this. She is dispassionate. There are some objects that are notable by their absence from the trees. There is nothing that can be done to dispatch them. Little wombless, I say to the baby, but I cannot finish. There is no finishing.

Is it over, Grady's breathing asks.

No, I am always answering.

The baby smells like bread. They take her away, down the dark hall. *I can't think of anything right to do,* Grady had said, his words rising with the engine's singing. The driving lamps swam against the curve ahead. *There is nothing that's right that's left to me.* I touched his hand. His hand was on the shift knob, closed against me. And then his eyes closed too. But I could see myself already beyond the curve and walking. Walking away and on the road back. Even then.

43

I turn on the radio. A woman is saying,

"I hope you will not think me vulgar."

"Not at all," "Action Line" says. He sounds a little halting, exhausted. He sounds a little querulous himself.

"My husband can only become sexually excited if he feels that some part of his body is missing."

"Yes," "Action Line" says.

"A finger or an eye or a leg. I have to pretend it's not there."

"Yes," "Action Line" says. "Nature is one vast mirage of infinite delusion."

44

The day after the tragedy, the housemother is standing on a street corner, waiting for the bus. Everyone is talking about Doreen. The town, or at least that part of it which deals with the college, is shocked. The feeling is that there must be some mistake. The entire incident is outlandish and certainly will mark the end of electing queens.

The housemother has had a fascinating day in town, talking to salesgirls and waitresses about it. She has had tea in six different restaurants and is exhausted. She is uncomfortable. She stands at the bus stop in brown low shoes, brown support hose, brown skirt and brown nylon blouse. She waits like an enormous brownie.

She cannot get over the fact that this has happened to one of her girls. She never expects anything to happen to them. Those that have graduated and gone north write and tell her that they have husbands and babies and live in carriage houses in Connecticut. She wonders what a carriage house is and why anybody would want to live in one. It seems a nigger could do better than that.

Her chin begins to move up and down. It has been doing that recently. Sometimes her entire face moves back and forth as though she is halfheartedly refusing something. When she realizes that her head is shuffling around like this on her neck, she immediately acknowledges it and turns the action into something she wants to do.

Waiting at the bus stop, the housemother sadly shakes her head. Of all her girls, Doreen seemed most eligible for a happy future. The housemother is becoming depressed. She thinks of the inaccuracy of life, of the folly and injustice of it. She thinks of the greediness of people, their rudeness and lust. All those people in Miami and Mexico and New York City, healthy and wealthy and doing sick things.

She is becoming exasperated waiting for the bus. She peers up the hot street. She does not like this part of town. It is almost in the area called Frenchtown, the *colored section.* Opposite her is a fruitcake factory where a northern lady was abandoned by her husband two years before. He, a gentleman in a white Oldsmobile, went to park the car and never returned. People said that the lady had stayed in and outside the factory for three days, being raped casually by roving bands of youths, and then finally and alone, had taken the train back to Forty Fort, Pennsylvania.

The smell of sugar and candied fruit hangs in the air. The housemother shifts her weight. She has to go to the bathroom. In the fruitcake factory is a machine like a printing press, pushing out loaves. Farther up the street is a bar called Daddy Meaning's. Music drifts toward her from a record player.

> My mother often told me
> Angels bonded your life away
> She said.

Inside, men are sitting on stools, staring at a jar full of eggs. No one walks in the street. The housemother goes over the tragedy again in her mind. She is thinking how she will relate it in a letter to her best friend, a blue-haired widow who lives in a condominium in Sun City. Last night, before the Serenade, before poor Doreen went out to wow the boys, the housemother had begun her weekly letter. She was having a difficult time. There was not much to relate. She told her friend that she had *in the act* caught the cook stealing a box of graham crackers and a 100-watt bulb. She told her about the new novel she was reading, *a warm and tender love story (but with some dirty words) that will touch your heart.* She has difficulty reading because of her eyes. Many words are not clear. She thinks she may be misinterpreting some of them.

At last she sees the bus approach. In the last few seconds that she waits, she falls. She has broken her hip. But it is not when she falls that she breaks the bone, it is while she still stands. The hip has simply worn out. It's tired, out of calcium and out of luck. They will tell the housemother this later in the nursing home. They will reassure her that it is not an exceptional occurrence.

45

I KNOW THY WORKS THAT THOU ART NEITHER COLD NOR HOT: I WOULD THOU WERT COLD OR HOT.

I met my love in a movie theatre. A silent film. Dim interminable images. It seemed as though I had been there for hours in a plushy seat leaking out its dreadful contents. Every place I put my hand it would come away *with something on it*. Thread or foam or gum rubber or whatever.

It was directly after Father left. A hot day. Imagine Father coming down by train in all that heat in his black wool suit, black blouse, black hat. With only a tiny tab of white at the throat to throw the costume into relief. It was soiled. Nodules of hair low on his neck. His hair was sweetly island ragged, like a boy's, and he smelled like a boy too as he introduced himself to me. SO THEN BECAUSE THOU ART LUKEWARM AND NEITHER COLD NOR HOT, I WILL SPEW THEE OUT OF MY MOUTH.

Grady's dead. In the operating theatre. Men in lime smocks and a few wine vests watching from the balcony. A few women too. And I swear I saw several taking notes.

Grady's dead. They gave me the word but not until after it had happened. I expected as much from them. I expected no better.

46

Any changes in the information on the birth certificate must be made within six weeks, they'll tell you. These corrections will be made for a fee of five dollars per correction. After six weeks, corrections will not be made.

They have released us from the hospital, the baby and me. The day is hot and still. The sky is full of rain. Every afternoon now it rains punctually at four. There is a sale on white whiskey. There is a sale on hams. There is a dead egret lying in the gutter. A man walks past us with his little girl.

"It must of been sick or it wouldn't have come into town," the man tells her. "It must of been sick or it wouldn't have been hit." This seems to comfort the little girl. She doesn't look at it.

The first warm drops of rain fall. A guilt beyond memory. A threat that is not fulfilled by the rain. I walk into a department store, into Infants Wear. I buy a back pack, six little shirts, three dozen diapers, four little gowns. Nothing else is necessary. The baby is so weightless on my hip. It is as though someone has bandaged the crook of my arm.

We leave the store and walk through the rain to the grocery. I take a cart. We orbit through the aisles. Behind the delicatessen counter is a man in a white apron, packing potato salad into a plastic bowl.

"They got that nigger," he says to his customer.

"Thank God," the customer says.

The man in the apron bends over the counter and looks at us. "Why if that ain't the cutest child I've ever seen," he says. "Lookit all that hair."

I wheel the cart back through the aisles. I have forgotten something. We travel past the same foods and bottles and boxes again and again. I have forgotton something irrevocable. I put a jar of peanut butter in my cart, a loaf of raisin bread. I have a great desire for ice cream. I must have ice cream. But I have no place to go. It will melt before I get there. My forgetfulness! The cart wobbles. The wheels will not turn. I abandon the cart and get another one. Blame must be placed. One of us has made a mistake. I put in another jar of peanut butter, another loaf of bread. The wrapper is torn. There is a small scissure in the crust. I continue shopping. There is bubbling in the canned fruit. There is movement in the yellow corn meal. There is sugar on the flour and glass on the cream pies.

I release the cart. Something terrible has been happening. Someone is responsible.

What have they done with my Grady? I ask this now but I did not ask it then. I had just been released, you understand. I inspire innuendo, if not slander, I know. But the door closed behind me and the tumult, before it did, only served to stupefy me. The paperwork, the bills that must be satisfied, the statements that must be signed. And I wanted to ask. It was up to me to contact the proper authority, I know, but the context of their conversation precluded it. There seemed no way it could be brought up. And it was not simply a question of transition or tact. I have difficulty in keeping up my end of a doctor's dialogue. There seemed no way it could be phrased in a meaningful fashion. And then the door closed shut behind me and they watched me from the air-conditioned inside until, I suppose, I was out of their sight.

Lost. The heat followed me in a small traveling stream of silence. The baby's eyes were squeezed against the sun. Her diaper stayed dry for hours and hours. Gone. In what parasitic place.

I did not ask a soul. And the accident was not mentioned. I never saw his friends after the accident. Even if I had seen them, the Fern Fellow and his wife, they probably would not have referred to our absence at dinner that night. They would have been hurt and insulted at our failure to show up. The man is particularly sensitive to slight. He would have put our unused glasses and plates back in the cupboard without a word. Larger servings for themselves would have salvaged the evening nicely.

I did not ask and no one spoke of Grady. Nothing on the radio. I gave them a day. I confess I expected some report, if only a line. The first night there was nothing. The second evening, I caught my Answer Man, my Action Line chum saying,

"The zone of life, the area which not only all that live and breathe and move inhabit but in which all vegetation is contained is a mere twelve miles."

I turned it off, feeling a bit mollified. One has to learn to deal with the unspoken. As it turned out it was the only information offered. The newspaper was indecipherable as always. Something about a traffic light erection. Something about children milkeholics. Our own story was lost in overset I suppose, but I should have inquired further.

Thrown back upon myself, upon my own devices, I went to his room. 17. It was empty as I feared. I lay on the bed for a moment with the baby, although I was not tired. When I got up, I smoothed the sheets. I do not mind criticism but it seemed important that I leave the room at least the way I found it the last time.

They released me in three days. I might have mentioned it. Another holy number, fixed as any race. Its implications arose immediately. Father would have noted it. The three that bear record in heaven and the three that bear witness on earth. I could go on and on. The angel flying through the middle of heaven said, "Woe, woe, woe, to the inhabiters of earth"—and three angels were yet to sound their trumpets and by these three, fire, smoke and brimstone, was the third part of men killed, and those not yet killed failed to repent of three things, their sorceries, fornications and thefts. And three unclean spirits came out of the mouth of the dragon, and the dragon and the beast and the false prophet constitute three.

Oh, I could have gone on and on but the door closed behind me. And I realized I had failed to ask where they put my Grady. In what terrible cold ground, his sunny arms.

47

I have left something behind. I have lost something and cannot find it. I am in a grocery. I clutch my stomach but the baby is in my arms. My hunger leaves me forever. The meat bleeds into the freezing coils. Body hair falls from the endive.

Everyone smiles at me as I start to leave. They smile at the baby. I am calm, for the baby has pinned my hands fast to her round chest. I pass the delicatessen. There are other customers now but the mangler is the same. He throws corned beef onto a scale.

"It's just as well he won't be seeing court," he says. "It's just as well for him it was done quick rather than long."

"More mercy shown to him than to that lovely girl."

There's a woman there so short her head hardly musters past the onion buns. "Onct lovely," she corrects.

"That's right," the man in the apron says. "They have got to take the skin off the tops of her legs and put it on her face." He looks at me. "That sure is a cute new baby," he says, "fresh out of the oven."

Lost. The blood is pounding in my head. So thirsty. And they've shot all the poor beasts, I'll learn as well. Carriers of disease. Torn the place down. Nothing to it. Dry wood termites. Seven minutes with two sledge hammers. The air has to turn no corners out at Bryant's any more.

The rain has stopped and hasn't left a trace upon the town. The heat is smothering. I walk outside and right away into a liquor store. Men are sitting at tables drinking blend. I buy two quarts of gin.

"Barfield must have been practicing because he only fired but three times." The rhythm of the man's words is soothing and confident. The sweat dries upon my lip.

"He only fired but three times," he croons. "The first shot got the nigger in the knee but he kept running right toward Terry worse than a mad dog. And the second shot got him in the other leg and then he went screaming and foaming and then he started crawling toward Terry and the third shot got him right in the rig and that was that."

The bartender coughs, jerking his head at me. The men shuffle and cough.

"You want anything else?" the bartender asks.

"Where can I buy a train ticket?" Milk is drying in dark circles on my blouse. In dream, the baby jumps a little in my arms.

"Right here," he says. "I can sell you one right here to get on the train. And then when you get on you buy another ticket for wherever it is you want to go."

"How much is it now?" I say.

"Fifty cents," he says. "You only need one. A baby in your arms don't need a ticket."

"I suspected it," I say.

48

The quickening train speeds past the junk yard. Pressed back against my seat, a Jaguar is in my range for just a moment, a Jaguar traveling toward me from the very edge of Glick's boundaries, from the very corner of the world, through the flowers and the sparrows, its doors peeled off, its trunk and hood indecently flung open, caroming sideways. Broken. Gone.

My head rests on a clean white napkin. The baby is nursing. Fifteen minutes on the left. I shift her to the right. Ten minutes. She falls asleep.

Her cheekbones. Her cheekbones are Grady's, I think sometimes. But I've left that all behind me, the bringing up of things that were. I won't bring them up again, I assure you. Grady and Corinthian and Mother and baby and sister and others over the years that I haven't kept up with.

People go, you know. It's only you that remains. That's the way it will be. That's certain at least.

It takes years to learn to be still.

At another time, for instance, you might have expected something to fly up from that wrecked Jaguar as we passed. Butterflies perhaps. Or insects. But there was nothing. Nothing.

I run my fingers along the ridges of the baby's cheeks which

are high and hard. She opens her eyes, her deep and perfect
eyes that don't believe in anything.

A man in a uniform comes down the aisle of the car, an
employee, asking me my destination. At another time this
might have led to something. But I am still now. I am collected and the baby's head is cool upon my breast. I feel cool
all over from the baby's head, and I tell him. While he is
punching out the tickets, I say, "I'm going home." I smile. I
take money from my pocket. I am a young mother going
home. A satchel beside me filled with simple necessities. Clean
and cool, my hair combed nicely, my little baby with a yellow
ribbon on her wrist. I am calm and neat. The baby is powdered and her diaper is tight and white and dry. I am responsible. A *good risk*.

"Well, that sure is nice," the man says. "That's what's so
satisfying about working on the railroad. You take so many
people home."

"It must be very rewarding," I say.

"It sure is," he says. He goes to the only other people in
the car, a man and woman sitting several seats away. They
buy a ticket for a place a hundred or so miles up the line.
The woman has a bag full of hamburgers. She has a long and
nervous and aggressive face. The man is handsome, with a
generous suffering mouth. One can tell immediately that
something is wrong between them. Something empty, long
familiar to them. The woman takes a small bite from her hamburger, looks savagely at the bun, takes another bite. She
pushes the mutilated hamburger into the man's hand and turns
away from him, watching the fields and the muckland soar by.
The man eats the food slowly, looking straight ahead. He is
facing me. I can hear his dry swallowing. I can see his eyes.
Just before he finishes it, his wife opens the bag and takes out
another hamburger. She begins to eat it, but becomes bored
again, annoyed, punitive. She hands it to him to finish. The

process is repeated again and again. Tears begin to roll down the man's face.

I know that nothing is expected of me in this situation. I am well groomed, sitting straight, holding my baby, going home. There was a time when I would have offered myself to this man. But now I see the impropriety of it. I see that it's just a dream. To know that it is all dream! To know that one has become free not to enter into it at last!

49

. . . And I am in Father's house at last, all the journeying behind me, all the times the others paid for. Just before I arrived, my Answer man was there, but the words were gone, as I knew they'd have to be, and his head, wide as the night sky, became the night sky at last, as I knew it would.

One more thing. When I arrived at the house with Father at the window, I found something, some small mammal on the lawn. Recently dead. I was relieved. If I had arrived sooner it might have still been hopelessly surviving, in need of action, of some sort, on my part. One cannot simply put an injured thing in the shade of a bush if convenient or turn its head to face its nest if ascertained. One cannot simply do that. I am grateful that the choice continues to be not mine. Some would call it luck, I suppose. I would not.

Father has the baby now. He is downstairs with her and I am upstairs, resting. I can hear him speaking with her. At another time, I might have thought the sound was only wind. But here there is no wind. It is a still summer night. Even the sea is silent.

I lie on the bed. I banish each thought softly. There are no more memories to resist. There is only the baby. I think of her with abandon but then more and more carefully. I remove everything but the fact of her. She is outside with Father, swimming in his arms. I let that go. I let almost everything go. I concentrate upon something deep within her, deep within all that remains after I have let everything go. I am left with almost nothing, but I enter it. I enter it.

What peace.

JOY WILLIAMS grew up in Maine but has lived, for the most part, on a Florida key for the past twenty years. In 1980, she won the National Magazine Award for Fiction for her short story "The Farm," and in 1974 *State of Grace* was nominated for the National Book Award. She is also the author of a story collection, *Taking Care*, and *The Changeling*, a novel. Portions of *Willie & Liberty*, her novel in progress, have appeared in *Esquire* and *The Paris Review*.